READER REVIEWS FROM AROUND THE WORLD

NIKITA

"Finally.....an author who delivers us a strong female heroine. We need more of this in our books and in the movies. I loved this book and Anna Masterson!"

Denise R. - Chicago, Illinois

"Nikita is a quick read with short chapters and loads of action. This book is destined to become another success in Bodell's arsenal of mysteries."

Carl B. - Nashville, Tennessee

"Bodell has the ability to allow the reader to feel as if they are right there in the action."

Paula, Q. - Zurich, Switzerland

"Bodell knows where our deepest fears lie buried in regards to the most powerful positions held in the U.S. government. There is no end to his creative imagination displayed in Nikita."

Roger C. - Leicester, England

"Nikita is one great read! It is a fast-paced plot that will grab you from page one. I couldn't put this one down!"

Duane N. - Rochester, New York

"I was already a Bodell fan after reading his first two novels: Treachery in Turtle Bay I and II. Nikita, his third work, proves he has mastered the art of writing page-turning bestsellers!"

Sarah V. - Washington, DC

"The writing is crisp and light. The Mastersons are the most likable characters developed by an author since Agatha Christie! I hope to read many more Masterson mysteries from Bodell."

Beatrice P. - Palm Beach, Florida

"Nikita includes every element of a good tale: great plot, strong characters, interesting dialogue, and lots of action. It is a real page-turner!"

Megan K. - Kilkenny, Ireland

THE ANNA & HUGH MASTERSON MYSTERIES

"...reading about a couple who are like Mr. and Mrs. 007 super smart and always covering all the bases is fantastic. It makes me feel like everything will be all right. I just have to cover all the bases. ...the fact that they have been together forever and are still in love is an extra bonus.

I must say that I sincerely hope that you are planning the next book, and the next book and the next book..."

Edwina van den Heuvel
MSc Criminology and Criminal Psychology
The Hague, Netherlands

"I enjoyed the first book of the series... actually I read it over a four day weekend. However, I could not put the sequel down and read it in its entirety on a flight to Kolkata. As the crew prepared for landing I began the epilogue, as the wheels touched the tarmac I realized that the scene depicted was written in 2008 and is eerily on target for the US domestic and international crises we find ourselves in mid 2010. I do not know where Bodell gets his material, but his fiction walks a precarious tightrope with real events."

Former United States State Department Official

NIKITA

By

G. Hugh Bodell

AN ANNA & HUGH MASTERSON INTERNATIONAL MYSTERY

SPRIG MEDIA GROUP

Library of Congress – Cataloging Data
Nikita
by
G. Hugh Bodell

Library of Congress – Control Number: 2011938584

First Sprig Media Group Trade Paperback Edition

Web Site: www.sprigmediagroup.com

Published by Sprig Media Group - 2011

Designs and Photos by Sprig Media Group

For information about bulk purchases
E-mail: nikita@sprigmediagroup.com

ISBN-13: 978-0615539263

ISBN-10: 0615539262

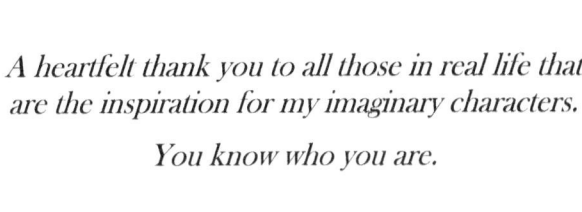

A heartfelt thank you to all those in real life that are the inspiration for my imaginary characters.

You know who you are.

Prologue

In a private conference room, in the Iranian Presidential Palace, Vladislav Dubnikov sat across a beautifully inlaid conference table from Heydar Vahdani, the President of The Islamic Republic of Iran.

They were the only two people in the room. Vahdani had dismissed his bodyguards and sent them to wait outside the door.

"Mr. Dubnikov, the United Nations has once again sought to insult our country by publicly justifying your appointment and intrusion into our nuclear program as, and I quote, '...the IAEA has completely bungled the oversight responsibilities for the aggressive nuclear activities of Iran. There appears to be no improvement in sight. In order to avoid more horrors in the Middle East, I am appointing a special envoy, reporting only to me, with the full power of the United Nations office of the Secretary General behind him.'

"After that insult from Pham Dac Kien, the Secretary General himself, I am supposed to welcome you, afford you every courtesy and open access to our progress in developing nuclear energy.

"What do you want to do, Mr. Dubnikov, crawl around our construction sites and assure yourself that our efforts are only to produce energy?

"I have said it before and I will say it again, my country wants to have access to nuclear technology. We want the security of sustainable energy.

1

"The most important issue of the world of tomorrow will be energy and it is my obligation to assure that the Iranian people have available to them energy, clean energy, endless energy.

"Do you understand?

"The United Nations or the puppeteers controlling the United Nations are not going to interfere with that.

"Do you understand?"

Calmly, Vladislav Dubnikov responded.   "President Vahdani, I do not doubt for one minute your determination to protect your people from decline due to lack of energy to power their homes, businesses, schools, hospitals and transportation.

"I believe that your country's investing in sustainable nuclear energy is not only intelligent and far sighted, it is admirable for its daring in requiring you to stand up to those afraid of you.

"No, President Vahdani, I applaud this initiative of the Iranian people to head off a future disaster long before your country will be impacted by fossil fuel shortages. Further, Mr. President, it is a far wiser strategy to sell your substantial reserves of oil into what inevitably will be a rising market, while your country flourishes relying on a twenty-first century energy alternative."

Vahdani's eyes narrowed and he said, "Is that the official position of the United Nations?"

Vladislav Dubnikov had decided that he would waste no time being politically correct. He knew what Vahdani wanted and he had it.

"President Vahdani, I do not know, nor do I care what the

official position of the United Nations is. The esteemed Secretary General, Pham Dac Kien, is on my payroll and has been since his first day on the job. I received this appointment because I told him I wanted it. If you will be so gracious, you may have your Minister of Energy write the reports I will send back to the General Assembly. No Mr. President, I do not want to crawl around construction sites. My mission here is concerned with further protection of your people."

"Really, Mr. Dubnikov, and how is that?" he said with a sneer.

"I wish to revive the nuclear armament relationship your country had with the former Soviet Union prior to 1993."

"How do you propose to bring that about?"

"Mr. President, you have been manufacturing Shahab-3 ballistic missiles for almost three years now and have stockpiled over one thousand of those efficient little rockets.

"Now as you are aware, your Shahab-3 is a modified version of North Korea's Nodong missile which itself is based on the Soviet-made Scud. There are, sitting in underground warehouses in my mother country, Russia, over four thousand nuclear warheads for the Scud missiles.

"My colleagues and I think that they are wasted sitting there since our mother country has over twenty thousand warheads for other missiles stockpiled.

"President Vahdani, we would like to see those four thousand Scud warheads put to better use.

"We feel your country may be a likely destination for some of our orphaned warheads. Further, maybe some of your

3

allies, like North Korea and Venezuela, may be interested in those you do not want."

"Mr. Dubnikov, your knowledge of our defense systems is interesting and your proposal is attractive, but I have two major issues with your entire proposition."

"And they are, Mr. President?"

"Mr. Dubnikov, in view of the unusual way you arrived in this post, I assume you really do have a hold on the UN through their Secretary General. But the UN is not my major concern."

"Who or what is, Mr. President?"

"The United States of course."

"Mr. President, I told you that Pham Dac Kien, Secretary General of the United Nations, is my employee. Well, my group and I are about to hire another influential figure."

"And who would that be?"

"The next president of the United States has been, is currently and will remain on our payroll, hopefully for eight years."

"How, Mr. Dubnikov, do you expect to pull that off, the elections are not for another ten months and it appears to me that everyone who can raise a few dollars is running for the job."

"Ahh, but Mr. President, that is just the issue, in order to win the Presidential election in the United States you don't need to be smart, brave or the best person for the job. What a candidate needs is to have access to a lot of money to buy a lot of media time to make the American voters think you are smart, brave and the best person for the job."

"So!"

"My colleagues and I own one of the candidates."

"Which one, there are so many?"

"Sorosh Saji."

"The Afghan?"

"First generation Afghan American, his parents are from Afghanistan. He was born in the US, a requirement to be United States' President."

"Right, so just how do you own him?"

"One of my colleagues has funded and overseen his development from childhood, beginning with his eleventh birthday party on to his political rise to US Senator.

"To assure his Presidential victory we have assembled a campaign war chest of over five hundred million dollars. These funds will be trickled into his campaign treasury, through small contributions from individuals, via the internet. As we speak, the databases are being built to insure that the contributions appear to come from over 10 million little people, a requirement if he is to be put forth as the candidate for everyman."

"And if he loses, you and your partners are out five hundred million US dollars."

"He will not lose, Mr. President."

"And you are assuring that how?"

"His only competition is another member of his party, the Democrats, who has been made independently wealthy with the caveat that he withdraw from the race for personal reasons. He will do that when it is only he and Sorosh Saji fighting over their party's candidacy and it is too late for another to enter the fray. Then it is simply a lot of advertising and wait for November 4th."

"November 4th?"

"Yes, their election day. Saji's party would win, if they put up a trained monkey. The American public hates the current President and for the most part will just vote against his party, the Republicans, and Saji, our man, shall be the next man in the White House."

"Well, Mr. Dubnikov, we too hate the American President, although I am sure Iran's reasons are quite different than those of the American public. He has been a hindrance to all of our expansion and nuclear initiatives for eight years, we will be happy to see him go.

"But tell me, how do we gain from your control over the US President? Your objective is to sell me nuclear warheads. The new US President is not going to look on that any more favorably than the current pain in the ass. What's in it for us?"

"Mr. President, when Sorosh Saji is elected the next President of the United States he will keep at least one of the promises he makes during his campaign. His first act will be to withdraw all US forces from Iraq in under six months."

"And do what with them, Mr. Dubnikov?"

"He will move them into and along the borders of Afghanistan, Pakistan and Turkey, Mr. President."

"Why would he do that, the outgoing President's plan succeeded, Iraq is showing signs of peacefully becoming a democracy, why in the world would he pull out now?"

6

"Because, Mr. President, we will tell him to do so and by that time he will know where his funding has come from since he was eleven. That knowledge will force him to see that the interests of his sponsor are unequivocally his interests."

"And those interests are somehow connected with Afghanistan, Pakistan and Turkey? The only thing those three have in common is ..."

"Smack, Mr. President!"

"Smack?"

"An American slang expression for heroin, the source of the enormous cash flow that has been put at Mr. Saji's disposal since he was eleven years old.

"Explain to me again, just what you get out of this?"

"Mr. President, let us not forget the primary objective of all this is to open the way to sell to your country four thousand Scud nuclear warheads at the bargain basement price of twenty-five million US dollars per nuke."

"Twenty-five million per nuke, one hundred billion dollars, that's rather steep don't you think?"

"Considering Mr. President, that you could sell half of them with the missiles to your oil rich neighbors at four times that price, you will not only recoup your investment, you will make a very healthy profit and I will be glad to function as broker ... for a small percentage of course."

"Of course, Mr. Dubnikov, but tell me, how do I know that this whole conversation is not garbage or your wishful thinking?"

"Because, Mr. Vahdani, if you receive me with great

fanfare and welcome me as the solution to the ongoing distrust of Iran's nuclear program by the UN and its American and European puppeteers, I will see to it that within a week, one of the four thousand Scud nuclear warheads is delivered to the destination in Iran that you designate."

Vahdani silently stared at Vladislav Dubnikov for about two minutes then reaching into his breast pocket pulled out a cell phone, pushed a button and said simply "Come into my conference room," and disconnected.

Within minutes, the door opened and a distinguished gentleman entered. "This is my Minister of Energy, Jalil Rastinpour.

"Jalil, this is Vladislav Dubnikov, United Nations Special Atomic Energy Oversight Envoy to The Islamic Republic of Iran."

Jalil Rastinpour looked both angry and unhappy.

Vahdani went on, "Please plan a rally at Azadi Square, right at the base of the Azadi Monument to welcome Mr. Dubnikov. The theme should be 'welcoming him as the solution to the ongoing distrust of Iran's nuclear program by the UN and its American and European puppeteers'. Make sure that there are more than two hundred fifty thousand people attending and have all the foreign media invited.

"Please have someone see to appropriate accommodations for our guest. Since he will be here for an extended stay, arrange a villa with appropriate staff.

"Thank you, Jalil."

Jalil turned to leave and President Vahdani interrupted his

departure, "Two final points, Jalil, Mr. Dubnikov will be having an item shipped here in the next week or so, it is radioactive and should be handled accordingly, please work with him to make appropriate arrangements. Finally, Jalil, the reports to the United Nations on the findings of the United Nations Special Atomic Energy Oversight Envoy to The Islamic Republic of Iran will be prepared for submission by you; Mr. Dubnikov will provide the format."

For the first time since his entering the room, Jalil Rastinpour had something to say, "Mr. President, am I to understand that I am preparing these reports for his review and changes?"

Dubnikov smiled and said "Jalil Rastinpour, unless you are a poor speller, there will be no changes."

Vahdani and Rastinpour both laughed at this comment and Jalil Rastinpour left the conference room a relaxed and happy Minister of Energy.

President Vahdani turned to Vladislav Dubnikov and said, "Shall we have lunch, we have much to discuss."

"An excellent idea, Mr. President."

Anna Masterson, Hugh Masterson's wife, walked out the French doors opening onto the terrace of the main building of their Long Island, New York compound. Anna, who had been told by Paulina the Masterson's maid at the Long Island compound, that Hugh was having breakfast on the terrace, headed quickly to join him.

Anna and Hugh are partners in Cayman Covert Cyber Reclamation, Ltd., the company through which the Mastersons' operate their business of recovering stolen funds for corporations, organizations and governments. Interesting and definitely rewarding work, but sometimes very dangerous work since essentially what they do is steal back money from bad guys and return it to the good guys.

Anna has been working tirelessly on a theory as to how to keep track of the whereabouts of the Russian villain that the Mastersons had labeled the Sinister One, aka Nikita, whose real name was Vladislav Dubnikov. Nikita hated Anna and Hugh and past efforts to kill them had made it clear that he would go to any end to destroy them.

~~~

On January 18, 2008, in the early morning hours, Nikita launched a rocket attack against the Mastersons' Cayman Brac villa complex, Villa Serenity. The motivation for this arguably insane move was the recovery by the Mastersons of over forty billion of loot that Nikita and his partners had relieved the United Nations and its agencies of over the preceding thirty years. They had pulled this awesome villainy off with the cooperation of a long line of UN senior officials. Fortunately, the villa was (and still is) well protected with an array of weapons including defensive rockets. The attack did not fare well for Nikita and by the time it ended, the Russian's reasons for hating the Mastersons had expanded considerably. Anna and Hugh had no doubts that Nikita would be 'gunning' for them and spent a great deal of time attempting to keep track of his activities and location. Unfortunately, his new role of United Nations Special Atomic Energy Oversight Envoy to The Islamic Republic of Iran was totally out of character for Nikita's career choices. Anna was convinced it was a post he had arranged not only to regenerate his massive wealth, but also to gain a powerful level of global influence and of course to bump off the Mastersons.

A critical weapon in their defense against any new vicious attacks he may launch was tracking his movements.

Anna's efforts were centered on creating a tracking link to a communications device, something like a satellite telephone that Nikita and apparently his co-conspirators carried with them at all times and more importantly they were on at all times. The device, called a Weltall-Kommunikationen Tragbarer Sender-Empfänger-Prototyp Ein, loosely translated Universe Communications' Handheld Transceiver-Prototype One, was a remarkable piece of engineering. A concept product, developed by the German electronics and communications giant Weltall-Kommunikationen AG, it is best described as a walkie-talkie on steroids. Anna, always efficient, tagged the device with the far simpler name, Nikita's Megaphone.

It measures three inches long by two inches wide by one-eighth inch thick and looks more like a credit card with buttons than a satellite communications device.

There are six buttons on the face plus two miniscule holes covered by a fine grill. The two miniscule holes are at the top and bottom of the long side of the device and are for speaking and hearing. One of the six buttons turns the device on or off, powering it and raising or lowering the tiny antenna. Three of the remaining five buttons are for connecting to the other holders of the device individually. The fifth button connects the caller to all of the other three holders in a conference mode.

The sixth or final button is special, when pressed the device is essentially destroyed, not physically but technologically. Pressing that button erases the memory chip in the device.

This was exactly the condition that Anna had received one of the devices from a long time colleague, Patricia Finnerty, from their consulting days, who was now a special advisor to the Florida State Police. Patricia had received the gadget as part of the contents of the pockets of a very wealthy German businessman who had been murdered in a rather spectacular way on Christmas day 2007 at a beach party in Palm Beach. The Florida State Police labs could make nothing of the erased memory so when they suggested farming it out for research by experts in data recovery Patricia immediately thought of Anna.

Anna has been for many years world renowned for her innovative application of technology to a broad spectrum of challenges including security, data recovery and transaction tracking using artificial intelligence in very creative ways.

~~~

Anna was obviously excited about some accomplishment and since she worked well into the night starting again early in the morning, concentrating on tracking the sociopath bent on destroying them, Hugh assumed that she had achieved some success.

"Good morning, you look like the cat that ate the canary! Am I correct in assuming that we're closer to pinning a tail on Nikita than we were last night when you finally came to bed?"

Anna had barely sat down when she began describing, with her eternal passion and enthusiasm, her success overnight.

~~~

Through a process she had patented two years earlier, programs had been running for days digitally 'peeling' back layers of blank memory on the chips in Nikita's Megaphone forwarded by the Florida State Police labs. Anna's program digitally scans the gallium arsenide (the material now used in extremely high speed, super miniaturized memory) chip in the communicator searching for remnants of data. The data is accumulated at each new 'level' of the chip and via another artificial intelligence driven application, assembled into an ever-expanding library. The ultimate objective is to recreate as much as possible of the applications and information that were originally on the chip.

~~~

"I've identified the signature ID of Nikita's Megaphone," she said with pride and animation, "and I've locked in on the satellite that the device uses as its global link. Now get this, Nikita communicates with his buddies by way of a satellite launched by the Russians at 4:31:59 on July 9, 1999."

"That's great," Hugh, said, "I thought…" but he didn't get a chance to finish.

"Wait, Hugh, let me finish, that was the launch of Raduga Gran # 34. The Raduga satellite program was begun by the

Soviets in 1974 and taken over by the Russians after the breakup of the Soviet Union and # 34 was the last launch in the program."

"Yeah, so, Nikita's a Russian who, like the Raduga Satellite, used to be a Soviet," Hugh began to laugh at his own joke, "what difference does it make who owns the satellite? You found the link and now you can track Nikita's movements."

Laughing, not at Hugh's pun but at Hugh laughing at his own joke, Anna once again interrupted him, "Hugh, wait, listen, according to Roscosmos…"

It was now Hugh's turn to interrupt, "Who the hell is Roscosmos?"

"It's the Russian Federal Space Agency, something like our NASA. Anyway, according to Roscosmos the launch of Raduga Gran # 34 self-destructed at 4:33:44 on July 9, 1999, exactly 1 minute and 45 seconds after launch. It appears our boy Nikita and his brotherhood of Russian villains has their own private communications satellite."

"Wow! You talk about secure communications no one even knows the satellite exists so no one would ever even try to hack into it, that is, no one except my beautiful genius. Now what? How do we keep track of the guy wanting to snuff you and me?"

"Well, since about 5:30 this morning, I've been scripting a program that tracks his movements in and around Teheran or anywhere else on the globe that he is, and further, via satellite imaging I'm literally looking at the streets he's on."

"You're amazing, Anna, too bad we can't get those satellite

images real time, we could see who the hell he's with."

"More importantly," said Anna, "after breakfast I start work on a program to monitor and capture the conversations he's having on the device."

"Holy shit," said Hugh, "this could be very interesting."

Anna and Hugh are working at their respective workstations in the office complex of the Masterson Long Island Compound. Anna, wearing oversized sound reduction headphones, is focused intently on her computer screen. Hugh is deeply engrossed in researching wire transfers related to a new client of their company. Suddenly, Anna starts to talk louder and louder, "You have got to be kidding me, my God Nikita, show a little respect at least, after all, he is the Secretary General of the UN."

Realizing that trying to get her attention by talking to her is useless with the earphones on her head, Hugh gets up from his workstation, crosses to the opposite wall and taps Anna on the shoulder.

Anna, being completely in 'her zone' nearly jumps out of her chair, then laughing, goes back to the screen, keys in some commands and takes the earphones from her head. Simultaneously voices come alive in the wall speakers on either side of the 60-inch LCD screen on the north wall.

"What am I hearing?" asks Hugh.

"Our nemesis Nikita having a very interesting conversation with none other than Pham Dac Kien," answers Anna, smiling, with a triumphant look on her face. Hugh, his eyes widening asks, "The Secretary General of the United Nations?"

"None other!"

"Anna, you mean you've worked out the protocols to tap into the conversations to and from Nikita's Megaphone?"

"Sure have! It was tricky. Every time I thought I had it straight, I had to wait for there to be activity on the device.

Problem was, if I could hear nothing I never knew if I was off track or there just was no conversation. Three weeks ago, I started a method where I would set up my program to 'listen' for conversations then move onto another protocol to break into the secure communication channel. I would then do the same on a slightly different protocol, all the time letting the previous listening continue. The script included the capturing of the conversations, if and when the program found one.

"Well, after three weeks, I have one hundred nine experimental hacking protocols working at the same time and each morning I check to see if I've captured any communications.

"This morning when I checked the files of each of the tests I was blown away. Wow did I capture some interesting chatter. Fortunately, they are both using English otherwise the conversation could be in Russian or Vietnamese, neither of which I speak. If that were the case, I wouldn't know who was chatting via Nikita's satellite."

"Anna, this means that not only will you know where Nikita is most of the time, you'll know what he's up to. Fantastic, you're one unbelievable genius!"

"Well now that I've zeroed in on the channel that Nikita's communicator uses, I'll set up an application to monitor it twenty-four/seven and capture all of his communications with whoever is holding other similar devices. This will also give us the capability of tracking the other users on Nikita's network and listening to their conversations, even if they're not talking to Nikita but are talking to each other. That way we'll ultimately identify all of the important folk in Nikita's Club."

Almost 1.8 million people crowded into the National Mall and the surrounding streets to witness Sorosh Saji, a first generation Afghan American, being sworn into office as President of the United States.

~~~

Sorosh Saji grew up in the ghettos of San Francisco, specifically in The Richmond, the vast region north of Golden Gate Park.

He led what appeared to be a charmed life from the age of eleven, particularly for a boy from the ghetto and the child of uneducated immigrant parents from a third world country, Afghanistan. Both of Sorosh's parents worked as unskilled labor for a very wealthy Russian, thought to be the most powerful leader of the Russian crime syndicate in the US, a ruthless man named Vilen Ovinko.

Ovinko met Sorosh Saji May 5, 1979, the day Sorosh turned eleven, actually at a small birthday party his parents were giving him at their home. For whatever reasons, either good intentioned or calculated, the Sajis invited their boss, Ovinko, to the humble affair.

Again, for whatever reason, either good intentioned or calculated, Ovinko attended and spent hours talking to the eleven year old. He returned to the Sajis' home on Tuesday and Thursday afternoons for four weeks, engaging the young Sorosh in three and four-hour conversations covering a wide range of subjects. For another four weeks, he sent his limousine for the boy on Friday afternoon and had him brought with one of his parents to his magnificent estate overlooking the bay in the Sea Cliff area of San Francisco. Once again, Ovinko's motives for introducing basically what could be described as a slum child, to the opulence of his life style, were unclear at the time to all but Vilen. For Vilen, he had found a diamond in the rough that with proper development and control could become an unbelievable asset. His objectives were as clear to him as the processes he used to plant, nourish, harvest and convert the poppy seeds in Afghanistan to the high grade heroin he manufactured to maintain his multi-billion dollar US drug distribution network, his empire's cash cow.

Ten weeks after meeting him, Vilen Ovinko arranged for the eleven-year-old future politician's transfer from his public school in The Richmond to the one hundred and forty year old internationally acclaimed Victor Mueller School for Boys in the Bay Area. The Mueller School was the educational resource of choice for the sons of the powerful in both industry and politics, not only in California but globally.

Sorosh Saji would remain in The Mueller School through high school and his record would indicate academic achievements placing him in the top ten graduates in 1986. He could have attended any Ivy League university, but Vilen's plans for his future called for him to remain in California. California was Ovinko's base of operations and power and it happened to be the port-of-entry for eighty-percent of the heroin he imported. From his first encounter with Saji in 1979, it was Ovinko's plan to 'manufacture' the most powerful politician in California for the simple objective of protecting and enhancing his empire.

Saji earned both a Bachelor of Arts and a Law Degree from UCLA and on graduation in 1993 returned to an appropriate apartment in the Presidio Area and immediately started on the path of a stellar, if not conventional, political career.

A little over seven years later, his mentor, Vilen Ovinko, considered him ready for his first election. After a rise through community based organizations, all of which were funded by Ovinko, he ran for his first meaningful office, President of the Board of Supervisors for San Francisco.

At that time, the election process for that post was unique in that the Board of Supervisors was elected 'at-large'. That is, all candidates running (which could be as many as sixteen or twenty), were all on the ballot. The candidate who received the most votes was elected President of the Board of Supervisors, and the next four or five (a function of how many seats were to be filled) were elected to seats on the board. In 2000, the year Sorosh ran, there were eight candidates for five seats, three very popular incumbents, four fringe candidates and Sorosh Saji who had a campaign bankroll big enough to run for Governor of California.

To the shock of a vast percentage of the citizenry of San Francisco, but not to Vilen, the three incumbents announced their withdrawal from the election at 3:00 PM, Monday November 6, 2000, sixteen hours before the polls opened for the November 7th election. The only name left on the ballot that the majority of the voters had heard in the preceding two months was that of Sorosh Saji. Most people did not bother to vote, but of the 147,653 ballots cast Sorosh got the lion's share, 128,431, almost 87%.

Sorosh Saji was the President of the Board of Supervisors but more importantly, Sorosh had learned from his mentor the secret of winning elections, have more money than any other candidate and use any means at your disposal to get rid of the other candidates.

The team of the puppet, Sorosh Saji, and the puppeteer, Vilen Ovinko, moved fast in an unprecedented climb through the California political labyrinth winning the special 2005 election for US Senator to replace the incumbent who drowned in a freak boating accident. Sorosh squeaked through by a narrow margin to become, in 2006, the United States Junior Senator from California.

As stated, the methodology was simple, using money and an orator's tongue, Sorosh managed by Ovinko, assembled a vast group of supporters to whom he promised everything, committed to and apparently delivered nothing and as a final safeguard eliminated the competition by one means or another. For the 2005 election, the day before the election, every media outlet in the US carried photos of Sorosh's much favored opposition meeting in a restaurant on San Francisco Fisherman's Wharf with a known heroin street dealer from The Richmond. No one heard her protestations of 'setup' and although her claims of innocence were later proven true, it was too late to save the election. She lost.

Next stop for Vilen Ovinko's custom designed professional candidate, The White House.

~~~

To the shock of tens of millions watching on television and those in the mall, Saji's media entrancing demeanor seemed to slip away from him.

The oath, as prescribed by the US Constitution and administered by the Chief Justice of the Supreme Court is 34 words long. Repeating the words after the Chief Justice recited them, Sorosh Saji flubbed his lines by word four! The expected reaction for the 40 year old, the youngest

President to take the oath, would be some level of nervousness. Surprisingly however, in the words of three different network commentators, the new President appeared of all things, to be distracted. At one point, it was so obvious his wife, standing next to him, had to nudge him to pay attention.

Anna came running into the conference room on the first floor of the western tower of the Mastersons' complex on Cayman Brac, Cayman Islands.

The large circular room has four 60-inch plasma screens, one each on the North, South, East and West walls. Hugh, together with the two men who head the Mastersons' security team, Alberto Martinez and Roger Taylor, are watching the inauguration of Sorosh Saji as 44th President of the United States. Each screen has a different perspective because each screen is tuned to a different one of the four major US networks.

The expression on her face is a mixture of fear, pride and anger. She hits a button on the conference table, which turns off the network coverage on the huge flat panel TV on the western conference room wall.

Since Anna had resolved the issues with security and encryption in monitoring the conversations involving Nikita's Megaphone in late October 2008, the computer banks in the Mastersons' Long Island compound had been capturing every conversation between Nikita and the close-knit group of villains sharing the very sophisticated communication method. Most of the conversations had to do with deals for narcotics and nukes amongst Russians, Afghanis and Nikita. Anna had taken her eavesdropping system one-step further; the conversations, once captured, are converted to text, almost instantaneously, using extremely sensitive and highly reliable voice/text conversion software.

Hugh wanting to know what the problem is said, "You look like you've seen a ghost." Anna didn't reply, instead she hit some buttons on the panel in the conference room table and the plasma screen changed to show a text message on the screen while the speakers produced extremely clear voices in the background.

Sorosh Saji *(angry and agitated)* – "Yes, who is this? I received this device this morning from one of my Secret Service people who said I am never to be without it and it is never to be off. Don't you know who I am? I'm about to be sworn in as the President of the United States!

"I'm not really interested in who you are or why and how you arranged to have this strange device delivered to me, but I can assure you it will not be with me and on at all times, in fact, it will not be with me at all in about 30 seconds!"

Nikita *(calm)* – "Sorosh Saji, please just be calm for those thirty seconds and listen.

"Your education, your campaigns, your elections, your marks in school, your jobs, your funding, hell your underwear have all been arranged and paid for by Afghan heroin money, a fact that has never been a secret from your Mamma and Poppa.

"Didn't they ever tell you, Sorosh? They apprenticed you to my friend, colleague and brother-in-law, Vilen Ovinko, at the tender age of eleven. Did you never wonder why he has paid for and directed your every move for these past 29 years or did you just never let your brain go to the unusual nature of that relationship?

"I understand he will be joining you and Mrs. Saji, on the party rounds tonight. Feel free to discuss this conversation with him. Oh, if your Mamma and Poppa tag along ask them about why Vilen was invited to your eleventh birthday party, he and I have always been curious about that.

"Anyway, Sorosh, every bit of Vilen's funding and directing of your life since you were eleven years old has been documented. In fact, we have some lovely home movies with you and Vilen, but more about that at another time.

"Vilen's ambitions for you were not as grand as mine, but once you reached the US Senate you became interesting to me and my colleagues.

"When you get back to the White House tonight there will be a video in the DVD player in your bedroom. Make sure to watch it with Mrs. Saji, it will make it quite clear to both of you how devastating is the information we could provide to the media. It is a kind of retrospective on your rise in less than fifteen years from a law school graduate to the role of the most powerful leader in the world. Once you and Mrs. Saji see it, try to imagine just how quickly will be your fall from that role.

"Congratulations on your new and prestigious position. Enjoy it. Tomorrow I will talk to you, and we will start the process of shaping the United States to fit mine and my colleagues needs…no correct that, desires. Goodbye, Mr. President, relax and enjoy the ride. We will tell you what to do regarding every aspect of your new job just as Vilen has been doing for the past 29 years.

"Don't worry you are in good hands, our hands. Oh and, Sorosh, do not, I repeat, do not do anything with that strange device as you call it, other than have it with you and on at all times."

Nikita's Megaphone went silent.

Hugh, Anna, Alberto and Roger stared at the screen in horror.

PART ONE

Anna and Hugh Masterson spend November through April at their magnificent retreat, Villa Serenity, on Cayman Brac in the Cayman Islands. This evening they are sitting in the gazebo, on the beach in front of the main house, just finishing dinner.

This enviable getaway is nestled on oceanfront property with a private sand beach on the southern coast of the island overlooking Hawksbill Bay.

~~~

It was not always this way. For twenty years, the Mastersons were moderately successful entrepreneurs. Then in 2006, Anna and Hugh got involved, unintentionally, in uncovering corruption, murder and general mayhem at the United Nations while consulting to that organization. Hugh's curiosity about an alleged suicide in a park near their New York City apartment dragged the two of them into an intrigue surrounding the massive theft of $29.7 billion from the corruption plagued UN run 'Iraq Oil for Food Program'.

It was a rather drastic move from their technology based consulting business to sleuthing on a global scale, but at the end of the adventure, things had changed for them forever.

They were rich, they had made some nasty enemies and they had come to the attention of the national security establishment in the United States Government.

They also realized from the 'Oil for Food' saga that they had a unique skill. Using sophisticated technology, they were good at finding and very quietly taking money from people and organizations.

Thus, in 2007, Anna and Hugh formed Cayman Covert Cyber Reclamation, Ltd. and began offering their unique services, at a fee contingent on recovery, to get back funds stolen. The stealing villains include dictators, rogue governments, greedy business enterprises or just plain crooks. The Mastersons track the stolen funds, reclaim them and return them to the rightful owners, thereby letting the good intentioned folk have another try, but this time with a little more smarts and a little less naiveté.

The interesting twist in their unusual enterprise is that in the course of stealing back from the crooks, they frequently find an opportunity to net out their personal form of unique justice often resulting in the untimely demise of the greedy villains.

When they committed to the new business, a major aspect they had to plan for was security, both physical and cyber. After much consideration and research searching for appropriate Cayman headquarters, they settled into 6.3 acres of waterfront property on the fourteen square mile Cayman Brac, an island just under ninety miles northeast of Grand Cayman. The property is not only aesthetically perfect it is isolated and eminently defensible. It fronts on a private sandy beach, on the southern coast of the island, overlooking Hawksbill Bay, which in turn opens onto the Caribbean. The main house is set back from the water two hundred feet and is two hundred feet from the main (and only) road. The horseshoe beach fronting the original acreage is as wide as the property, almost five hundred fifty feet. In other words, the villa house itself was in the center of an almost square piece of land five hundred by five hundred fifty feet fronted by water and backed by a single entry road and Caribbean jungle land on either side. The staff housing is in its own building east of the main house.

After a serious attack in January 2008, the Mastersons bought ten additional acres, five each of the Caribbean jungle property on either side of the original piece. This gave them an additional four hundred thirty-five feet of buffer property and beachfront on either side of the original compound where they could locate additional defensive security equipment.

The compound is completely self-contained with its own electrical generators that can, when needed, replace all the power provided by Cayman Energy. Further, there is an onsite water purification plant should Cayman Water Company Limited fail to provide adequate water.

Some other details that will make for improved visualization as this saga continues: the main house is fourteen thousand six hundred square feet; has six bedrooms, eight bathrooms, a two-story living room and an eighteen-foot bar in an entertainment room overlooking Hawksbill Bay. It includes a huge office area with satellite communications and about two million dollars worth of cutting-edge technology equipment. Outside there is a twenty by twenty-foot gazebo with wet bar, a swimming pool and a four car detached garage.

The layout of the villa is interesting in that it somewhat resembles a castle. The main body of the house is a two-story rectangle one hundred foot wide by sixty foot deep. On the southwest and southeast corners rise three-story round towers a little over twenty-three feet in diameter.

The eastern tower is for guests with suites on the third and second floor and a library, sitting room and small gym on the first floor. There are more guest accommodations on the eastern half of the second floor.

The western tower is Anna and Hugh's domain with their sleeping and living quarters on the second floor and their private working environment on the third floor. The third floor is set up with two identical work settings; one covering the eastern arc of the circle and half the southern arc, the other taking up the western arc and the other half of the southern. The area is full of the tools of their trade, technology. It appears reasonably simple on the surface. Each work area is equipped with three screens and associated keyboards, telephones with speakerphones, plus printers and other peripherals.

Each work place has a seventy-two by forty-eight inch white electronic copyboard mounted on a partition behind the workstation area chair. These are the modern version of the old standby black board using colored erasable markers on a white laminate surface instead of chalk on slate. In addition, everything written or drawn on the board is digitally captured to a server. Each is located in such a way as to be visible to both work areas.

Finally, there is a sixty-inch LCD screen on the north wall at a point that it can be seen from both work sections.

The first floor of the western tower is a circular conference room twenty-three feet in diameter with a ten-foot diameter circular conference table in the center surrounded by eight very comfortable conference chairs.

There are four, sixty-inch LCD screens, spread evenly around the walls of the room.

Embedded in eight positions on the conference table, in

front of each chair, is a control panel including keyboard, roller mouse ball and a sub-panel that resembles a very complex video remote; plus Ethernet jacks for notebook PC connection.

The first floor of the main part of the villa includes kitchen, breakfast room, living room, dining room, sitting rooms, den/entertainment/media room and bathrooms.

A further security feature; the building is concrete and steel construction.

East of the building is a two-story staff residence containing four one-bedroom apartments. This is where the four Caymanian members of the villa staff live full time: Della Watler, age 42, the housekeeper; Twila Bodden, 38, the cook; Jennifer Ebanks, the 24-year-old maid and Wayne McLaughlin, 40, gardener/handyman/driver.

Finally, there is the nerve center of the Mastersons' defensive security at the Cayman compound. They have created a very complex security infrastructure that is as close to impregnable as possible. It includes not only monitoring capabilities, but also an impressive arsenal of very modern weaponry. These were obtained by their security team leads: Alberto Martínez, an American of Puerto Rican descent from the Bronx, (a borough in New York City) and Roger Taylor, an African American also from the Bronx. Alberto had ten years in Marine Force Recon before joining the Mastersons and Roger spent ten years as a US Navy Seal before becoming part of Cayman Covert Cyber Reclamation, Ltd. Without giving away their defense secrets, they have everything from small arms to mobile field grade missiles.

The surveillance systems are state of the art thermal

infrared technology. They monitor and record activity throughout the property and its perimeter twenty-four/seven.

All of this equipment is housed in a building on the west side of the grounds, on the opposite side of the original compound property from the staff housing, about three hundred feet from the beach. It includes a kind of war room where all of the systems are controlled and where any activity can be carried out in a conference room like atmosphere. It looks like a miniature of the one in the White House that every American has seen on TV or in the movies; large LCD screens on the walls, monitors, and all the bells and whistles.

In addition, on the second floor, there is a two-bedroom apartment for the security folk on duty since coverage is twenty-four/seven.

After the January 2008 events, the Mastersons determined that they needed an expanded security staff. Alberto and Roger recruited specialists in several fields from various branches of the U. S. Armed forces and by November 2009, the compound boasted a compliment of ten security personnel, eight specialists led by Roger and Alberto.

To house this group, a concrete and steel ten-unit apartment complex was built to the west of the security building connected by an underground tunnel.

However, the real pride of Roger and Alberto is behind the main structure, but reached through a concrete and steel passageway. It is a bunker built partially into a low hill on the property. This bunker's contents are confidential, but have already saved the lives of many if not all the compound's residents.

The whole security complex, as noted above, is built of steel reinforced concrete. However, to maintain the serene aesthetics of the beautiful Caribbean paradise, it is covered in a veneer to blend with the other buildings on the Cayman Brac south shore.

This compound, together with the complex on the North Shore of Long Island, New York, is paid for and maintained with funds earned through the recovery of stolen loot.

One or more of the over one hundred five organizations under the United Nations' umbrella are usually involved in each cash recovery project of Cayman Covert Cyber Reclamation. Generally when describing their business the Mastersons usually say, "We recover tens of billions of dollars stolen from or through the United Nations by villains working for or with the United Nations. It is an extremely profitable and an endlessly self replenishing market."

~~~

This evening before the US Thanksgiving Day holiday, Anna and Hugh were sitting alone in the gazebo looking out on the calm Hawksbill Bay as the sunlight was slowly sliding towards dusk.

"Well, this will be the biggest group we have had here for Thanksgiving since we took over the villa," said Anna.

"And not one relative; it should be a very relaxing celebration," replied Hugh with a smile.

"Yeah, the whole group is looking forward to it," replied Anna laughing. "Della and Twila started preparing around Halloween. First, they had to study up on what Thanksgiving was then spent two weeks planning the menu and getting all the supplies from the States for a 'real New England Thanksgiving' as they have announced it to all.

"Alberto told me that the eight new security specialists think they died and went to heaven. All of them spent at least the last three Thanksgivings in less than desirable places: Iraq, Afghanistan, Korean DMZ, Pakistan border. Hell, Kateri hasn't been home to Massachusetts in six years."

"Anna, did I hear her arguing with Twila and Della about the Thanksgiving menu yesterday?"

"Yesterday and every day since their planning began. She points out that the books they are reading and the recipes are not the real Thanksgiving. She wants them to make the menu more like the original."

"Which was what?"

"Fish, lobsters, eels, vegetables, fruits and nuts, but she does agree that there was probably wild turkey and maybe duck. However, she is adamant that there was a lot of seafood and definitely no potatoes."

Laughing, Hugh, who had been looking out at the Hawksbill Turtles heading for their nests around the bay, turned towards Anna saying, "What the hell got Kateri so adamant on this little search for accuracy?"

"Hugh, she is very proud of her Native American heritage…"

"Yeah and I'm very proud of my Pilgrim heritage…"

Anna burst out laughing, "Pilgrim heritage? In November 1621, your ancestors were probably sitting in a one room, stone cottage next to a bog near Dublin drinking Irish whiskey. On the other hand, Kateri is a descendent of the

Wampanoag, the Native Americans who were at the first Thanksgiving. If anyone knows, what the Pilgrims ate and drank that day, my bet goes with Kateri.

"Anyway, last I heard we are having all the dishes, those from Twila and Della's historical recipes and those from Kateri's ancestors."

"Wow, this is going to be some feast, I'm getting hungry just talking about it. Are we eating outside?"

"Yep, right here on the beach, just like the Pilgrims and the Wampanoag Indians."

Anna got up from her chair and walked around the gazebo and turning towards Hugh said, "Hugh, it's ten months since we uncovered the reality of the forces behind the new American President and we have never discussed it again since that day. Roger and Alberto have approached me several times asking if we have any plans."

"What do you tell them?"

"I turn the question back on them and say simply that when they have any ideas as to just what the hell we do with this devastating knowledge they should let me know because I haven't got a clue."

"They ask me the same thing weekly. My response, in my usual wiseass way, is that my role in this team is to keep track of what Mr. Vladislav Dubnikov, known to them as Nikita, is up to regarding any evil he may be planning against our expanding group. Further, thanks to you, I not only know where he is, I know who he's making plans with and what the substance of those plans is. If, at any time, I conclude that his attentions are veering towards injuring our group in any way, shape or form, I will call a planning

35

session to launch defensive as well as offensive measures."

"I know, Hugh, they tell me what you tell them as I am sure they tell you my answers. The problem is all ten members of our security force are true patriots and since every week more devastating crap is happening in the US as a direct result of Sorosh Saji's action…"

"Or inaction," Hugh interrupted.

"…or inaction and it is really upsetting them all. I don't know if all ten of them know what we learned on January 20th, since we never told Roger or Alberto not to share with them, but if they do, we have ten young patriots that I am sure are chomping at the bit to put an end to the charade playing out in Washington, DC."

"This means, my Anna, that we had better come up with a plan of what the hell we do with this gem of knowledge that has fallen into our laps."

"Well it didn't really fall into our laps," Anna responded. "I spent about three thousand hours cracking into the communications network that Nikita uses to manage his puppet in the White House, but I understand what you're saying."

"OK, please sit back down and let's talk about what each of us is doing," said Hugh, "and see if a go forward plan emerges from our accomplishments to date. You're working on redistributing the billions we recovered. I spend every day analyzing what Nikita is up to, where and with whom. Maybe we should develop a plan for both endeavors that the whole team can understand and participate in."

"You mean like we used to do in the consulting days;

where we are, where we want to be and how do we get there, right?"

"Exactly, let's give each other a synopsized version of where we are now, right here, tonight. Then we can set a schedule for each of us to come back with the where we are, where we want to be and how do we get there plans. After that, we bring in our ten specialists for their input and we lock down a go forward strategy. What do you think?"

"Great," said Anna, "I'll go first."

~~~

"Well, the escrow account in Regal Bank of the Caymans contains the funds recovered for the last President from the US\UN run Iraqi oil industry debacle plus the additional funds found in the 'Sinister Three's accounts. All other funds from recovery projects have been turned back to the rightful owners."

"How much is in there now?"

"Well, for whatever reasons, Cranebrook never got back to us on where he and the White House wanted us to transfer the ten and a half billion directly related to the Iraqi oil business fiasco."

"Maybe they were waiting until after the election so they would know where to put it in order that they could control it. It's somewhat tough to hide ten and a half billion bucks if you're a couple of unemployed former politicians. They sure as hell don't want it turned over to Saji's administration and watch it disappear down that rat hole. I guess they thought it safest to leave it with us and then call us the next time their group is in control of the US Government."

"Yeah, right," answered Anna, "let me know how that works out for them. Anyway, that ten and a half billion is sitting there with the thirty-three and a third billion we happened on in Nikita's and the other two guys bank accounts. That makes it almost forty-four billion that has been sitting in Regal Bank of the Caymans earning interest at the whopping rate of 1.25% since January 2008."

"Poor Stuart Jefferson, he thought when he got the original forty-four billion dollar transfer that he would spend the rest of his life playing golf as President of the largest one office bank in the world. That is until we told him we wanted interest on the escrow balances at 1.25%. He now spends every waking hour searching out secure places to invest it to make a profit for the bank."

"Ahh, he's doing OK. He just turns around and lends it through the US Fed and the Bank of England to healthy banks in the US and the UK for as much as he can get over 1.25%."

"Anyway, Hugh, the account now has almost forty-five billion in it counting the interest since January 2008."

"Wow, that's a lot of dough!"

"You're telling me. I'm trying to break it down and link it to the hundreds of scams that those three pulled off over almost forty years starting with the three million in 1967 from UNOPID in the Congo."

"Yeah, UNOPID, the United Nations Organization Promoting Industrial Development; that little scam they pulled off was the training ground for their development into crooks on a global scale and billions. I wonder if that was the kind of industrious development the United Nations had in mind when they set up UNOPID?"

"Probably not, but if the UN had such good intentions why is it these three could find crook buddies inside all the hundreds of organizations and projects? They stole over thirty-three billion bucks from those organizations and that's not counting the Iraq ten billion buck oil scam. Moreover, while we're on that topic, why are the controls so loose that they could get away with the scams for almost forty years?"

"Crook buddies! I love you! That's so cool, Anna; it would make a great reality TV show: the Sinister Three and their crook buddies clean out the UN coffers; tune in next Tuesday at …"

"Enough, Hugh, you get wackier by the day. Are we going to continue with our synopsized 'where we are' discussion or should we just …"

"Sorry, you're right. Back to your …shall we say challenge. What are you doing trying to assemble a history of the scams and how much for each?"

"Exactly! I literally started with that first three million bucks the bastards stole from the seriously poor folk in the Congo and started tracking the UN organizations they moved to. That was not as difficult as it would seem since we have the United Nations Pension Fund's UN Human Resource records from 1949 through 2006 when our consulting contract ended. It gives me not only where they worked, but what they did and how much salary the UN paid them. Of course, the salary was small change compared to the take from their villainous endeavors."

"How long did they stay with the UN?"

"Get this, all three stayed on the UN payroll right up to their retirement at sixty. They retired between 2003 and

2005, one a year. The icing on the cake, of course, is that they are all receiving their pensions. Well, at least Nikita is. In the case of Charles and Konrad, since they're dead, their wives are getting the monthly checks.

"That absurdity aside, the history of their posts within the UN has given me a baseline to research projects and the accounting associated with those projects for the first seventeen or so years they were UN employees. In the last twenty years, since 1984, they must have had a lot of UN senior management on their payroll. All three were liaison officers between UN high cost projects all over the globe and the various Secretary Generals and the General Assembly during those twenty years. An interesting element of their jobs, they reported only to the Secretary General. I think the last two are not the only ones made wealthy by the Sinister Three. Anyway, for those twenty years I hacked into the UN archives and lifted every one of the five hundred sixty eight reports they filed. Add those to the projects they were directly involved in between 1967 and 1987 and our industrious trio have had their fingers in nine hundred ten high end projects between 1967 and 2004."

"Hell, Anna, assuming that the money they stole earned income over that forty years or so, they probably ripped off the UN organizations for about twenty-five billion bucks directly. That's a little over twenty-seven million per project."

"Right and then you realize that in that same forty years the UN pumped over a trillion bucks into the African programs alone. It's no wonder that watchdog organizations never caught on."

"Plus, Anna, the fact that they shrewdly included as their

crook buddies, senior officials in both the UN and the countries involved, it's easy to understand how it went on so long un-noticed."

"Anyway, enough of the trip along the crooked yellow brick road of the Sinister Three, back to my process of distributing their ill-gotten loot.

"I've assembled vast details about the nine hundred ten projects that were the source of the thirty-three billion not related to the Iraqi oil rip-off and have allocated the thirty-three billion across all the projects based on their original size. I've sorted the list by date, oldest first, and I'm now beginning the process of analyzing them in that order to determine where the funds should go to do the most good. For instance, the first embezzlement, the UNOPID in 1967 for three million bucks, was part of a ten million dollar project to build a children's' hospital in the Niari region of the Republic of the Congo. There were so many crooks in this endeavor that the only thing built was a small building for approximately one million dollars. There was no hospital and children continued to get sick and die with no facility to help them. However, forty years later, in 2007, the Maryhill Missionary Sisters sent one lone nun, Sister Kathleen Todd, to attempt the creation of a health facility in this poverty-stricken area of Africa. The small building built in 1967 was unoccupied and decaying, but this 64-year-old Sister Todd organized the people in the area, got the building cleaned up and functioning. Now this one nun is unrelenting in getting contributions from people and companies, volunteer medical people and students and turned the place into a working clinic. Three million bucks will go a long way in helping and will certainly put a smile on the good sister's face."

"How are you controlling getting the money exactly where you want it to go?"

"I contacted Arthur McCauley and he has assigned one of his staff attorneys to work with me in assuring that the funds get used for what we plan. In Sister Todd's case, the funds will go to the Maryhill Missionary Sisters in trust for the clinic run by Sister Todd and she is the controlling trustee. All this hasn't happened yet, but as you can see the details have all been mapped and ready to roll."

"When will you start actually paying out money?"

"I am going to give the Maryhill Missionary Sisters their three million Christmas week. After the first of the year as I resolve where to spend each of the remaining nine hundred nine shares, I'll dispense more of the funds."

"Are you holding back our 2.5% fee?"

"Of course, dear, but it will not cost the beneficiaries anything. I am only distributing the original thirty-three and a third billion as it came out of the Sinister Three accounts. It has earned about six hundred twenty-five million in interest in Regal Bank of the Caymans and by the time it is all distributed that sum will reach the eight hundred twenty-five million dollar 2.5% fee."

"I don't mean to sound greedy, Anna, but this is one hell of an expensive operation we have undertaken."

"I know, but remember we have the other ten plus billion and I have a funny suspicion no one is coming looking for that any time soon."

"No one but Nikita!"

"Yeah, Hugh, that crossed my mind. If he gets wind that we are spending what he perceives is his billions, he's going to be one pissed Russian and I think we will become more important to his agenda.

"OK; that's what I spend my days doing and will be doing for pretty much all of 2010. Bring me up to speed on tracking Nikita and monitoring the conversations."

~~~

"First, let me tell you that after you broke the code for Nikita's Megaphone in October 2008 and we decided that we had to monitor and analyze his conversations to keep one step ahead of him, I figured it would be a one day a week effort for one of us. That all changed with the conversation between him and Saji the day we learned the President of the United States was a puppet of international arms and drug dealers."

"I know, Hugh, I thought we would take turns at tracking Nikita and both concentrate on distributing the thirty-three billion, but when we uncovered that bombshell what choice did we have. Like I keep telling Alberto and Roger, I still don't know what we're going to do with what we keep learning, but we've got to keep listening. Don't you agree?"

"Yeah, but it has become a full time job."

"Why? Do they talk that much on their walkie-talkies?"

"No. It's not so much the volume of the conversations as figuring out the meaning behind what they are saying. I may listen to a five-minute exchange, but then I will spend eight hours researching the subject matter of that conversation to piece together the implications. Also, there has been an interesting development."

"What's that?"

"Remember that you determined that three of the six buttons on the phone were for communicating with three other devices? We figured out there were only four people on the network."

"Yeah, we guessed it was Nikita, his two partners, Charles and Konrad plus the Secretary General of the UN. We could never prove that Charles had one, but we knew that the one Pat Finnerty sent me belonged to Konrad. I would say that when I found the satellite communications link and broke in on the conversation between Nikita and the UN Secretary General, Pham Dac Kien, it confirmed that the fourth villain on the network was the UN Secretary General. So, since we have one of the original four there were probably only three bad guys on the network."

"Yeah, that's what I expected to find, but that is not the case."

"So, Hugh, what are you saying, there are four people you hear on the network? Maybe they replaced Konrad's device and recovered the one Charles probably had. Who are the four?"

"That's just it, Anna, there are more than four."

"How many?"

"Thus far, I have identified nine including Nikita himself."

"Nine! Well they must have come out with a new generation of Nikita Megaphones," Anna went on. With the original model, the buttons used to connect with each other were for single channel connects. The conference button simply connected with the three channels on the direct dial buttons. Either it's a much bigger device or they've added buttons to let them put in combinations to connect to a larger number of villains. Like four buttons will let them have twenty-four combinations; five buttons one hundred twenty; six …"

"OK,' said Hugh, "I get it, but somehow I don't think the inner circle will even reach twenty-four. I don't care how they reach each other as long as they don't change the frequency they've carved out of the satellite. As long as they stay on that frequency, we're tapping into unencrypted communications between the phones on the network. If they move to a different frequency or worse a different satellite, we're through. Remember, we found them because we had one of the devices and you brilliantly reverse engineered the communications protocols."

"Don't worry, Hugh. They think that no one is even aware of the existence of the satellite so they ain't going anywhere."

"Yeah, you're probably right since someone designed and manufactured a new generation of Nikita's dynamic walkie-talkie."

"OK, Hugh, who are the nine in the club now?"

"Anna, it is one scary group. Individually they are a bunch of gangsters, but when you put them together, you have the makings of one hell of an evil cabal.

"Thus far, the nine members of Nikita's gang are of course: Nikita and his closest buddy, Vilen Ovinko; his son, Vladimir Dubnikov; his Russian lawyer, Cheslav Bocharkov and Boris Batkin, Chairman of Bank Snachala Dlits'a; Nikita's private Russian bank. Those five are just a normal bunch of bad guys in the global drug trade, but when you add in the other four you have a very frightening group and the nucleus of an organization that has unprecedented power."

"OK, Hugh, enough dramatics. Who are the other four?"

"First to come up on the network was Pham Dac Kien, Secretary General of the United Nations. The next guy I encountered in a conversation was Heydar Vahdani, the President of the Islamic Republic of Iran, and, of course, Nikita now communicates quite frequently with our esteemed President, Sorosh Saji. Those conversations would be great for a sitcom were they not so horrifying…"

"What do you mean 'great for a sitcom'? How so?"

"Nikita tells the leader of the free world what he will do next and President Saji whines and weeps."

"Weeps? You mean Saji cries?"

"Yep, you got it. He cries as he complains that he can't implement any of his ideas."

"And what does Nikita say?"

"He tells him he has no ideas."

"OK, enough about that mess. That leaves one more member of the club. Who is that?"

"Ah, the voice of the man it took me a week to track down and identify; Dimitri Demochev. He's a former buddy of Nikita and Ovinko from the Soviet days who now holds the post of Director General of RFTABO."

"What the hell is RFTABO?"

"Rossijskaya Federaciya Tehnologicheskoye i YAdernoye B'uro Oploshnosti; translation: 'the Russian Federation, Technological and Nuclear Oversight Bureau'. This guy has absolute control over every class of nuclear and biological weapons system owned by the Russian Federation.

"Well, once I figured out who the guy was I began to wonder why is the United Nations' Special Atomic Energy Oversight Envoy to The Islamic Republic of Iran talking to the guy who controls the largest nuke arsenal in the world?"

"Did you find out why?"

"Yeah, but let me continue explaining the process I've been following since that fateful day in January when we learned who is really running the US Government. That way it will make more sense and then you will know everything I know.

"When I first started to spend a lot of time eavesdropping, your system was generating files of the conversations faster than I could keep up with cataloging them. It wasn't always clear who Nikita was talking to. He would connect and just start talking and the other guy would jump in without identifying himself. There was no reason for either of them to use names as they each new who was on the other end of the line. Sometimes it would get really confusing because Nikita would bring in a third and occasionally a fourth party. Fortunately, your program differentiates in the text transcription documents so caller one is always the guy initiating the call. For all the calls I have cataloged, Nikita is the initiator. I haven't found any that were started by one of the other nine. Anyway, caller two is the first person Nikita calls, caller three the next, and so on. That at least clearly identified for me both sides of the conversations, thanks to you.

"Now, keep in mind that I had no idea who Nikita was

communicating with or how many there were. However, early on, listening to the voice files I determined that there were more than three or four. My method from that enlightening moment was simple. I spent weeks listening to the voice files and creating a cast of characters. Each new character I isolated, I created a voiceprint for and gave them an identifier: BG01, BG02, BG03, etc. By April, I had a master database of Nikita and his eight buddies with their voiceprints, very extensive voiceprints. Then I was ready to roll."

"OK, I bite, Hugh. What does the 'BG' stand for…no let me guess 'Bad Guy'."

"Ahh damn! How did you guess?"

"Oh God, you are so predictable; such simple structures from such a complex brain."

"Anyway, I wrote a program that essentially listened to every one of the conversations. By May this year, we had over sixteen hundred on the server. The program then compared them to Nikita's and the other eight voiceprints and separated them into groups: Nikita, who was labeled BG01 of course, and BG02, Nikita and BG03, etc. If it were a conversation with more than two participants, the group would be Nikita and BG03 and BG06 or whatever.

"Once I had every conversation categorized it became much clearer what was going on. Nikita's conversations break down into four major groupings: heroin, nukes, money and political destabilization."

"Political destabilization, what do you mean?"

"Simply put, in order for Nikita and the inside group to make the huge amounts of money and power they are pursuing by way of nukes and drugs, they must keep the eyes of the world distracted. Their method is to create new bursts of havoc in those countries and organizations that may want to stop them."

"Who makes up the inside group?"

"Well first off, it took a lot of analysis and listening to a bunch of narcissistic villains being interviewed or making speeches. To replace the bad guy codes with names, I listened to dozens of conversations between Nikita and one of the bad guys and tried to identify from the substance of the talks, who it could possibly be. Then, I would search archives all over the world for interviews and conversations and run the voiceprint of who I suspected that particular bad guy was against the voice from the archive. One by one, over months, I identified all nine.

"The inside six are: Nikita; his son, Vladimir; his long time buddy and drug czar, Vilen Ovinko; his lawyer, Cheslav Bocharkov; his banker, Boris Batkin; and finally Dimitri Demochev."

"That's the guy controlling the Russian nukes, right?"

"Yep, and he is the guy that is the conduit to the merchandise that in the end is going to make them unbelievably rich if the early discussions are any indications of the money involved."

"How much are we talking about?"

"Hang onto your hat, one hundred billion bucks minimum!"

"What the hell are they selling and to who?"

"I am still putting together the details, but from the pieces I have picked up so far Nikita is the middle man selling four thousand nuclear warheads at twenty-five million a pop to Iran. Then, he will act as broker selling two or three thousand of them to other countries like North Korea, Syria and Venezuela at a healthy profit to Iran, and a healthy commission to him and his cartel."

"Holy shit," said Anna. "And in order for this to go down, he has to keep the world concentrating on other things, any other things.

"So the non-insider group of three is: his customer, Heydar Vahdani, the Iranian President; Pham Dac Kien, the UN Secretary General; and our own illustrious President, Sorosh Saji. What a cast for Nikita's sideshow.

"They can keep stirring the flames and create major fires, two and three at a time, to keep the US and its few active allies scrambling to put them out. The rest of the world will pull the covers over their collective heads and pray for the 'bad things' to stop."

"Yeah, but there's more I think. I'm putting together the conversations Nikita has with Saji and I am beginning to see a pattern."

"What kind of pattern?"

"I'm not sure because I'm still analyzing it. I should have something in the next week or two."

"My God, Hugh, we are sitting on a global, nuclear powder keg. What's your idea on where we go from here?"

"I think you should stay on distributing the thirty-three billion. Not only will we get the money back to the originally intended recipients, but also, as you keep peeling the onion we keep learning more about Nikita's connections and colleagues. In addition, we get more insight as to what his agenda is.

"I'll concentrate on monitoring and analyzing what the Nikita group is up to. I think this is critical now because once he gets wind of the fact you are giving away billions he perceives belongs to him, things will really heat up for us.

Along the way, of course, it may prove wise and valuable to keep on top of their progress in spreading nukes around the world."

Sunday night's weekly grand party in the east room of the residence didn't end until almost three AM Monday morning. As the last of the revelers made their way through the entrance hall and out the north portico to their waiting vehicles, Sorosh Saji and his wife, Lucile, took the family elevator in the entrance hall to the second floor living quarters. On exiting the elevator, the President went directly to the master bedroom. Mrs. Saji looked in on their two sons in the east and west bedrooms just down the center hall from the Sajis' bedroom.

By the time Mrs. Saji got to the master bedroom, the President was lying face down diagonally across the king sized bed, his tuxedo still on.

~~~

Lucile Saji, Sorosh Saji's wife and thus the First Lady, was born Lucile Maria Regina Ramirez Mendoza. She was third generation of a Mexican American family of significant wealth. A graduate of UCLA & UCLA Law; she met Sorosh while doing pro bono work in San Francisco. Their backgrounds could not have been more different.

Lucile Saji was raised in aristocratic, genteel surroundings where the trappings of wealth and power were played down. Partying took the form of small dinner parties or Sunday afternoon barbecues on the family's magnificent estate in the west San Fernando Valley. The guests included the sub-group of the rich and famous who, like Lucile's parents, protected their privacy.

Prior to moving to Washington to take up the duties of First Lady, she was the youngest partner in the San Francisco law firm, Beregovoi, Zhukov, Conroy & Salazar.

She went to work for the prestigious group of lawyers on graduating from UCLA law in 1995. Her abilities, enhanced by her tenacity and clear thinking, resulted in her moving rapidly up the ladder to partner status by 1999.

Two minor footnotes; Beregovoi, Zhukov, Conroy & Salazar handled all of the legal work for Lucile's family enterprises and all of Sorosh Saji's patron, Vilen Ovinko's, work.

While taking on some of the firm's pro bono work for various community organizations, Lucile met Sorosh Saji.

Three significant events in Lucile's life occurred in 2000. She was made a full partner in Beregovoi, Zhukov, Conroy & Salazar, the youngest since the firm was founded in 1853. Her family announced her engagement to marry the up and coming community organizer, Sorosh Saji. Finally, the law firm placed her in charge of all their work for Vilen Ovinko's many community endeavors.

However, Lucile was only occasionally brought in on issues involving Ovinko's business enterprises. These were handled by a team of nine partners and eighteen associates, comprised mostly of criminal lawyers, a somewhat unusual condition, but one that Lucile seemed perfectly at ease with.

They were married in June 2001 and by the time they moved into the White House the Sajis had two boys; Victor (Sorosh wanted to name him Vilen after Vilen Ovinko, but Victor was the closest Lucile would go) and Peter, a solid Christian name to please Lucile's mother.

Victor was six in 2009 when they moved into the second

floor of 1600 Pennsylvania Avenue and Peter was four.

~~~

"Are you sobbing, Sorosh?" asked Lucile, not really surprised.

"That party was a disaster. I don't want to have any more of them. Those people are all ungrateful and worse than that, they are all disrespectful."

"Well, the food was great, the wine even better and the entertainment was absolutely out of this world. As for the guests, fortunately, being First Lady doesn't stop boozed up actors, musicians and millionaires from flirting. I had a great time. Maybe you would have a better time at parties if you talked to more than wonks from the media. We're here, Sorosh, you can stop campaigning. In fact, I have no idea why you and that weenie Press Secretary, Jack Tatter, invite any of the media people to our Sunday night festivities. They are arrogant and besides that they are very boring."

"They got me elected. They only asked the questions Vilen's people supplied them with and never once exploited the times I screwed up the answer. They only aired or printed what Vilen's people had told them to and never a word more. Besides Vilen says I must invite them."

"OK, OK. So what has you upset this time?"

"They're saying I'm making them look like fools because they did nothing but tell the voters all the great changes I was going to make. Instead, the country is slowly slipping into the sewer."

"Sorosh, dear, did someone actually say that 'the country is slowly slipping into the sewer' or are you being a bit dramatic?"

"Cal came up to me while I was talking to that dynamite singer. Wow she is…"

"A whore, Sorosh! Anyway, you're talking about Cal Thompson from VPNN? He said this to you in front of that messed up girl?"

"No, no, he came up to me and said quietly that, 'we had to talk'. She didn't hear a word she was too occupied…"

"Talking about herself I'm sure. Stay on topic, Mr. President, I know it's difficult without a speech from Vilen's people, but try this could be serious. Now go on. Did you meet him to talk?"

"Yeah, he left and as he passed me he told me he would meet me in the Green Room. I waited a short time and left as if I was going to the bathroom and went into the Green Room. There he was with two other anchors from different networks and some guy I didn't recognize."

"Four of them…you met alone with three media talking heads and a guy you don't even know? Vilen Ovinko did you no favors keeping you in a goddamned protective bubble from your eleventh birthday.

"Well, you met with them. It's too late to do anything about that, Sorosh. Tell me what went on."

"They show no respect, none!"

"Sorosh, please, give me specifics. What happened after you went into the Green Room? Who started talking first?"

"Thompson, Cal Thompson, he started talking as soon as I was inside the door. You won't believe it. I walked into the room and one of the others shut the door and...."

"Who shut the door, Sorosh?"

"Carlton Moore."

"The guy from AATN?"

"Yeah, he's the anchor on the six o'clock news on the African American Television Network. You remember he had us on the week before the election for that special interview. It was fantastic, we...."

"Yeah, Sorosh, as did every other first and second tier network that Vilen paid off. Get back to the conversation. What did Thompson say after Moore shut the door? Wait, where was Secret Service during this little ambush?"

"I told them to wait outside, that if I needed them I would yell, then we all laughed and that's when Moore shut the door."

"OK, back to Thompson. He started talking right away, what did he say?"

"He said I was embarrassing them. That they had gone out on a limb not only endorsing me, but also giving me an unprecedented amount of airtime and all without a single hardball interview. I asked him how I was embarrassing them. I said I had done nothing wrong since taking office. Then Moore piped up and said, 'It would be more accurate to say you have done nothing period since taking office.' The nerve of that bastard and after all Uncle Vilen has done for him."

"Sorosh, Vilen is not your uncle he is more like your pup... Never mind, continue with the comments of the talking heads."

"Thompson said I have been in office over nine months and have only proposed four of the fifteen cabinet posts and none of them terribly important. He wanted to know what the problem was since the four I proposed were approved in record time, as would all the rest since we control the Senate. When he said, 'Jesus, Mr. President, you control the goddamned Senate', I almost fainted. I thought he was referring to Uncle Vilen's solution for uncooperative senators and congressmen. Anyway, I pointed out that for the eleven critical areas of Agriculture, Commerce, Defense, Education, Energy, Health and Human Services, Homeland Security, Housing and Urban Development, Interior, Labor, and Treasury, I had appointed an interim czar. That way there is no pressure on the Senate or me to rush appointments.

"Hell, Lucile, that is what Uncle Vilen told me to do and that is what he told me to say if anyone asked about the use of temporary appointees instead of filling the Cabinet posts."

"Stop calling Ovinko your fucking uncle," shouted the First Lady! "He is no relative of yours. He is simply the man who pulls your strings. What has happened to you, you appear to be completely out of control and…?"

"Out of control," shouted Sorosh Saji sitting up on the bed, "out of control you say! It's not only me that's out of control, it's the whole goddamned country that's out of control. I can't take any more of this. I had some good ideas when I was on the campaign trail and a plan to introduce them over eight years, but no go. Vilen and this new guy, Nikita, want everything at once, now, in the first two years."

"Get back to Thompson and Moore, what else did they

say?"

"Actually they weren't the ones to drop the bomb that really upset me. It was some guy named Ward Bailey who I thought was from one of the networks."

"He is not from a network, he's the Executive Director of COGI."

"What the hell is COGI?"

"You are scaring me, Sorosh. COGI stands for Control Our Government, Inc. It is a think tank providing you with data supporting every item on your campaign agendas. Everything from your campaign for Senate through your speech last week on shifting troops from Iraq to the Afghanistan/Pakistan border. You've met with him and his staff at least fifty times over the last four years. What is the matter with you? What's happening to you?"

Sorosh Saji, youngest President of the United States ever to occupy the White House, laid back down, rolled over on the super big king sized bed and began once again to sob. "I can't keep this up, Lucile, everyone is starting to pick up on the chaos surrounding my presidency. I have been in office less than a year and the country is sinking into a state of confusion. Nothing I started is working. Unemployment is now moving up almost one percent per month. The government has spent more money in ten months than FDR spent fighting the entire Second World War and we have nothing to show for it. The presidency is slipping from my control."

"Sorosh, I think you are losing it. You're acting as if you were this brilliant statesman going to step into the Oval Office and fix everything. In a few words, Sorosh, you believe your own bullshit. We both know how you got here, for Christ's sake there is a goddamned DVD from Nikita in our safe-deposit box that tells it all. You were a poor student at best. A rather good speechmaker as long as Vilen and his folk provided the speeches and completely without any of your own ideas as to what you should be for or against. You have performed perfectly in your role as implementer for Vilen's privately held mega business, American Heroin Incorporated. Now you need only to slip into that role for this new guy on the block, Nikita."

"That's the problem, Lucile. Vilen's agenda was simple to understand. All I had to do was make sure nothing interfered with the free flow of heroin into and around the US. As long as I did that, he wanted me to do things the people liked. For instance, the earmarking of federal highway funds to build playgrounds in all the cities in California with over twenty-five thousand children under the age of 18."

"Yeah, Sorosh, as long as you designated the construction companies he named as the contractors from San Diego to San Jose. Never mind that, so what is the problem now?"

"The only time I hear from Vilen now is when he wants a personal favor or to pass on instructions from Nikita that Nikita doesn't want to tell me directly."

"Do you hear from Nikita directly? Does he have many ideas or suggestions?"

"Shit, Lucile! Nikita calls me at least once a day on this damned walkie-talkie." Pulling out the credit card thin device from his inside coat pocket he continued, "And it's not with suggestions or ideas, it's with goddamned orders: 'Sorosh appoint this person czar of education. Mr. President, make this woman czar of homeland security'.

Last week he called and said 'Saji send $250 to all the fifty-eight million people on Social Security. It will make them very happy and it will make the other one hundred forty million working Americans hate them'. When I asked him why he wanted working people to hate retirees he simply answered, 'chaos, Sorosh, chaos,' and disconnected."

"What the hell does that mean, Sorosh, chaos?"

Sorosh was now lying on his back and the sobbing had subsided. He was now unburdening himself on Lucile who had been the 'fixer' of all things bad in Saji's life since the wedding in 2001. He said, "Everything he makes me do is to keep the government and the economy in a continuous state of confusion. He wants the country to be anything but focused and united. He wants chaos and a chaotic US means a chaotic world."

"Why?"

"So he can negotiate the sale of four thousand SCUD rocket nuclear warheads in Russian Republic warehouses to Iran, Syria, Venezuela, North Korea and a few others. He wants to pull it off without it coming to the attention of the US and the rest of the nations that will be directly threatened by a dozen nuclear armed pissed off countries."

"Sorosh, how do you know this is what he is doing?"

"He told me."

"He told you that he wants you to keep creating deeper and deeper chaos here so the world is distracted from his arming every whacko dictator with nukes and you just go ahead and do what he tells you to do?"

"Yeah, Lucile," said Sorosh, getting out of the bed and walking around the room. "You bet your ass that is what I am doing. You want me to be the first American President tried for treason. You want Victor and Peter to watch on TV as the FBI drags their father, a father that mind you they think is king of the world, out of the White House in handcuffs at gunpoint. If Nikita or Vilen release the videos on that DVD or the conversations they've had with me since I took office, you can be sure that is exactly what will happen. I, for one, do not want any part of it.

"I took this job to have a fantastic time for eight years after which I figure I would leave office to great fanfare and regrets by my fans that I couldn't serve a third term. Moreover, I would leave this lovely home with you, the kids and a couple of hundred million bucks. I'll write my memoirs, plan my library and generally live out my years as a brilliant former President. Nothing, particularly a few old nuke warheads sold off by those two old Russians, is going to interfere with that script.

"Thank you, Lucile, as usual you have made everything clear and put me back on the path of understanding my own worth. I am going to get a glass of milk and some cookies."

"Before you go, you said there were four people with you in the Green Room. You only told me who three of them were. Who was the fourth? You referred to him as the guy from the third network, who was he?"

"I don't know, I think he was from some public television station, but I can't be sure. He never introduced himself."

"And you, the President of the United States, never thought to ask who he was listening in on three wonks chastising you?"

"No not really, it didn't seem important at the time and it

still doesn't."

As Sorosh Saji walked down the corridor to the elevator to descend to the White House kitchens, Lucile Maria Regina Ramirez Mendoza Saji walked towards her dressing suite with a very angry look on her face.

Lucile thought as she undressed for bed, "Hopefully, Sorosh, you are right and the fourth wonk was just another talking head. But, chances are we will never know, at least not before it's too late. For a guy who is the central character of the greatest scam of all time, you're becoming increasingly careless and that's scary."

If you were nearby and listened very closely, you would have heard the First Lady whisper to herself, "Vilen, I hope you and your buddy, Nikita, know what the hell you are doing. We all have a great deal depending on a very fragile, not too bright, egocentric puppet."

Anna was in the kitchen discussing the Christmas plans with Della Watler, the housekeeper and Twila Bodden, the cook. Twila was laughing and asking Anna, "Now do we have a relative of Santa Claus in our group that is going to insist on historical correctness in what was served on the first Christmas?"

"Actually, Twila," answered Della, "they would have to be relatives of Jesus to know what the first Christmas meal was. Really honey, I don't think we have any relatives of Jesus Christ in this unholy group."

With this, the three burst into hearty laughter.

Hugh walked into this scene. He was not even smiling much less joining in the laughter.

"I'm sorry," he said, nodding at Twila and Della, "I'm afraid I have to steal Anna from this little get together. Something quite serious has surfaced and I need her advice…urgently."

This was a good approach when dealing with the household staff. They loved Anna who was always fair, a straight shooter and most of all fun…Hugh, not so much! By indicating, that he needed her help, he triggered Twila's response. "Go Mrs. M, Mr. M needs you, Della and I will work this out and give you our ideas later today."

Hugh was already exiting the kitchen onto the terrace and heading for the gazebo, their favorite spot for planning and serious discussions. Anna smiled at the two, turned and followed Hugh down the beach.

"Wait up! Hugh, this must be serious to have you so worked up. What's going on?"

"I can't believe the cesspool the American Presidency has become. I don't think more than a handful of people know what is going on. Sorosh Saji is a tool in the hands of a very well organized group of very evil people. I am now absolutely convinced that the process to bring this about called for every aspect of Saji's life to be managed, by this sinister group, since it first started with Ovinko when he turned eleven."

"What has happened to get you so passionate now? We've known all this since we picked up the conversation Nikita had with Saji on the day he was sworn in as President."

"We knew that Nikita and Ovinko had the President of the US in their pocket. What we did not realize was that this marionette is the central character in a scripted play in which all the other players are employees of central casting...Nikita and Ovinko central casting."

"Hugh, it sounds like you've found that someone else in the White House group is part of the Nikita gang. Who is it?"

"First of all, there is no doubt that this little production had its off Broadway run in California under the direction of the ruthless Vilen Ovinko. When the show was brought to Broadway...The White House, Ovinko turned over the director's role to Nikita with a full cast handpicked by Ovinko..."

"I get it, Hugh. Who is the newly discovered member of Ovinko's cast?"

"Lucile Maria Regina Ramirez Mendoza Saji! Our beloved First Lady is not only from central casting, she is number ten on the Nikita Megaphone network."

With this, Hugh opened the notebook computer he was

carrying and sitting down, indicated that Anna should sit next to him.

"I picked this call up from yesterday's monitoring of the network. The conversation made it clear who was talking to Vilen. Just to be on the safe side, I ran Mrs. Saji's conversation through the voice analyzer and compared it to several of her speeches and interviews. No doubt, it's Lucile Saji talking to Vilen Ovinko and get this, she has a code name, Sister M, and she initiated the call. Sit back and listen."

After Hugh keyed a few commands into the notebook, the first voice, female, came loud and clear from the computer's speakers while the text transcript flowed across the screen.

Lucile Saji *(sounding grim)* – "Vilen, it's me, Sister M. We have a situation here that is growing graver and more dangerous by the day."

Vilen Ovinko *(calm)* – "I gather it is quite serious for you to reach me this way. Start at the beginning and give me all the details."

Lucile Saji – "It began over two weeks ago, early in the morning after the Sunday night bash November 30th. Apparently, Cal Thompson, Carlton Moore, Ward Bailey and some fourth guy, Sorosh doesn't even know, suckered him into the Green Room. They started blasting him for not producing anything he promised in his campaign, not filling cabinet posts and being a general screw-up as a President. They pointed out that they had believed in him and supported him without question and he was now an embarrassment.

"From what I got out of him that night he didn't over react, however, when he got to the residence he broke down sobbing. It appears he has become a believer of his own bullshit and he thinks he is some kind of a genius and his brilliance is being ignored. I thought I could deal with it and get him back on track. I pointed out he is in the right place at the right time to get a lot of publicity, make a lot of speeches, be the guest of honor at numerous dinners and parties and along the way make a couple of hundred million bucks.

"This worked for him that night, but apparently more and more of the bastards riding his coattails for the past year are turning on him. Kind of like abandoning the ship before it starts to sink. Well anyway, he goes through the same routine almost every night, sobbing, kicking his feet, pitying himself and howling that everyone around him is ungrateful and disrespectful.

"By the way, he has connected the dots and realizes he is in the job to be 'the cat amongst the pigeons' and create domestic and international chaos while you guys peddle nukes.

"Now here is the really scary thing, that role doesn't bother him at all. His concern is loss of celebrity status before he is ready to retire as a senior statesman."

Vilen Ovinko – "What's your response? Whatever you're doing, it must be working. I've heard of no scenes with our Sorosh cracking up on camera (a muffled laugh)."

Lucile Saji – "The same thing, every freaking night, 'Keep perspective, Sorosh; more parties and money than you ever dreamed of, Sorosh; keep perspective.' It soothes him and he goes and gets cookies and milk or a brandy depending on whether he feels like a child or a sophisticate. He's driving me up a wall, Vilen. This better pay off very, very big for me and Dad or I am going to be one pissed off former First Lady."

Vilen Ovinko – "Lucile, it's already paying off big for you and your father so let's not go there. I know you have a solution up your sleeve, let's hear it."

Lucile Saji – "I want to take him on a world tour for three months, visiting thirty countries, making speeches to huge crowds, promising away the US sovereignty, wealth and security to great applause and fanfare. This will feed his insatiable ego for ninety days. The more applause he gets, the less inclined he will be to return to Washington. If he is away from Washington for ninety days, the government will grind to a halt. He won't give a shit because the sound of applause is like 'five lines of coke' to him. He will be on a three-month 'bender'.

"We on the other hand, will sit back and watch the escalation of chaos beyond our wildest dreams, both here and around the rest of the globe. It wouldn't be any better if the head of the most powerful country on earth were a 'cokehead' who couldn't be relieved of power or replaced. That is where you come in, Mr. Ovinko."

Vilen Ovinko – "Let me guess. You want Nikita and me to see to it that he embraces this idea of a three-month sabbatical from governing. Then when he checks with you, which he inevitably will, you'll say it is a wonderful idea. Am I right?"

Lucile Saji – "You've got part of it. I also need you and Nikita to see to it that no one attempts to have him declared incompetent, impeached or removed from office. That is imperative!"

Vilen Ovinko – "I'll talk to Nikita and get back to you tomorrow. It sounds to me like a win-win proposition. By the way, tell your papa that thanks to the ever-increasing state of depression overtaking the US population, demand for heroin in the states is outpacing the supply capabilities of the Afghanistan-Pakistan producers. It will be necessary to increase the volumes from the Mexican supply channel. Give him my regards and ask him if he can help us in this, our hour of need (another muffled laugh)."

The transcription ended and the screen on the notebook computer went blank.

"I trust I didn't wake you, Vladislav Dubnikov," Vilen Ovinko said into the tiny satellite communications device he had activated seconds before.

"Not a chance, Vilen. This is a Muslim city and the first of the six calls to prayer is about 5:30 in the morning and believe me it is heard by everyone in the city. It is good, I get up early and since the last call to prayer is around 7:30 in the evening, I generally go to bed early. It may not be bringing me any closer to God, but the ritual is definitely making me live a healthier life. So what is new on your side of the world, my friend?"

"Earlier today I received a call from Sister M. She has serious concerns about Sorosh's state of mind. He feels he has lost the respect of the American press and people and that they do not acknowledge his brilliance. They no longer are embracing his innovative ideas."

"What the hell is the matter with him? Is he believing his own bullshit and forgets his brilliance and innovative ideas, which by the way were meant to multiply not fix the United States' problems, were bought and paid for with our money?"

"Hmmm, Lucile's words exactly. I guess he's rewriting the history of his ascendency to power. Anyway, Sister M is fearful of his cracking up in public, although that might not be a bad thing. However, the chaos that would follow a public breakdown would not be long lived enough to cover our needs. We would have to come up with some other distraction, not a good idea. If all is to go as planned, we must steer the eyes and minds of the world away from Iran, Russia, nukes and us, at least for all of 2010. That means

69

keeping our boy in place for at least that long. Do you agree?"

"Yes. I would like to have all of the merchandise here in Iran by September of next year. However, I think it wise for us to have a margin to allow for unanticipated bumps in the road. Remember that 2010 is the year of midterm elections in the US and the outcome could definitely create some bumps."

"Nikita, my friend, I have good news on that front, but first let us get Sorosh's melt down out of the way. I think Mrs. Saji has a very good solution, one that works for us on many levels.

"She suggests Mr. President go on a ninety-day grand tour of thirty countries, a round of parties, speeches, TV appearances and general fanfare."

"You mean stay out of the US for three months?"

"Yes, radical but it just may work."

"Yeah, Vilen, that could work, precisely because it's so off the wall. He can promise everything to everyone, everywhere, but at home in the US. The American public will be frustrated and angry that they are losing jobs and getting poorer and can't even bitch to their President. His supporters will question the sanity of their support and start to argue amongst themselves.

"Everybody will be pissed off at everybody else and no one will trust anyone. That's just what we need to make sure that no one notices a few poor Russian boys trying to sell some old nuke warheads.

"Tell Lucile that her idea works for us. By the way, I still can't believe you got her to marry him."

"Her father had more to do with that than I did. I knew Sorosh better than anyone did; I couldn't ask her to marry him. No, her father appealed to her sense of keeping the Mendoza family strong."

"Well, we owe Raul a debt of gratitude, not to mention Sister M. I'll take care of giving Sorosh his mission and getting him hyped about it in the process. Now what good news do you have concerning the 2010 US midterm elections?"

"We're out in front on that one. There's no question that the Democrats will lose many seats in both houses of congress. However, those seats haven't been the source of chaos in the US Government. Two people have been the driving force, the Senate Majority Leader and the Speaker of the House."

"And what happens, Vilen, when they are swept out in 2010 by the angry American voters?"

"That's just it, Nikita, they won't be swept out. We have known and have considerable visual evidence for some time that these two old degenerates have rather unusual appetites. We felt it was time to make a deal with them going forward. For our part, we'll make sure they hold onto their elected offices and their party's leadership roles. In return, they agree to put forward bills that are ever more radical, beginning immediately. This tactic will further antagonize the Republicans and assure a confused and chaotic government. It will become a country too distracted to pay any attention to little things like nuke and drug sales."

"When will you put this plan into motion, Vilen?"

"It is done, Vladislav Dubnikov, the details were all

worked out this afternoon in a special meeting called by Saji at the White House and attended by advisors provided by Beregovoi, Zhukov, Conroy & Salazar. One of the advisors is Tony Mendoza, Raul's son."

"The First Lady's brother?"

"Right. He had all the legislation documents already prepared and simply gave them to Sorosh and our two most recently acquired lapdogs to propose when the politicians come back to work next January. Zhukov called me at dinner time to tell me all went perfectly and Mendoza told him, thanks to a Democratic control of both houses, the seven bills will be passed before April 15th next year."

"You're sure you can get those two reelected at the midterms?"

"If my people and I have anything down to a science, it's winning US elections. Looking at who is in the White House and how he got there, I feel solid that we can keep a Senator and Congressman in office."

"You have balls, Vilen, I know why my sister, God rest her soul, married you. We're well on our way to a very big win, probably the first of many now that we are perfecting the formula. By the way, are you going to Saji's Sunday night bashes?"

"No, do you believe the arrogant bastard said that having me at social functions was not good for his image. One of the media people may connect me to the drug trade and that would be devastating for his reputation. What reputation? The media geniuses he invites are all on my payroll and half of them take their pay in various drugs. Nikita, my friend, by the end of two terms, the voters won't be the only ones that will welcome his melting into the history books."

"My fear, Vilen, my friend, is he won't last eight years. We have got to get the level of chaos as high as we can so that everyone in the US is distracted from what Iran and the rest of the Middle East are up to with our nukes. If the US is in chaos, the rest of the world will follow.

"Have a good night, Vilen Ovinko."

"Have a good day, Vladislav Dubnikov." They disconnected.

"Sister M," Vilen spoke into the tiny satellite communications device, which once again he had activated only seconds before. However, this time his voice was far softer. "Thank you for picking up, Lucile, I assume that you are alone."

"As alone as I ever get in this role. My lead Secret Service shadow, Heather, is here with me. She's amusing herself trying to fix the zipper on one of my backpacks.

"What, Heather? Oh, Heather wants me to wish you a very Merry Christmas."

"Wish her the same and let her know that we will miss her at the annual organization's Christmas party. Her father and brothers have told me they think it wiser for her to pass up the festivities, at least as long as she is with the Secret Service, and I agree. We will miss you too, Lucile. This endeavor we are all involved in definitely has its down side, but the payoff will be worth it.

"Now why I called, Nikita will call Sorosh, give him his instructions, and get him worked up about the whole idea of the grand tour. He thinks it's a stroke of brilliance on your part. After he gets him excited about this fantastic opportunity to carry his campaign to the globe, Sorosh will come to you with his usual, 'Lucile, what do you think?'

"Do one of your magnificent performances and convince him it is a great idea. It will enhance his image globally preparing him for a role of international statesman and savior of global peace and prosperity. With him doing the Sorosh Saji road show for three months, we have a clear shot at moving all the nukes to Teheran before the end of 2010."

"Consider it done; he wants to get out of Washington anyway, so emphasizing his place in history plus playing up to all the applauding fans will send him on his way."

"Great, I'll watch the news for the announcement. Let me know if we can do anything to help."

"Wait, Vilen, before you hang up, I want to give you Daddy's answer to your 'need'.

Where is it? I have it somewhere around here. He made me write it down word for word, here it is. 'We'll start immediately to increase production of Black Tar and China White. These are the American teenagers newest FHF.'"

"What the hell is FHF?"

"Daddy predicted you would say exactly that, FHF is the newest texting term meaning 'Favorite High Forever'.

"I'll talk to you as soon as things start moving towards the grand tour planning. Goodbye for now, Vilen."

"Goodbye, Sister M," Vilen Ovinko said laughing heartily as he disconnected.

Anna was sitting on the veranda, overlooking Hawksbill Bay, studying the screen of an open notebook computer on the table in front of her.

Hugh walked through the French doors behind her. "You have got to come and hear this right away. I don't know how long we can pretend we don't know what's going on in Washington."

"Hugh, we are not pretending we don't know what's going on. We're just not doing anything about it and I don't know how we would go about doing anything or even if we should."

"OK, fine, but come listen to the conversations we've captured over the last twenty-four hours. It sounds more like a wiretap on a mob social club rather than the conversations of the President's wife."

"Who is Lucile talking to?"

By this time, they had reached the first floor conference room in the west tower of the villa and Anna took a seat at the conference table. Hugh pressed a few buttons, opening a sliding panel on the conference table, in front of a chair opposite where Anna had sat. As he began to punch in information on the keyboard that had been exposed when the panel receded, he spoke to Anna. "The participants in these two scenes are Nikita and Vilen in the first conversation Friday night at 9:45 San Francisco time. The second conversation is between Vilen and the First Lady with an indirect Christmas greeting to Vilen from Heather Boyd via Lucile Saji."

"Who is Heather Boyd?"

"Sorry, this has me pretty hyped. The cabal going on at 1600 Pennsylvania Avenue is so pervasive that if I were not hearing the players' conversations directly, I would never believe any of it."

"This is one of the reasons we do nothing. Whom would we go to and who would believe us? Anyway, who's Heather …what's her name?"

"Heather Boyd is the First Lady's lead bodyguard. While Mrs. Saji was talking to Vilen, Heather asked her to pass on Christmas greetings to the country's largest heroin merchant. She's a Secret Service agent for Christ's sake! The top of the First Family's protection team and she is sending a 'Merry Christmas' to a fucking heroin dealer…a mega fucking heroin dealer.

"Anna, the US is going to hell in a hand basket. We may be the only non-involved citizens in the world that know the size of the conspiracy in place at the highest level of the government. We can't sit back and let it happen."

"Hugh, I don't think we have any other choice but to sit back, continue our monitoring of the situation and see to it that our group is safe and secure. If we trust anyone and expose what we know, how do we know they're not one of the villains? If we pick the wrong person to confide in, the security and safety of our team is compromised. I'm not ready to take that chance, are you?"

"Not really, but after you hear these conversations you tell me if you still feel the same."

Almost two hours passed as they listened and re-listened to the two conversations. Finally, they turned off the feed and Anna said, "Well it appears that you were right on target Friday, when you said that Sorosh Saji's life has been managed, in every detail, since he was eleven years old. I wonder how early in the process did Vilen and Raul Mendoza decide that Raul's daughter would ultimately be Mrs. Saji."

"The whole thing is creepy, Anna."

"Creepy and quite scary, Hugh. Essentially, we have a drug dealer, a drug dealer's daughter and an international nuclear arms dealer running the United States Government. If we wanted to do anything about it, where would we start?

"We can't go to any of the high ranking officials in the Federal Government. Most of them are interim Saji appointees or czars who are probably on the Nikita/Vilen payroll.

"We can't go to any of the organizations under the Homeland Security umbrella. That amalgamation of disorganized fiefdoms is kept in a state of chaos by the Homeland Security czar, Madeline what's her name, the former Portland community organizer.

"No, Hugh. I still feel our priority is to keep our team safe and secure. Should this Washington farce play out in such a way that it places us in danger, then we'll have no choice but to act on our obviously superior knowledge and information. Until then, we stick to our plan of returning Nikita's stolen funds and making sure he isn't planning evil towards us. By the way, once we disclose our knowledge of these conversations, there goes our ability to stay one-step ahead of Nikita. They will shut down the satellite communications network instantly."

"Yeah, Anna, as usual you're right, but it just feels like we should do something."

"I feel the same way and God knows that our ten patriots will feel the need to do something far more strongly than us. However, we have to keep our heads straight and focus on the team's safety, security and survival. We'll discuss all our findings with them after the New Year; first with Roger and Alberto and then with the other eight. They're all very bright and levelheaded; we'll come up with a strategy that makes us all happy, I'm sure.

"Now about Christmas. I thought we would celebrate Christmas Eve by gathering everyone in the household in here and let everyone participate in the first distribution of Nikita's booty. The presentation of the three million bucks stolen from the UNOPID Congo project forty years ago, to Sister Kathleen Todd of Maryhill Missionary Sisters. What do you think?"

"I think that's a great idea. How will you set it up?"

"I'll contact Arthur McCauley and let his office set it up. Hey, you know what would be great? Conference his law offices in on the presentation so the people who have been working with me on the research can celebrate also."

"That would make a nice tradition for each of the nine hundred plus presentations. It's going to take years so it will keep everyone's interest up as you plod through the billions. Ask Arthur what he thinks."

"Great, I'll call Arthur now and tell you at dinner what the plans are."

"Hell, we've been at it for over three hours. We missed lunch. I'm going to the kitchen for a snack to carry me to dinner, want to join me?"

"You better believe it."

Everyone living in the Villa Serenity compound was assembled in the huge entertainment room overlooking Hawksbill Bay. It was the beginning of the Christmas celebration for the entire team. The celebration would continue through to Sunday evening, since Christmas Day fell on a Friday, and everyone was excited about the coming three days of festivities.

Much had been planned, including a large party on Saturday, the day after Christmas, to which over one hundred local residents of Cayman Brac had been invited. The guest list included a real cross section of the inhabitants of the island. There was Stuart Jefferson, President of Regal Bank of the Caymans, with his wife and three daughters; local merchants and their families, the extended (and extensive) families of the four members of the Caymanian staff, among others. It would be a Christmas weekend to remember.

However, the entire household was thrilled to be participating in the historic event planned for that afternoon. Cayman Covert Cyber Reclamation, Ltd. would return the first installment of the thirty-three billion dollars, stolen by Nikita and his band of villains from needy communities around the globe.

It had taken some serious logistical planning to arrange a teleconference for the event. Included would be the team from Arthur McCauley's office, the law firm of McCauley, Berger, Grasso and Picarski in New York, together with all the other participants.

Arthur's staff had pulled off the impossible. Connecting in the Mother Superior and her staff at the Maryhill

Missionary Sisters Mother House in Terre Haute, Indiana with, and this was the big accomplishment, Sister Kathleen Todd at her under staffed, poorly equipped clinic in Mossendjo. The city, in the Niari Valley, Republic of the Congo, has about ten thousand residents.

This whole ceremony was to present the recovered funds directly to the dedicated woman, on the scene, in this seriously poverty entrapped farming area. The trust that Arthur's firm had established gave Sister Todd absolute control over the funds. The Mastersons wanted the whole team to see real life effects, of all their efforts, in maintaining and protecting the mission of Cayman Covert Cyber Reclamation, Ltd.

No one was disappointed.

The technology went off without a hitch. The massive screen in the villa's entertainment room was partitioned into four sections each showing one of the four groups participating in the presentation. Of course, everyone was deeply affected by the scene presented of Sister Todd and some of her patients.

Anna wondered how Arthur's people managed to get the technology components, necessary for Sister Todd to participate, into an isolated building in an area with little or no electric service, never mind communications facilities. They apparently asked Roger and Alberto for advice. Shortly thereafter, a United States Army Mobile Self-Sustaining Satellite Communications Unit was flown in from Technical Base Complex Centurion which is just south of Pretoria, South Africa. The good Sister Todd was told by the crew, who set up the unit and was operating it, "It's a test of the rapid deployment capabilities of the unit."

While the sixteen permanent residents of Villa Serenity stood watching, Arthur McCauley explained why Sister Todd was receiving the funds and the source of the three million bucks. He went on to point out the only restriction was the funds must be used for the Maryhill Missionary clinic in Mossendjo. Within that restriction, she was to have total authority over the use of the funds, a condition that was confirmed by the Mother Superior.

Sister Kathleen Todd began to cry. The children surrounding her, all of whom were patients of the clinic, began to cry. Not because they understood what had just happened, but their Saint, Sister Todd was crying…therefore they must cry.

There wasn't a dry eye amongst the participants in Terre Haute, New York City or Cayman Brac.

Merry Christmas and Happy New Year greetings were exchanged. The connections shut down and three days of partying began in a beautiful villa on Hawksbill Bay in Cayman Brac, Cayman Island.

It would be the last celebration for some time to come.

"Volya, are you there?" Nikita asked his son, Vladimir Dubnikov, via the satellite communications device.

"Yes, Papa, we are all here. No need to take attendance." Vladimir giggled, a sound his father heard clearly via the stratosphere in Teheran, Iran.

"Vladimir Dubnikov, you giggle like a school girl. How the hell am I supposed to know who is on since there are so many now on the network? The original version of these great little devices only had four of us on the network and we each had a button. The button changed color if that person was on line. Now there are ten people on the network and a much bigger phone with several more buttons. How do I know who is on line?"

"Papa, see the little window at the top?"

"Yeah."

"OK, just hit the down arrow next to the window and a new name will come up each time you hit the arrow; just like when you dialed us all. Anyway, if the name has a red star next to it that means that person is live on the network."

"Thank you, Volya, I did not know that. Tell me son, what color is the star if they are dead on the network?" Nikita laughed heartily at his little joke then said, "That is how you should laugh, Vladimir, if you think something is funny; not giggle like a young girl."

"OK, Papa, but one more thing. When you scroll down the list of callers, if you initiated the conference call you can drop any one of the parties by simply displaying their name in the window and press the disconnect button once. Press it twice and the conference call ends and everybody drops off."

"Enough of this technology lesson," shouted Dimitri Demochev, Director General of RFTABO, the guy with all the nukes. "It is a simple satellite phone for a network with some interesting security features. I am sure we all know how it works."

"Actually, Dimitri Demochev," interjected Cheslav Bocharkov, Nikita's Russian lawyer, "I want to thank Vladimir Dubnikov for his taking the time to provide the training. I have not been clear on how it works since receiving it and since I have made no outgoing calls thus far, I never had to deal with anything but answering it."

"My God, Cheslav Bocharkov, I thought all lawyers were…" but Dimitri was cut off by Boris Batkin, Chairman of Bank Snachala Dlits'a, Nikita's private bank and a friend of Nikita's since before Vladimir was born. "Dimitri Demochev, I too am glad that Volya took the time to educate us. We are not all as fortunate as you to have such familiarity with all things technical."

"Enough, enough," said Nikita, "since four of the five I dialed have decided to discuss my ignorance of the operating procedures for the new communicator; I know you are live on the network. I see from the window that my long time friend and brother-in-law, Vilen Ovinko, is also on the network. His silence is proof that he is obviously too bright to participate in the conversation." This was followed by hearty laughs from Nikita and Vilen.

"I assume since everyone is on the call, we now can get started. I have gathered you all, in this cyber meeting, to go over the Iran deal and each of our roles in the months to come. I think it will be best for all involved if the entire inventory of four thousand warheads is moved into Iran before mid-year. That way, we can make the second level sales and wrap up the entire transaction before year end."

"Vladislav Dubnikov, there are thirty-nine hundred and ninety-nine left in my warehouse," interjected Dimitri Demochev. "You already have one, shall we say on consignment, for which my group awaits the payment of our share for one nuke, twelve and a half million bucks."

"Right, Dimitri. As we agreed, funds will be transferred to your designated account for that sample warhead with the payment for the first shipment, which brings us back to the logistics and planning.

"Since Iran is buying the entire lot of four thousand, Iran's President, Heydar Vahdani, and his Minister of Energy, Jalil Rastinpour, think the maximum they can handle is two hundred nukes a week though the Ghale Morgi Airport in Teheran."

"That's a military airport just outside the heart of the city," said Dimitri, "do you think that wise?"

"I don't understand, Dimitri," responded Nikita. "Are you suggesting they come into a commercial airport? It would be far more difficult to keep the public from snooping in a commercial airport…"

"No, no, you misunderstand. Should something happen, like the plane crash on landing, two hundred exploding nukes would level Teheran and kill over twelve million Iranians."

"Shit, Dimitri," piped up Vilen, "are you saying that a crash could detonate these nukes?"

"Vilen Ovinko, it is not supposed to be possible. Let me

explain. These warheads were built many years ago and are of a class known as pure fission weapons. They use a type of detonating method called 'gun assembly'. The nuclear material in all of them is uranium, U-235, to be specific. The bomb is inert unless one piece of U-235 crashes with great force into another piece of U-235. If that happens, then bang, you have a nuclear explosion.

"To prevent that type of thing happening, while two drunken warehouse workers are moving them around on forklifts, the warhead and the trigger are in two separate pieces called a gun assembly. In that kind of warhead arming, the bullet in the gun is not attached to the target part of the detonation mechanism until just prior to launching. After it is attached and launched, sensing mechanisms detect when it is at the point in its travels that detonation is called for. The triggering mechanism goes off, the bullet piece of U-235 is fired into the target piece of U-235, and when they meet, bullet and target, you get a nuclear blast."

"So, what you are saying Dimitri, is that there are safeguards and a negligible possibility of accidental detonation," said Vladimir Dubnikov.

"Yes and no. That is the way they are designed and the casing of each of the components, the bullet and the target, are expected to withstand any accidental crashing into each other. Remember, U-235 is in both so a critical mass can be created if target crashes into target, bullet crashes into…"

"Yeah, yeah, Dimitri, we got it. What's the problem? They're safe to transport, right?" replied Vladimir.

"They are old, quite old, most between thirty and forty

years old. I cannot guarantee the integrity of the metals used to manufacture the casings. In the case of a bad crash, the casings could smash into each other with sufficient force to create critical mass and explode. This type of event could create a chain reaction setting off all others in the shipment."

"I don't think this matters," said Nikita, "each of these warheads is a fifty kiloton nuke, more than twice the destructive power of the Hiroshima explosion. Two hundred, fifty-kiloton nukes, going off anywhere in Iran will suddenly get the Americans out of their state of induced chaos very quickly and they will wake up the rest of the snoozing world. Then Iran is in the shit pot and if Iran is in the crapper, our deal is dead. Once the world finds out where the nukes came from, we are all in the crapper.

"We are either in this business or not and I say we are in it. It makes no difference where the hell we deliver the nukes. All that matters is that we deliver them and we get paid.

"Anyone disagree?"

No one spoke.

Finally, Dimitri piped up, "It appears we are in the business, so I would like your opinion on a delivery plan that my people and I have worked out. I think you may find that our alternative may be a good idea considering that President Vahdani has placed a limitation of two hundred warheads per delivery requiring twenty trips to get all the nukes into Iran. The more trips involved, the greater the chance of getting the United States' or the United Nations' attention."

"I think we have those two organizations chasing their tails.

However, I agree with you, the more shipments the greater the probability for a screw-up. Let's hear it, Dimitri Demochev," said Nikita.

"There is a scheduled shipment of automobiles from Tolyatti destined for Bushehr, Iran in March of this year."

"Ladas?" asked Vladimir Dubnikov.

"Vladimir, what the hell difference does it make what kind of cars are being shipped," growled Nikita into the communicator. "I think I know where Dimitri is going with this, shut up and let him continue. Go on Dimitri."

"Actually, the shipment will contain somewhere between three thousand and thirty-five hundred Lada 4X4s leaving a considerable amount of space on the ship which generally carries five thousand vehicles. There is a railhead at the port in Tolyatti and we can transport the warheads by rail, from their current location, and load the containers directly on the ship. It will go unnoticed since the largest Lada factory in Russia is in Tolyatti and the port is always busy."

"That is one shipment, how many nukes do you intend to put on that ship in March?" asked Vilen.

"Thirty-nine hundred ninety nine, Vilen Ovinko. That is all that remains in Russia of that particular class of nuclear warhead. Bushehr, Iran is also a hectic port and like Tolyatti has a railhead in the port complex itself. The containers can be moved from the ship to railcars and shipped wherever President Vahdani wants them stored.

"Now the really perfect element in this plan is that Bushehr is the port supporting the Bushehr Nuclear Power Plant in Halileh about ten miles south of Bushehr. If for any reason, the Americans or anyone else is watching the area by satellite or with a man on the ground and pick up indicators of radioactive material, what better place for it to be than up the block from a nuclear power plant?"

"That is one ambitious plan, Dimitri. You don't anticipate questions from the shipping company?" asked Vilen.

"The owner of the shipping company is in our group and can taste his share of our fifty-billion US dollars. It was his idea. In fact, he says that even if AvtoVAZ wants to put more Ladas on the ship at the last minute, he will reject their attempts saying it would require a complete unload and reload in order to reposition a larger shipment correctly."

"I think it is a very good idea," said Nikita softly, "and I think President Vahdani will also like it. He can take his time moving the nukes to where he wants them stored without arousing attention. How long will the ship stay in port?"

"As long as President Vahdani feels appropriate. My partner said he will have nothing in the schedule for the use of the ship and will not assign it until President Vahdani wants to release it."

"I personally like the idea," said Nikita. "It is neat and efficient and runs the least risk of interference or mishap. Even if the US or the UN woke up by March and suspected something, what the hell are they going to do, board a Russian Republic flagged ship mid ocean? Once it's in port in Bushehr, if they have any suspicions, the US will contact the UN to ask for an inspection. My trusted employee, Secretary General Pham Dac Kien, will assure the world that he will have it looked into immediately. Who will look into it? Me, the United Nations Special

Atomic Energy Oversight Envoy to The Islamic Republic of Iran." Nikita burst into loud laughter joined by all on the conference call.

"Unless any of you disagree, I will discuss it with President Vahdani this evening over dinner and get back to all of you tomorrow."

Murmurs of approval could be heard from all. Nikita said with obvious enthusiasm, "Until tomorrow, gentlemen," and pressed the disconnect button twice, closing down the conference call.

As he placed the device in his pocket, he smiled and said to himself, "That's fifty billion from the initial purchase by Iran, add about ten billion or so brokerage fee for selling half the four thousand nukes to North Korea, Syria, Venezuela and a few others. Vilen, Vladimir and I will have sixty billion US dollars in our pockets. Let me not overlook the UN Secretary General and US President which we also have in our pockets," once again, Nikita roared his hearty laugh. "There will be nothing we cannot accomplish...absolutely nothing, including vaporizing the Mastersons and their group!"

He left the villa and went off to get an afternoon massage before preparing for what he expected to be a very productive dinner with Heydar Vahdani, President of The Islamic Republic of Iran.

"Vladislav, let me make sure I understand the proposed delivery plan," said Iran's President Heydar Vahdani as he and Nikita enjoyed the dessert course of their dinner, Ranginak, a rich Iranian pastry. "Sometime in early to mid March of this year, thirty-five hundred Lada 4X4s and thirty-nine hundred ninety nine Scud nuclear warheads that can be easily adapted to our Shahab-3 will arrive aboard the same ship, in our port city of Bushehr. On the arrival and inspection of the nuclear cargo, the Islamic Republic of Iran will wire one hundred billion US Dollars into your account at Bank Snachala Dlits'a."

"Correct, Mr. President. Since I'll start lining up buyers for two thousand of those warheads immediately, by the end of 2010, you will have recovered all of those one hundred billion dollars."

"What's the price you intend to offer those two thousand nukes at, Vladislav?"

"Fifty-five million dollars a warhead. That's fifty million per nuke for you and five million for my group as brokers. I believe that Syria, Venezuela and North Korea will take eighteen-hundred, the remaining two-hundred will go to a dozen or so ambitious heads of state around the globe."

"I trust you'll be able to keep the UN and the US distracted for the balance of this year. I certainly don't want to read headlines showing my country as the shipping depot for a nuclear weapons stockpile."

"Yes, Mr. President. Between the midterm elections of most of the US Congress and the leader of the free world leaving on a three-month good will tour, the last thing on the minds of the people in charge of the United States

Government this year is the trade details between Russia and Iran. Further, Iran's interaction with a half-dozen of her trading partners will be the last thing the politicians will want to hear about. Unless, of course, they could figure out how to make money for their campaigns from that trade activity.

"Tomorrow I will be 'suggesting', to the United Nations' Secretary General, that he join Sorosh Saji and the First Lady on this global tour. This will further demonstrate the deepening of the relationship between the US and the UN. I've hired a very connected publicist to travel with Saji on the tour. He is to make sure the emerging love affair between Saji and Pham Dac Kien gets lots of press coverage particularly in the US Media. If the American public gets it in their collective heads, the UN will have more and more say in their national affairs, there will be rallies and riots. Our trade event will never be noticed."

"Vladislav Dubnikov, I am glad you are on our side in this episode and I want to keep the relationship that way. After we have completed the warhead transaction, I would like you to act as broker for our soon to be retired Shahab-3 as we introduce the longer ranged and more accurate, Shahab-3-C & D, into our defensive arsenal.

"Also, we may want you to continue brokering nuke warheads since our programs to produce plutonium and enriched uranium have successfully accelerated and we will start producing clones of what we are getting from you. Of course, we owe this enhanced production capability to the diligent efforts of our very own, United Nations Special Atomic Energy Oversight Envoy to The Islamic Republic of Iran.

"Shall we invite my energy minister, Jalil Rastinpour, in for tea and bring him in on the Russian/Iranian nuclear trade agreement?" At which the laughter could be heard reverberating through the halls of the Presidential Palace.

"I can't believe this shit," shouted Sorosh Saji as he stormed around the living room on the second floor of the White House residence, a bourbon Manhattan in one hand and a Cuban cigarillo in the other.

"What is it now, Sorosh honey," replied Lucile in a calm steady voice. She was sitting at the end of the sofa, on the west wall, with her hands folded on her lap and a look on her face as if she were listening to a child whining to his mother about how the kids were picking on him.

"Nikita, the Russian bastard, called on the damned satellite phone and all but ordered me to go on a tour of thirty or more countries spreading good will and promoting a new world order with the United Nations at center stage. When I'm back on US soil, the Congress plus my Cabinet and czars will be after my head for leaving them here to take the heat from the country for me traipsing around the world glad handing politicians and dictators. In the meantime, the government will have come to a standstill since I won't be around to sign any new laws or push through any legislation. I won't have a friend inside the beltway, never mind the three hundred six million Americans outside the beltway. Ahh shit, Lucile, I should never have left San Francisco."

"Now how do I handle this with surprise and sympathy but still guide him into enthusiasm over the grand tour?" The First Lady thought to herself…and then the proverbial light bulb went on in her devious brain.

"Take them with you, Sorosh."

"What take three hundred six million Americans on the tour? I don't think that is practical, Lucile."

"I do hope that's the bourbon talking and he didn't really think I was suggesting we wander the globe like some ancient tribe of three hundred six million nomads," she thought to herself.

"No, honey, I meant the Cabinet, the czars and their spouses or significant others.   Think of the display of commitment to a new world order.   You are bringing your entire government to each of their capitals to show how deeply you believe in equality and the philosophy of 'from each according to his ability, to each according to his need'. You will show the world that you stand ready to bury the ill gotten concept of American Exceptionalism and contribute the assets of the United States to the effort to elevate the entire world order."

"That should tickle his ego and turn him around," she thought.

Sorosh Saji, the forty-fourth President of the United States, swigged down the last of the bourbon and vermouth in the glass and poured himself another Manhattan from the pitcher on the coffee table.   He took a drag from the cigarillo and looking up at Lucile began to smile. Taking a sip of the freshly poured drink, he said enthusiastically, "You are a genius, Mrs. Saji. You always manage to make the sweetest lemonade from the sourest lemons.   I could emerge on the other side of this grand tour as the likely leader of the new world order." Taking another drag on the cigarillo, Sorosh plopped himself into the large winged easy chair opposite the sofa where Lucile sat.

"Wow, he didn't say emperor of the world, thank heaven for little things," Lucile mused silently.

"You know, Lucile, you just gave me an idea. We will do

just what you suggest. We'll take the four cabinet members I appointed and their spouses, or significant others, plus the same for the thirty-one czars. Now get this, we will call it the President Saji's End of American Exceptionalism World Tour. What do you think, Lucile, and is three months enough?"

"Holy shit," she thought, "do these two Russian gangsters realize what they are unleashing on the world? To keep their cash flow robust and move their drugs and nukes they may ignite a civil war in this country and then their cash and our lives will be worth bupkis. And that fucking name; President Saji's End of American Exceptionalism World Tour. We won't make it to Air Force One alive. I've gotta control this whacko."

"Honey, I don't think we should be so, shall we say aggressive, in selling the idea of a one world order and the end of sovereign nations to the American people just yet. They will have to be educated and eased into the benefits of the change. I believe you can accomplish that, on the grand tour, by stimulating the outpouring of goodwill for the United States from the thirty or so nations we will visit. Good, well managed media coverage fed back to the United States and the rest of the world each night will promote positive attitudes towards the one world concept."

"It's not a concept, Lucile; it is the way of the future. I believe that. I know you believe that too. However, I think you may be right, a less aggressive title for the tour may be better. You have any ideas?"

Once again, Lucile was saying more in her brain than with her voice. "You believe in this one world order crap, me not so much. I am here to make sure you keep the good old USA misdirected and confused. You are here thanks to two Russian gangsters to keep that misdirection and confusion pumped up. Jesus, Vilen, you and your brother-in-law wanted chaos. I hope we don't get pandemonium. Shit, I seem to be having more and more of these conversations in my head as this project moves along."

Speaking now to Sorosh, "How about, 'President Saji's United States Good Will World Tour' and then when we return and all America is turned on to the Saji Global Order we can rename the tour. How does that sound? If it is going well and three months aren't enough, we can just continue for another three months."

Once again, silently to herself, "Probably we will not be able to get back into this country after the tour and we will have to wander the earth. Let's see we'll call that tour 'The Sorosh Saji Government without a Country Tour'. Christ, I am getting as whacky as he is."

"You know what would be really great, Lucile honey, if somehow, Secretary General, Pham Dac Kien, could be on the tour with us."

"Yes, that would be nice. Finish up your drink and let's go to bed. You have major planning ahead of you and the next weeks will be hectic getting ready."

"Lucile, I want this trip to start on January twentieth, the first anniversary of my presidency. We will have to work fast that is only six days from...oops; it's Friday already. Then that is only five days from now."

"Yes, dear, January twentieth it will be."

As she walked down the hall to the master suite shaking her head, she thought, "OK, Vilen and Nikita, you wanted chaos. The President of the United States packing up his family and his government and taking them on a three-month grand tour in five days. That should really rain a shitload of chaos on the United States and for that matter the entire world. Watch out world, here comes the next emperor of the globe and his band of merry folk.

"Daddy, I told you when you asked me to marry this ego maniac that I would do anything to protect the Mendoza family and our business. I just hope we will have a country to do business in."

The Secretary General of the United Nations is provided with a five-floor residence on what may be arguably referred to as the most affluent two blocks of real estate in the world. The wide, but short, avenue runs from Fifty-Seventh Street to Fifty-Ninth Street overlooking the East River. Past and present residents of the two-block enclave include the names of the world's richest and most powerful families: Vanderbilt, Morgan, Kennedy, Grace, Ford, Onassis, well, you've got the picture.

The largest single-family residence on the block is the UN Secretary General's residence.

At 7:15 on this brisk, clear morning in New York City, Pham Dac Kien, the eighth Secretary General of the United Nations, the first Vietnamese to hold the office and the fifth to be on the payroll of Vladislav Dubnikov, sat at his desk in his private study on the third floor of the mansion. He held in his hand the tiny Nikita Megaphone that more and more world leaders seemed to be in possession of these days and he listened to instructions from his employer, not the UN, but none other than Nikita.

The look on his face was a mixture of hate, disgust and a kind of helplessness.

"Stop, Nikita," he said into the tiny cell phone like device, "or at least slow down. You're telling me that I must drop everything, pack my bags and accompany Sorosh on a three-month world tour of thirty plus countries. Do you realize the howling this will generate from my enemies and the enemies of the UN?"

"Shut up, Pham. You are supposed to be the supreme ambassador of international good will and the leading supporter of the one world order. Well, now you and the leader of the nation that loses the most from that absurd concept are going to go around the world patting each other on the back and prophesying the soon to be created global government."

"It is not a concept, Nikita, it is…"

"Bullshit, Mr. Secretary General, pure stinking bullshit. You go on believing that your world order of people, sacrificing for the greater good, will be realized in the not too distant future. Me, I'll play it safe and listen to the words of a true survivor, 'the only real power comes out of a long rifle,' realpolitik from a man who understood power."

"Whose advice is that, Nikita?"

"Joseph Stalin!

"Now contact Saji and start making the arrangements. I gather he wants the tour to start on January twentieth, the anniversary of the day they swore him into the job we bought for him, just as I bought yours for you. I want both the United Nations and the United States distracted and in as much chaos as the two of you can generate. Remember, Saji really thinks this global government crap is going to happen and he is going to be emperor. Play that angle up it will score with most of your member nations and it will bring the Americans to the brink of civil war. That, Mr. Secretary General, will give us just what we need to complete our trade transactions.

"If you pull this off, Pham, and we are successful, there is a hundred million dollar bonus in it for you. You can pay off your wife in Vietnam, take that Latvian whore, Taska Meierovics, off to some hideaway, and live out your life in comfort and leisure.

"Fuck it up, Pham, and I will once again turn to Comrade Stalin's solutions and both that wife in Vietnam and the Latvian whore can mourn your passing."

~~~

Pham Dac Kien sat in his study staring out at the East River in front of him and the corner of the United Nations building nine blocks south to his right, for at least ten minutes. This abandonment of his responsibilities, as Secretary General of the United Nations, to create an atmosphere in which his benefactors could make billions through the sale of drugs and nukes would bother a less focused individual, but not Pham.

His mind wandered back to some fifty years earlier in 1960 when he, at the age of fifteen, had begun his carefully calculated climb out of the slums of Ho Chi Minh City, then known as Saigon. He was obsessed from childhood with the accumulation of wealth; the weapon he had observed repeatedly determined the winner of every struggle.

~~~

Pham Dac Kien was born in 1946, the year in which the First Indochina War between Viet Minh and the colonial French forces that had occupied Vietnam since 1885 began. By the end of that long conflict in 1954, both of Pham's parents were long dead and Pham himself was an eight-year-old street-smart urchin living by his wits in the horrific slums of Saigon.

Not being big of stature, Pham learned early on to study conflicts in the streets and attach himself to the individual or group that was destined to come out on top. He would then make himself useful to the new group in charge until a new conflict emerged. At which time, the process would begin all over again. The secret of his surviving as a young man without allegiance could be attributed to his strategy of never being noticed. He never took credit for his accomplishments leaving the glory to those who soon became targets. His objective was to survive and being inconspicuous made that possible.

When the country was partitioned into North and South Vietnam in 1954, again, owing to his cultivated ability to go unnoticed, much like busboys in expensive restaurants, Pham traveled unimpeded between North and South Vietnam. He cultivated relationships in both the Nationalist South where Saigon, the place he thought of as home was, and the Communist North.

As he had done with the street gangs of Saigon, for the next six years, Pham studied who was to be the winner in the many conflicts between the Communists and the Nationalists. He then endeared himself to the group he anticipated would triumph.

In 1960, things changed. In that year, the United States' President John F. Kennedy authorized the use of paramilitary officers from the CIA's Special Activities Division to train and oversee raids and military action against the Communist North. This was a new factor in the equation that Pham was familiar with and adept at maneuvering. Thus, at fifteen years of age, Pham Dac Kien made the decision to play the role of a dim-witted street person, wandering aimlessly and non-threateningly among the North Vietnamese, the South Vietnamese, the Viet Cong and to his utter surprise the United States Armed

Forces.

He did simple things for all the players from running errands, to cleaning toilets and loading trucks. If all of the opposing forces in this free for all, carried on in a country two-thirds the size of California, could have heard each other, the phrase "Get Pham" would have been clear in Chinese, English, French, Russian, and of course Vietnamese. This multi-national clientele of Pham's menial services did not go unexploited by Pham. Once again, he was uncertain as to who would come out the victor in this multi-dimensional street war, but in his mind there would be one sure winner at the end of the conflict…Pham Dac Kien.

Pham had a long wait for the end to come, but by 1975 when the unification of Vietnam was finally achieved, two years after the United States forces withdrew from the country, Pham was a very different man than the boy who went into anonymity in 1960.

He was twenty-nine years old, had accumulated a considerable amount of money in multiple currencies, over two hundred fifty thousand if converted to US dollars, and he spoke and wrote fluently: Chinese, English, French, Russian, and of course Vietnamese.

By 1976, Pham decided he had observed the conflict for long enough and could clearly identify the players of the winning gang. That was the way he looked at all conflicts, beginning with his childhood days on the streets of Saigon, 'conflicting gangs'.

Therefore, at the age of thirty, with a neat apartment in Hanoi, money in the bank and an impressive, if not truthful resume, with university degrees and past experience, all unverifiable, unfortunately, due to the 'devastation of the war with the Americans,' Pham Dac Kien walked into the Office of Vietnamese Ministry of Foreign Affairs. Entering the magnificent historic building at 1 Ton That Dam, Ba Dinh, Hanoi, Pham explained to the officer at the security desk that he was there for a scheduled meeting with Mang Ba Toai -- the then Deputy Prime Minister and Minister of Foreign Affairs.

The security officer, on checking the roster of expected visitors, bowed and promptly escorted the elegant looking gentleman to the office of the Deputy Prime Minister.

Pham smiled and thought to himself "I probably cleaned the toilets and the boots of this security guard sometime over the past fifteen years." He was about to apply for a post as the special assistant for international communications to the Deputy Prime Minister and Minister of Foreign Affairs.

The meeting took three hours and by the end, Pham Dac Kien left with Mang Ba Toai for lunch as the new Special Assistant to the Deputy Prime Minister And Minister of Foreign Affairs for International Communications.

The languages, the understanding of the various cultures and habits of the people, the extensive reading Pham had done of popular books and magazines from the US, China, Russia and France deeply impressed the Deputy Prime Minister. So much so, that Pham was invited to a get together at the Minister's weekend retreat on nearby Cat Ba Island.

Later that night, the Minister explained to his incredulous wife that he had invited Pham because he found him to be the most cultured, self-possessed dignified young man he had come across in years. Besides, he was thirty and good looking while their daughter, Mai Thi Toai was twenty-eight, single, not so good looking and with no prospects in sight.

Pham's thirty years of scraping, observing, calculating and waiting were over. His fortunes were about to change. He never looked back.

By 1979, Pham had married Mai Thi Toai, the Deputy Prime Minister's daughter. By 1985, they had four children, and by 1990, he was acknowledged by all to be the third most powerful man in Vietnam. When the new Vietnamese constitution took effect in 1992, Pham's father-in-law filled the post of President\Prime Minister. Pham was then immediately appointed to the post of Deputy Prime Minister and Minister of Foreign Affairs.

That is when Nikita contacted Pham Dac Kien, on behalf of his group of three corrupt United Nations' senior officials: Gerhardt Durkheim, a German, code named Konrad, and violently murdered on Christmas day 2007; Jean-Luc Bazire, a Frenchman, code named Charles, also violently murdered on Christmas day 2007; and of course Vladislav Dubnikov, Nikita himself.

The group had been watching Pham for many years and admired his ability to go from chameleon for the first twenty-nine years of his life to powerful, celebrity-like politician since 1976. What they admired most about Pham, Nikita explained, was his absolute loyalty to nothing and no one other than his own survival and ability to accumulate money and whores.

Nikita pointed out, to the attentively listening Pham, that they would not be much help on the accumulation of the whores, but they could be great assistance in the money thing.

There was scheduled to begin, in 1993, a major undertaking by the United Nations' to assist in the development of the united Vietnam. These activities would be under the auspices and control of three UN organizations: UNOPID, (the United Nations Organization Promoting Industrial Development); UNFHWB, (United Nations Fund for Health and Well Being) and the UNCIC, (United Nations Central Investment Commission). The budget was one billion dollars US.

Nikita explained that with Pham's support and participation, one hundred million of those US dollars could find their way into designated foreign bank accounts, say twenty-five million apiece for each of the four of them.

Pham Dac Kien did not miss a beat. He responded simply that the project would be more attractive if the distribution was forty million to his bank account and twenty million each to the accounts of Nikita and his two partners.

A new partnership was born that day. The ten regional children's hospital\clinics to be launched, throughout the country, would unfortunately now be only nine.

By 2006, when the United Nations began the process to elect a new Secretary General, Pham Dac Kien, the choice for the post of Nikita and his partners became the choice of both the General Assembly and the Security Council. Of course, this swelling of positive feelings towards a man who had never worked a day inside the halls of the United Nations came about after Nikita and his partners spread a total of two hundred fifty million dollars among the esteemed members of both the General Assembly and the

Security Council.

And that brings us to Secretary General, Pham Dac Kien, sitting in his third floor study contemplating Nikita's orders and composing his thoughts for the conversation he was about to have with Sorosh Saji, President of the United States and his fellow employee of Vladislav Dubnikov, code name Nikita.

~~~

"Sorosh," Pham said, into the satellite communications device he had moments before disconnected from Nikita, "I wish to join your around the world in ninety days excursion. I understand that you want this adventure to kick off next Wednesday, the twentieth. If you agree to my joining the tour, could we possibly leave later, do a bit more planning and coordinate our announcements?"

"What planning, Pham? We will have probably more than six hundred people and a dozen or more jets. If you forget your underwear, I will send an FA-18 fighter back to New York to get you a dozen pairs…you do wear underwear don't you, Pham…?

"We leave on the twentieth; my people will call your people and coordinate the itinerary and the media spots. I want to have a very big sendoff event, at Andrews Air Force Base, at about noon next Wednesday. All our fellow travelers and the massive amount of equipment assembled will be displayed for the world to see that we are committed to the mission of the tour."

"What is the mission of the tour, Sorosh?"

"The mission of our joint world tour," Saji began, "is the ending of severe poverty in our time through international cooperation."

Pham thought to himself, "My God, it sounds like he's reading from a prepared speech," to Saji, he said, "An ambitious and noble goal, Mr. President.

"OK, Sorosh, Wednesday it is. Your people and our people will make all the arrangements. See you at the grand farewell celebration."

Pham Dac Kien pressed the disconnect button. As he rose from the desk heading for the dining room and breakfast, he muttered to himself, "Saji, you really don't give a shit what your fellow Americans think of you. Are you so self-deluded that you think flaunting the beginning of a global party that will cost them billions will go unnoticed. Not to mention the fact that the only way you will make a dent in world poverty is to distribute the wealth of the United States. The wealth that belongs to those people you are trying to impress with your launch show.

"I am glad we are leaving the United States. I doubt that once the consequences of your message sinks in, neither one of us will have a lot of friends here outside the United Nations' building.

"Well, Mr. Nikita, you made an excellent choice for President of the United States when you bought Sorosh Saji the job. What better instrument to create anarchy than a delusional narcissist. Chaos is what you want; chaos is what you are going to get...and I will get my hundred million."

~~~

Meanwhile, back in the White House residence, Sorosh Saji was shaking Lucile Saji awake and shouting, "You will not believe who just called…Pham Dac Kien, Secretary…"

"Sorosh, I know who Pham Dac Kien is. What did he want at this hour?"

"He wants to come on our grand tour. Can you believe it, just last night, I said how good it would be if Pham Dac…"

"Yeah, yeah, Sorosh, great. Now let me go back to sleep; it is far too early to face the day."

As Sorosh Saji, President of the United States, left the room, Lucile muttered into her pillow, "Jesus, does he really think that Pham just decided it would be wonderful to go on a grand three month world tour with the President of the United States. He knows Pham is on Nikita's payroll just as we are. Or does he block that small, inconvenient fact and just assume that people do the things he wants because he is such a grand chap," her last words before slipping once again into a deep sleep.

The scene could only be described as awesome…and cold. The temperature this winter day in Maryland was a freezing 29 degrees Fahrenheit, 12 once one factored in the wind chill.

Central to the display of the dimension of this joint world tour, of the President of the United States and the Secretary General of the United Nations, were the two Boeing 747-200Bs, Air Force One and Air Force One 'backup'. Alongside them, stretching across a quarter of a mile of airport tarmac, were four Boeing 787-9 Dreamliners configured to carry comfortably two hundred fifty passengers each. The newest addition to the Boeing luxury intercontinental family of airliners and the newest non-combat aircraft added to the inventory of the U.S. Air Force. These would transport the press and support staff for the President, four Cabinet members and thirty-one czars, a group announced to be one-thousand strong.

The four Cabinet members, thirty-one czars and their spouses or significant others would be traveling in Air Force One with the President and First Lady.

The United Nations support contingent, slightly smaller being only five hundred and fifty strong, would be traveling in three Boeing 737-900s. The Secretary General and his contingent of forty–nine Directors, Under Secretary Generals, Special Advisors and Special Envoys together with their spouses or significant others, would be traveling in the Boeing 747 designated Air Force One 'backup'.

In addition, in order to transport limousines, security vehicles and equipment, including extensive wardrobes for all those in the President and Secretary General's party, the airborne fleet included three Boeing C-17 Globemaster III air transport giants.

Behind this lineup was a Boeing KC-767 International Tanker, capable of refueling any or all of the aircraft mid-air should the need arise.

Finally, to round off this spectacular show of resources of the United States Air Force, at each end of this lineup were two FA-18 fighters, a security contingent of four supersonic state of the art fighter jets to protect the members of this grand tour.

Each of the aircraft (except the fighters) had been emblazoned in red, green and yellow letters along the entire length of each plane with the words, 'President Saji's End of Severe Poverty in Our Time through International Cooperation World Tour.'

In front of the aircraft line, stood the almost two thousand men and women that would make up the grand tour over the ensuing three months. In front of them stood President Sorosh Saji, his wife, Lucile Saji, Secretary General Pham Dac Kien and his wife, Mai Thi Kien.

Moments after the sweeping cameras took in this display, Sorosh put his arm around the shoulders of Pham and spoke clearly to the cameras, "The Secretary General and I embark this day on a mission of international…no global importance, my initiative, the President Saji's End of Severe Poverty in Our Time through International Cooperation World Tour. Together, we will do what it takes to achieve the elimination of extreme poverty in our time. If this takes the redistribution of the wealth of my great country, to supplement the productivity of lesser nations, than that is what we shall do. However, we will not stop until we have achieved our goal, 'global economic equality'.

"We will visit the poor and repressed in the darkest and poorest regions of the world and let those poor suffering, struggling souls know that they have friends and supporters in President Saji and Secretary Pham Dac Kien.

"Now I know you all want to get out of this freezing weather and into your respective aircraft so I will simply say that this is a working tour. We will all be putting in long hours in the worst of regions in the world. Seeking solutions and calling on economically advantaged nations to join with us in the personal sacrifices my fellow Americans are prepared to make to lift up their neighbors in South America, Africa and Asia. Come with us and document this pivotal point in history."

As Saji turned and with Lucile started towards Air Force One, Agnes Cavaliere, a reporter with VPNN shouted, pushing her cameraman (and part time lover) out ahead of the crowd, "Mr. President, a question. We have no itinerary. What depressed country will be our first stop, what part of the world, Malaysia, Central America, Africa, where?"

"Don't be impatient, Agnes, you will know when you get there," said the President barely turning his head.

However, Pham Dac Kien's wife wanted the hundred million bucks she knew her husband would get if this tour were the match that lit the fire of American anger. Stopping, she turned and shouted back at Agnes Cavaliere and thirty still running TV cameras, "Maui, Ms. Cavaliere, see you in Maui."

"What, Maui? Maui, as in the Hawaiian Island? Maui, the

fantastic resort in the Hawaiian Islands?"

"Yes, Agnes, that Maui. Is there any other? See you on the beach, dear."

"Mr. President, Mr. President," shouted reporter Cavaliere, "this grand tour is estimated to cost one billion dollars a week of American taxpayer money. Is it true you and your two thousand closest friends are starting in Maui? Mr. President, please explain to the American people, is this what you perceive to be…poor and repressed in the darkest and poorest regions of the world?"

Too late, Sorosh Saji and Lucile had disappeared into the magnificent interior of the primary Air Force One.

Two minutes later, the thirty videos of that brief but informative scene were being digitally transmitted via satellite to thirty global news and entertainment media outlets.

…and that is how the shit hit the fan in the United States at 1:29 PM, Wednesday January 20, 2010 and over three months of chaos and distraction was launched.

~~~

Throughout the afternoon and evening, all four networks and every non-affiliated cable and TV station carried that exchange repeatedly. Before the world awoke on January 21, 2010, it was being beamed to the TVs of every continent on earth.

In the United States, the scene was chaotic! The sentiments ran from "This party boy is finished spending or giving away my money," to "This will finally bring peace." The country was about equally divided pretty much down the center of the economic divide. The more prosperous half of the population vowed to defend their right to their property with their lives while the less prosperous half of the population vowed to use whatever means necessary to take the property of the more prosperous folk.

It would have probably erupted into a civil war had not a few of the more conservative media outlets pointed out to the angry factions that the President and Secretary General intended to take most of both groups' assets and distribute them to Africans, Asians and South Americans via the United Nations.

It would take weeks for the anger to be refocused. The result would be that three hundred six million Americans could give a shit less about Iraq, Iran, Afghanistan, Pakistan, Mexico, Russia and the drug and nuke trade going on with that diversified group. No one felt in charge enough to try to stop or recall the tour.

Since Mr. Saji had indicated he wanted every developed nation in the world to execute the same plan, and there were opponents and proponents in all those nations, the same chaos erupted around the globe. Of course, predictably, that was followed by the same disregard of happenings in Iraq, Iran, Afghanistan, Pakistan, Mexico and Russia and the drug and nuke trade.

Since the entire hierarchy of the United States and the United Nations were on an extended party, touring every depressed region of the world (amongst which there were a number of beach and ski resorts), Nikita and his band of rascals had a clear road ahead of them.

Nikita entered the villa in Teheran feeling invigorated and very optimistic about the future. President Sorosh Saji was soaking up the sun with Lucile and two thousand of their closest friends and colleagues on the glorious beaches of Maui. This was the first, 'poverty stricken', area in the world that called for the undivided attention of the most powerful members of the political and diplomatic world. The group was definitely off to a good start in their mission to "End Severe Poverty in Our Time…"at least as far as Maui, Hawaii was concerned. It was necessary to book entirely the four largest hotels at Kaanapali, one of the most beautiful and luxurious resort areas in the world. It got the reaction Nikita and his band of villains wanted.

Agnes Cavaliere filed daily reports with pictures of the group's diligent efforts to find solutions to global poverty…aboard sailboats, wave-runners, surfboards and just sitting on the magnificent beach, which in her cameraman's photos looked endless.

Along with Agnes, of course the other one hundred ninety-nine members of the world media filed similar reports to their outlets in Europe, Asia, Africa, Australia as well as North and South America.

The eruption of anger, and as a result chaos, was rippling around the world each day in lock step with the rising of the sun.

No one cared about the goings on in Iran and if that country and its neighbors were pursuing a more aggressive nuclear arms program. Hell, the only news on screen, radio or paper was about the largest globetrotting party ever assembled.

To Nikita, this was perfect. He walked towards the kitchen of the villa shouting for Svetlana Baikov, the Russian cook that his host Heydar Vahdani had arranged, and the smile on his face registered his absolute enjoyment at the way his plan was progressing. At that moment, his satellite communicator sounded in his pocket. Telling Svetlana to get him coffee and some pastry, he headed for the veranda.

He pressed the button activating an answer to the call, but failed to follow Vladimir's instructions and did not notice who was calling.

"Vladislav Dubnikov, this is Dimitri Demochev. I trust you are free to speak openly, if not, call me back when you are," said the man with warehouses full of nuke warheads.

"Dimitri Demochev, it is a pleasure to hear from you and yes, I am alone except for Svetlana, my cook. Have you seen the videos of the Secretary General and the President of the United States? They are party animals," at which Nikita broke into his hearty guttural laugh.

"Vladislav," interrupted Dimitri, "I had a meeting last night with my partners and we have some concerns. The reaction throughout the world to Sorosh and Pham prancing about the globe could backfire. Their actions are so outrageous that they may find themselves fired from their jobs, a complex process, but one that unfortunately will result in large, wide-scale investigations. That may just bring about a disruption to our transaction."

"Dimitri," answered Nikita, "it is essential we keep the two groups those partiers represent, looking in a direction other than the Middle East's nuclear programs and that seems to be working. Would you have me tell them to go home and get back to work? That would set off immediate curiosity from every media group in the world, a not so good alternative I believe. Thanks to your efficient plan, the entire transaction will be over in March."

"That is what caused the concern, Vladislav Dubnikov, our delivery plan. All thirty nine hundred ninety-nine warheads will be on that ship leaving Tolyatti in early March. For that to happen, we must start delivering them to the port by the end of February. I can guarantee nothing will go wrong up until the time that ship leaves Tolyatti. However, once that ship leaves Russian waters anything could happen. If the Americans, Europeans, or both suspect something, make a stink and board that ship, my group will lose what could be fifty billion US Dollars. That is not acceptable to them. Instead of being paid on arrival in Bushehr, we want to be paid on departure from Tolyatti."

Nikita said nothing for almost a minute, "Shit," he thought, "I don't have fifty billion bucks and even if I did I'm not taking that kind of risk. After waving goodbye to the ship, Demochev and his people have no skin in the game. They would've gotten rid of old nukes nobody wanted and have a cool fifty billion in the bank. Hell, they could put anything on that ship, tell us they were nukes, secretly sink the ship on its way to Iran and say 'oops, I guess you guys had a bad day'. Then I'm up shit's creek.

"Well, if Vladimir gets my forty billion back from the Mastersons, I'll risk part of it. This deal means a minimum of sixty billion in pure profit to Vilen and me."

"Are you there, Vladislav, or have you passed out?" said Demochev, who then had his opportunity to laugh.

"Dimitri Demochev, the fact of the matter is, I do not have fifty billion dollars to pay you up front."

"Get it from Vahdani. Iran's got plenty of dollars, it's the currency of the oil trade and they export about one hundred billion dollars worth a year."

"That won't work, Dimitri. He will think we are pulling a fast one and probably shoot me on the spot. Hell, he intends to have his nuclear weapons guru get on the ship in Bushehr and inspect every one of the thirty nine hundred ninety-nine nukes before he issues the one hundred billion dollar transfer. No, that won't work. I'll have to put up the money, but it won't be fifty billion. You can get ten billion when the ship leaves and the balance when Vahdani pays the one hundred billion."

"My partners will say 'leave them in the warehouses and look for another buyer'; forty billion is too great a risk for them."

"Tell them they would have never thought of selling the old warheads if I hadn't come up with the idea and the buyer. Your group is risking nothing but a bunch of old warheads. Do they really think they can find someone with one hundred billion bucks that wants them? Let me tell you, Dimitri Demochev, they are worth less than shit unless I make the deal with Iran so you are risking nothing. But you want me to risk fifty billion US dollars, fifty billion US dollars I don't have."

"Vladislav Dubnikov, my friend, we go back a long way together. My partners are the facilitators here in the Russian Republic that will make all traces of the nukes and their whereabouts disappear. I, no we, need them and they want money up front. Can you split the risk with us? We'll put up the nukes you put up twenty-five billion when they leave Tolyatti."

Nikita thought for a minute, "If Vladimir gets his hands on the money the Mastersons stole from me, I'll risk twenty-five billion to make a clear profit of sixty billion. I'll get Vilen to agree to cover half if it goes bad. If Vladimir fails to get the money back, it all makes no difference. I will have to go to Heydar Vahdani for the twenty-five billion and settle for a much smaller profit…so what the hell."

"Yes, Dimitri, I will have twenty-five billion wired into your account when the ship leaves Tolyatti. However, before I do that, I will have some of Ovinko's people in Russia check out the shipment."

"OK, Vladislav Dubnikov, my friend, we have a deal. I will get back to you with the exact date the shipment will leave Russia and you can work out the logistics with Ovinko. Have a nice day and tell Svetlana to make you something delectable for dinner."

The call ended.

"Shit," said Nikita to himself, now I have to make sure I can get my hands on twenty-five billion bucks by the end of February."

It was almost two hours before Nikita decided to make some calls and find out what progress was being made by his son, Vladimir, in his efforts to get back the forty billion. He knew the answer would not be a good one because one thing he was sure of, if Vladimir had made a breakthrough, he would have been on the satellite communicator immediately telling the world.

Nikita, therefore, did not want to call his son and listen to his stuttering, weak excuses and evasions. He needed to know exactly how great was the risk that he would not have twenty-five billion dollars by the end of February. After lunch, he made the decision to call Boris Batkin, another of his colleagues from the days of the Soviet Union. Batkin was now the chairman of his private bank in Russia, Bank Snachala Dlits'a. Boris was working with Vladimir on finding and getting back the forty billion, but Boris was a no nonsense banker and would give Nikita a status in few words that were only facts.

"Good afternoon, Boris Batkin, this is Vladislav Dubnikov…," before he could finish his greeting the banker cut him off. "I knew it was you, Vladya," using the very familiar form of Vladislav. "I learned how to identify the incoming caller from Vladimir's lesson the other day."

"Of course you did, Borushka," said Nikita, matching the acknowledgement of the closeness of the relationship by using the equally personal form of Boris. "I have no doubt that you have made it now an instinctive action before you answer that little device whenever it beckons."

"I have, Vladya, and I know you would expect nothing less of me. To what do I owe this pleasant afternoon call from my most influential stockholder?"

"Your only stockholder, Batkin, and my call actually has to do with banking. Has my son, and only remaining heir, significantly improved my bank balance?"

"I am afraid, Vladislav Dubnikov, that Vladimir has not improved your bank balance significantly or insignificantly for that matter. Considering his past life, Vladya, you should be grateful he has not diminished it significantly." At this remark, they both gave forth deep guffaws.

"On the serious side, Vladislav, he has been working very diligently; some days around the clock. He wants very much to make up to you for his past decadence and show you he is now a man you can have confidence in. As to the funds, he has not had any success. In his words, 'those bastard Mastersons have put every roadblock in the way to prevent hacking into the account.' They must have a great deal of influence in the Regal Bank of the Caymans. As Vladimir explains it, the only way into their account is through a specific IP address. That is what they call the numerical address of the Regal Bank's computers. Anyway, the bank apparently changes it several times a day, and on no particular schedule. Only after he has found the IP address for the time in which he is hacking, can he start to try to break their access security, which appears to include some biometrics. Enough from me, you must call him yourself. He has been without drugs, alcohol or as far as I can see, whores, for more than a year now. Give him a call, Vladya, and let him tell you of his progress himself.

"Vladya, by the way, do you know how to make an outgoing call on that device?" The laughter from Boris could be heard across the veranda that Nikita was sitting on in Teheran, if anyone had been there to hear it. Nikita, with a smile on his face that he could not constrain, simply pushed the disconnect button and then laughed himself.

"Hi, Papa," said Vladimir, as he answered his satellite communicator. "If you're calling for a status report on getting back your forty billion bucks, it ain't so good."

"Why ain't it so good, Vladimir?" said Nikita, with no attempt to hide the sarcasm.

"Three pieces of bad news and no good news. The IP address for the Mastersons' account changes at random times throughout the day. Sometimes it is the same for two or three hours during which I have a lot of time to try to hack into it. Other times it will change three times in a half hour and drop me off before I even had time to set up the password breaking software. However, bad news number two. Today I learned that access to the account is protected by biometrics. Getting inside the account to move the money requires an authorized fingerprint, which I assume is one of theirs, and if they both can access the account that's two prints out of twenty possibilities.

"The final problem…now don't get crazy, Papa. I picked up on a press release from the Maryhill Missionary Sisters, a Catholic religious order that has a Sister Todd working in a facility that was supposed to be a clinic built in 1967 as part of a UN project. Apparently, the project was run by some UN organization called UNOPID, the United Nations Organization Promoting Industrial Development and nothing was built, but the building. Nothing in it, just a building. Well, these nuns are trying to get a clinic going forty-three years later, but they ain't got much money and suddenly they get a windfall and you'll never guess from whom."

"The Mastersons, Vladimir, the Mastersons."

"Shit, Papa, how did you know?"

"Because, Vladimir, that was the first deal in which the United Nations shared their extensive financial assets with me. Let me guess, that windfall was for three million bucks."

"How did you know that?"

"Because, Vladimir, three million dollars is exactly the amount that the UN shared with my two partners and me forty-three years ago and it came from UNOPID.

"This is not good! This means they have started to return the money to the original sources or in this case the originally intended beneficiary of the UN's largesse."

"That was brilliant, Papa. Instead, you and your buddies were the beneficiaries of the UN's largesse. Can't we get back into that business; it sounds like it was fun?"

"We are still in that business, but we have a much bigger fish to fry. We have another big problem. Demochev and his people want twenty-five billion US dollars up front before the nukes leave Tolyatti."

"So, can't you get it from Vahdani? Iran has a lot more money than we have."

"As I told Demochev, when he made the same stupid suggestion, Vahdani will figure something stinks and have me shot. Worse yet, shoot me on the spot himself.

"No, Vladimir Dubnikov, I am afraid this is all up to you. You want me to believe you are no longer a drunken whore-chasing slug, you must get back our forty billion bucks and you don't have a hell of a lot of time to do it. The ship is scheduled to leave Tolyatti with the nukes the end of February, so I must have twenty-five billion by the last week of February. Now what is the problem getting around the fingerprint thing?"

"I can't get around the biometric security. I have got to satisfy it and go through it. I have got to somehow get the fingerprints of all twenty fingers or at least all ten, of one of them, and try each until I get into the account."

"So can't we duplicate the fingerprint with some kind of software? You told me that is probably how the Mastersons broke into my partners' and my accounts and stole our money. Why can't we steal it back using the same technique?"

"The way you break a password code is to generate passwords at an extremely high speed trying each until you find the right series of characters. This method can be made more efficient by feeding information, about the person whose password you are trying to duplicate, into the program. Information as simple as their birthdays and as complex as the telephone number of the first person they had sex with."

"How the hell would you find out the telephone number of the first person that Hugh Masterson had sex with…?"

"I am only using that as an example. Once you put as much data about the person whose password you want to steal in the system, the application starts creating possibilities. You let the software run as long as it takes until it finds the matching password. However, Papa, passwords are dealing with a finite number of possibilities. No matter how many digits in the password and using every key on a computer keyboard, the number of variations in that password can be calculated. Therefore, a software application can be created to list all of those possibilities.

"Fingerprints are different since there is no definable population of the shapes, size, pattern or position of the ridges that make up every fingerprint. That is why they are all unique. You can compare them to one another, but you cannot create one by assembling the pieces."

"OK, OK, enough of the technical education on fingerprints. Are you telling me I'm screwed? There is no way I can get into that account without getting the Mastersons' fingers, with or without them attached?"

"The Mastersons' fingerprints, not necessarily the fingers."

"Alright, Vladimir. You want me to ask you how we do that. OK, how are you going to do that?"

"I want to get copies of their fingerprints from some repository of fingerprints, a repository that I can hack into quickly and reasonably easy. Hugh Masterson has purchased guns in New York State so he had to be fingerprinted when he bought them. Law enforcement agencies have those prints on file, but I don't want to try to hack into the New York State Police computers or the US Bureau of Alcohol, Tobacco and Firearms' computers."

"So, where do you intend to get them?"

"From the computers of the retailers that sell the guns. My research indicates that they keep an exact duplicate of the documentation they send to ATF in their databases. I know that Masterson has bought some fancy guns. I have found newspaper articles about clubs he has been shooting at and they have pictures of him with his guns. Only one retailer sells two of his guns, a very classy store in Manhattan owned by the guns' manufacturer. That is where I'll start."

"That's very smart, Volya, very smart. It's too bad you spent so many of your years drunk and chasing whores, we may all have been in better shape now if you had used those brains in the first thirty-three years of your life.

"Vladimir, can you connect us with Pham Dac Kien on this communications device? I have an idea that may make this process easier and faster."

It took less than three minutes and the Vietnamese accented voice of the Secretary General of the United Nations could be heard over the satellite communicators of Nikita and Vladimir. The background noise sounded like the crowd at a soccer game.

"Pham," said Nikita, "does UN security fingerprint consultants when you hire them?"

Pham Dac Kien was all too familiar with his boss's less than socially acceptable telephone etiquette and knew when the best strategy was to follow his lead. "Not always, but if they are involved in areas of security or finance we do, why?"

"Would you have fingerprinted the Mastersons' when they were consulting to the United Nations' Pension Fund?"

"I was not at the UN when they were consulting to the pension fund. Considering the areas Hugh Masterson was in, I am sure they did a full security profile on him, which of course, includes fingerprints. She was never involved in that contract so I doubt that we have anything on her, why?"

Once again, Nikita simply ignored the 'why' at the end of Pham's answer and went straight to his point.

"Can you get us a copy of that file and particularly the

fingerprints in it?"

"Probably if I was in New York, but you do realize I am sitting on the beach in Maui. Our

President Saji's End of Severe Poverty in Our Time through International Cooperation World Tour began three days ago. I must say this ending poverty thing is really working for me. The food is great, the weather is exceptional and the accommodations are fit for a king. I always knew I hated poverty, but this…"

Nikita cut him short, "I don't give a shit about the tour. Have one of your people in New York get me those fingerprints…"

In an unusual display of brazenness, (he was probably feeling the wine that was continually flowing and he was continually drinking) Pham interrupted Nikita and with what sounded like a snicker, said, "I have no people in New York that I would trust with the assignment to get me the fingerprint file of a former consultant."

"Why the hell not?" piped in Vladimir. This must have pushed Pham over the edge because he replied with a definite edge to his voice, particularly for the number one diplomat in the world. "Because every last fucking one is here on the beach with me and Sorosh Saji giving our all to President Saji's End of Severe Poverty in Our Time through International Cooperation World Tour. And from the shitty state of my approval ratings, in the last twenty-four hours, successfully generating chaos around the globe."

Nikita said nothing, he simply looked at the device in his hand, scrolled down the corner window to the name 'Kien' and pressed disconnect.

"Vladimir, get to work on your idea and get us those fingerprints. We need that money." He then disconnected the call.

Anna and Hugh left the gazebo, on the beach, after breakfast and headed for the conference room on the first floor of the western tower. The monitoring of the conversations, of what now appeared to be ten members of Nikita's inner circle, had produced ever more frightening information about what was going on with Nikita. Even more disturbing was the fact that the President of the United States, his wife, the First Lady and the Secretary General of the United Nations were all on Nikita and Ovinko's payroll.

The Mastersons had decided it was time, since the holidays were in the past, that they bring Roger and Alberto up to speed on this conspiracy since it was getting ever more complicated and sinister. After letting those two in on everything, they knew they would then decide how much they would involve the other eight members of the security team. Anna and Hugh had decided the afternoon before, while kayaking around Hawksbill Bay, they would first have to assemble all they had gathered into a logical sequence.

After a half-hour of jumping from conversation to conversation, they decided how they would like to have the vast amount of information they had collected explained to them. If they were the audience rather than the performers, it would be in the form of a kind of story or narrative.

That is exactly what they put together over the next eight hours, having had a light working lunch right in the conference room. When they finished, they started toying with a title for the thriller...for a thriller it was.

They were scribbling titles on yellow pads, when Anna

said, "Nukes, dollars, diplomacy and the sinister one; a conspiracy of global proportions," they had a title.

It was six-thirty that evening, when they decided they would sit down with Alberto and Roger on Thursday, allowing two days to go over their narrative. Anna called them both and set Thursday, January 28th at 10:30 in the morning for show time.

Neither concealed their excitement at the prospect of finally getting the full picture.

Anna and Hugh had put several hours into assembling the saga they were about to present to Roger and Alberto. Assembled, were all the conversations and tracking information they had gathered since October 2008, when Anna had hacked into Nikita's satellite communication system. They had the identities, whereabouts, background information and photos of all ten members of Nikita's band of bad guys and a bad girl. In addition, where possible, they had assembled video footage of those in the ten who made public appearances where news bureaus got them on tape. It was from one of these appearances, the celebration in honor of the new United Nations Special Atomic Energy Oversight Envoy to The Islamic Republic of Iran in January 2008, that the Mastersons got their first live video of their nemesis, Nikita, known to the diplomatic world as Vladislav Dubnikov.

Therefore the delivery of the status of the conspiracy drama, the 'where we are' segment of the Mastersons' planning process, would be both audio and visual.

Alberto and Roger arrived in the conference room at exactly 10:30 and took seats next to each other at the large circular table. Since each of the walls of the conference had its own video screen, they would be able to see the video elements of the presentation no matter where they sat.

As they took their seats, all four video screens came alive with a gray and black background with the title, 'Nukes, Dollars, Diplomacy and the Sinister One - A Conspiracy of Global Proportions' in fiery letters across each.

The two young men showed the flicker of a smile to which

Anna said, "Hugh likes to be dramatic at times. The title is mine, but the graphics are his. However, what you are about to learn is far more sinister than the fiery letters could ever be.

"Sit back and relax because you probably will not be able to relax ever again after you know what we have been learning for the last two years."

…and so began the following presentation, delivered alternately by Hugh and Anna, with photos and videos related to the villain or event being described.

Hugh started, "It all began with our need to keep tight and continuous surveillance on Nikita and, if possible, his son. As you know, Anna perfected the technology to lock onto the satellite communications device that Nikita and his partners in the past had used to plan and execute their less than honest activities.

"While developing the protocols to listen to the conversations going back and forth, Anna turned up proof of what we had suspected. The United Nations' Secretary General was on Nikita's payroll. This did not come as a big surprise. Particularly after the news that Nikita had been appointed to the rather serious post as United Nations Special Atomic Energy Oversight Envoy to The Islamic Republic of Iran reporting only to the Secretary General, not the Security Council or General Assembly. Nope, he reported directly to Pham Dac Kien. A cozy situation since Pham Dac Kien works for Nikita.

"Anyway, as you guys remember," Anna said, smiling, "on the day of the inauguration of the President of the United States, January 20, 2009, we learned that he too was an employee of Nikita Incorporated.

"We discovered he had been groomed for the role he was about to play since he was eleven, by none other than Nikita's brother-in-law, the heroin czar, Vilen Ovinko. It was a bad day for us, but a far worse day for the United States. The head of the most powerful country on the globe and the head of the most influential political organization in the world both worked for two men whose only interests revolved around their own wealth and power." During this part of the narration pictures and videos of Sorosh Saji, the President, and Pham Dac Kien, the Secretary General, flashed onto all four screens creating a kind of macabre background.

Hugh jumped in, "We made a decision at that point, to simply monitor every conversation, twenty-four/seven, collect and catalog them. We were well aware that the two of you thought we should do something. However, we truly hadn't a clue as to what that something might be.

During the year just passed, we have separated our activities. I continue to monitor the movement and communications of every one of the conspirators on Nikita's network and we have successfully identified all ten." With this, one by one, pictures of the ten players in the conspiracy with their names and positions came up on all four screens:

1. Nikita, Vladislav Dubnikov; Lead Villain

2. Vilen Ovinko, Heroin King; Number Two Villain

3. Vladimir Dubnikov; Nikita's Son

4. Cheslav Bocharkov; Nikita's Russian Lawyer

5. Boris Batkin; Nikita's Russian Banker

6. Dimitri Demochev; Director General, RFTABO

7. Pham Dac Kien; Secretary General of the UN

8. Sorosh Saji; President of the US

9. Heydar Vahdani; President of Iran

10. Lucile Saji; President's wife; Daughter of Mexico's Heroin King (aka Sister M)

Anna and Hugh had scripted this presentation to bring these two up to speed quickly, but to lose none of the devastating implications of what they had uncovered.

When number six came on the screen, a large footnote appeared:

RFTABO is the acronym for the Rossijskaya Federaciya Tehnologicheskoye i YAdernoye B'uro Oploshnosti, translation: Russian Federation Technological and Nuclear Oversight Bureau.

At this point, Anna said, "This is the organization with absolute control over every class of Nuclear and Biological Weapons owned by the Russian Federation. Demochev, a former Soviet and long time colleague of Nikita, has absolute control over the RFTABO."

Then when the screens came to 'Heydar Vahdani, President of Iran', Hugh announced, "And this is the man that wants to buy four thousand nuclear warheads from Dimitri Demochev via Nikita. Warheads that were designed for Iran's Shahab-3 ballistic missile which in earlier incarnations was known as the Soviet made Scud ballistic missile."

At exactly the same moment, both Alberto and Roger exhaled muttering "Shit" under their breath. However, they continued to sit quietly and maintain a professional demeanor.

That all ended with the last picture and description. Alberto was the first to lose his composure, jumping to his feet when Lucile Saji, the United States First Lady, and her close relationship to the Mexican drug cartels appeared across each of the four screens. "What the fuck..." but he got no further. Roger grabbed his arm and pulled him back down into his seat.

Anna smiled and said, "The conspiracy in the federal government is far more sinister than we ever thought and runs very deep. We essentially have nowhere to go with the knowledge we developed from the Nikita communications network. Knowledge, which unfortunately you too are now burdened with.

"Alberto, Roger, this ownership of the President and the White House is well planned and has been in the works for some time. As far as we can deduce from the conversations and research on the participants, particularly: Nikita, Ovinko, the President and the President's wife, it all began with Ovinko. He managed every aspect of Sorosh Saji's life including who he would marry and when.

"Lucile Maria Regina Ramirez Mendoza – third generation Mexican American; graduate of UCLA & UCLA Law; formerly youngest partner in Beregovoi, Zhukov, Conroy & Salazar law firm; and now First Lady of the United States. This charming lady was handpicked by Vilen Ovinko together with her father, the esteemed Raul Mendoza, Jefe de Jefes to the Mexican heroin industry, to romance, marry and most of all manage the pathetic, narcissistic tool, Sorosh Saji.

"It would appear that when Nikita realized what his brother-in-law had created in this charismatic, self obsessed front man, who didn't even realize he was nothing more than a front man, he was determined to see Sorosh Saji in the White House. We suspect that Nikita put up the five hundred million dollar war chest and saw, shall we say, to the 'surrender' of his opposition. That is what got Saji into office.

"We have no idea how deep it goes, but we believe that every one of the four cabinet members and thirty-one czars is on either Nikita's, Ovinko's or Mendoza's payroll."

"Add to that a handful of key senators and congressmen," interjected Hugh, "and we would have no place to hide if they found out what we know. Worse, if they put two and two together and realized the only way we could know what we know is from their satellite conversations, they would shut that golden goose down. At that point, we would be as good as dead.

"Anna and I know your initial reaction is going to be 'there's got to be something we can do to stop this'. At this point, we don't see any way to stop Nikita and his crowd. We also believe that you will shortly come to that conclusion.

"Now let's go on. Why would these two go to all this trouble? What is the pot of gold at the end of the rainbow? Well, we figure it is not a single pot of gold. It's an initial big killing followed by unparalleled control of the government of the wealthiest, most powerful country on the globe, by really bad guys."

"Let me guess, the initial big killing is the nuke deal, right?" said Roger. "How much do you figure that deal is worth?"

"One hundred billion," answered Anna. Both of them whistled through their teeth, but Alberto couldn't help but make a comment. "Maybe, Mrs. M, we let the deal go through and you work your genius and grab the hundred bil. What do you think Roger, Mr. Masterson?" and then he burst out laughing.

Anna smiled and answered in a rather serious tone, "It could come to that, however, now let's get into as much of the details of that transaction as we've put together so we're all on the same page.

"Let me start with the joint actions of President Saji and Secretary General Dac Kien. I'm sure you have been watching the spectacle on TV, the President Saji's End of Severe Poverty in Our Time through International Cooperation World Tour, and know as we speak they are working diligently to end poverty in Maui. A performance that to the world looks like the actions of a couple of out of control teenagers. Coupled with the fact that by taking hundreds of bureaucrats with them, bureaucrats that keep the government and the UN functioning, they have essentially brought the UN and the US government to a halt. Seem crazy, well it's not!

"We have monitored conversations where Nikita and others are speculating on how long they can keep it up. The agenda is to create chaos to keep every political body in the world concentrating on their own problems and too busy to pay attention to nuke deals in the Middle East. Of course, an added benefit to this group is that stopping the drug trade is at the bottom of everybody's priorities. However, Demochev, the Russian with the nuke stockpile, has thrown a monkey wrench into Nikita's plan."

"Let me guess," said Roger, "he wants money up front."

"Right," said Hugh, "originally he wanted fifty billion

bucks, his group's share of the one hundred billion, but now he has settled for twenty-five billion. Nikita agreed, but doesn't have the money nor does he have anywhere to get it, but from us.

"We have put all of the conversations we've monitored and captured out on a secure server that you and Alberto can access. They are in sequence by date and time and if you bring up the associated text, it will identify the participants and their location. It is very interesting stuff. Particularly, when you realize it isn't a novel or a movie, but it is a group of real bad guys planning a real global crisis. One like no one has ever seen before. However, we want you to hear this conversation between Nikita and his son with a short participation by Pham Dac Kien from Maui. Believe me when I tell you, it is revealing and it has seriously elevated our need to be on high alert. This conversation took place last Friday, the twenty-second at three in the afternoon Teheran time. Nikita made the call to his son in Russia from his villa in Tehran, Iran."

The top of the screens then came alive with the pictures of Nikita, Dac Kien and Nikita's son. The bottom displayed the text of the conversation with the participants and their locations. Simultaneously, the audio came from the speakers on the four screens and the four listened to Nikita in his frantic scramble for twenty-five billion bucks and his intention to get his money back from the Mastersons any way he could.

At the conclusion of the conversation, Anna said, "That is the last communication we have monitored. The network has been silent since Friday. I guess the evil ten took the weekend off. However, in view of the fact that Vladimir seems to be getting smarter and his plan to lift Hugh's fingerprints from the shotgun manufacturer's computers may just work, we have taken some precautions. Friday afternoon, we moved enough money from the escrow accounts to our operating accounts to sustain us in a costly operation. We then changed the account access security for both accounts to iris scan and fingerprint scan. Now here is the kicker. The operating account only requires one of us to withdraw or transfer funds while the escrow, the one with the forty billion plus in it, requires iris and fingerprint scans from both of us. Those four scans must all be done within three minutes. Since they can't get our iris scans from anywhere, we think they are very effectively blocked."

"Which means as soon as Nikita's kid figures this out and tells his old man, their only recourse will be to grab the two of you, intact," said Roger.

"Well, it won't happen overnight, but it will happen quickly," answered Anna. "First Vladimir will figure out that security has graduated from fingerprint to both fingerprint and iris map. Then it will take him some time to figure out it requires both of us to get through the security wall. Then the shit will hit the fan."

"Oh boy, will it," said Roger, "and since Nikita knows you have started distributing the money he needs, to the original planned recipients, or at least people who will use it as was intended, he is gonna want to act fast."

"Hopefully," said Hugh, "Vladimir will spend a few days trying to get the fingerprints from the gun manufacturer's computers. Then if he gets them, another day or two trying to use the fingerprint to hack into Regal Bank of the Caymans before he figures out he's screwed."

"That will give us about a week or less to accomplish something Alberto and I have been discussing for about a month," said Roger.

"What's that," Anna said, looking somewhat surprised.

"We want to get you and Mr. M weapons, side arms to be exact," piped in Alberto. "We not only want you to get them, we want you to become proficient at using them. Kateri says she can turn you into very efficient gunslingers in a week, so we would like each of you to spend three hours a day with Kateri beginning tomorrow. Mr. M, you take the morning shift. Mrs. M, you do the afternoon, OK?"

"This is not only you two that want this to happen, Kateri is on board with the idea also?" asked Hugh.

Looking at each other, Alberto answered, "All of us are."

Roger continued, "We don't want anything to happen to either of you. This is a fun and good business you recruited us into and with the ever-expanding number of crooks in the world taking decent folks' money, it is a growth business. But, it is as you always say, 'stealing from the bad guys and giving back to the good'. Those bad guys are always going to want to get at you two and our team won't let that happen because that is what we do and we do it pretty damn good."

It was now Alberto's turn to pick up the conversation. "But we are not always right there with you, for instance when you want to be in the gazebo or on the beach or kayaking. You go there to be alone with each other. We keep an eye on you wherever you are, but if someone wanted to get at you when it's just the two of you we think they could do it."

"How," asked Anna?

"Well, that's how it all started," continued Alberto. "We were watching you follow the giant turtles in Hawksbill Bay, in kayaks one day, when we started to speculate on how we would grab you if we were the bad guys. By the way, that's what the bad guys would do, grab you not kill you. Because whoever they are, they want their money back more than they want you dead. Anyway, we figured they would wait until you were far enough away from your security team so they could grab you and get away. Now there are a lot of precautions that make that virtually impossible. We just decided that afternoon a nice lightweight '38' automatic would be the perfect deterrence. If they came after Mrs. M, in seconds, Mr. M would kill them and vice versa. We discussed it with Kateri and she said, quote, 'it has to be'. We then brought it up at dinner and it was unanimous."

"So," Roger added, "this is the perfect reason and the right time."

"Shouldn't we pick out guns that we like?" asked Anna. Seeing the looks on their faces she added, "You've already done that, haven't you?"

"We think we know you both pretty well," continued Roger. "Hell, we watch you twenty-four/seven, so we all got together and discussed it and came up with two handguns we think you'll really like and which will definitely provide protection."

"I trust without sacrificing style and comfort," said Anna, trying to suppress a giggle.

"Definitely not," answered Alberto, "we have selected for you, Mrs. M, a Ruger 380 LCP. Fully loaded with seven rounds of .38-caliber bullets it weighs less than a pound and is only slightly bigger than a smart phone, but it's deadly."

"Let me guess guys, you got Hugh a Walther PPK so he can continue to view himself as 'James Bond'," quipped Anna.

"Actually," answered Alberto, "we did, Mrs. M. A Walther PPK – 380 ACP, also a .38-caliber seven shot compact semi-automatic, but one that is a little bulkier and heavier."

He hardly got the words out when Hugh shouted, "Perfect, absolutely perfect, we'll start training on Saturday. Great, great, goddamn, a Walther PPK, I've wanted one forever. Did you get me a shoulder holster?"

The arming of the Mastersons being resolved, Anna and Hugh had one more issue to address.

Hugh started, "We have decided that the growing threat from Nikita is serious so we are splitting up what we do in our company. Anna will continue to analyze the source of the billions Nikita and his band stole via the UN and return it to the proper beneficiary of that long ago largesse. I'll concentrate on monitoring the doings of Nikita and his band of bad guys, particularly as it might relate to all of us and our need for additional security."

"Now for new business," said Anna. "We feel we each should have backup, just in case. In the event something happens to both of us, there should be others who know what we are doing. There are several peoples' lives and a lot of money involved and we feel the team and the business can go on. To get to the point, we have decided you two are our backup plan.

"You, Roger, will work with me and I will teach you what I do and bring you up to speed on where we are in understanding the history of the billions from the UN programs."

"You, Alberto," said Hugh, "will become my protégé, first in tracking the bastard Nikita and his bunch, while enhancing security.   After that is eventually resolved, learning how we track down stolen funds and the bad guys that stole them."

"What do you say, guys?" asked Anna.

"What an unbelievable opportunity, we will be forever grateful to you and Mr. Masterson," said an emotional Alberto.

"From the Bronx to this, it is all almost unreal," added Roger.

"Well, that makes three of us that got here from the Bronx and it still is surreal to me," said Hugh.

"OK," said Anna, "tomorrow we will sit down with the other eight and bring them in on everything we went over with you today.   Then we will reassign your responsibilities and organize them around our new business plan.   There are enough specialties amongst them that we will have the best-staffed funds reclamation company in the world.   Hell, we're already the richest.   Tell the others we'll meet at noon tomorrow in the war room and have lunch while we discuss and plan.

"Gentlemen, let's go to dinner."

Anna and Hugh arrived in the war room in the security building about fifteen minutes before noon. Allowing them time to set up the audio and visual components for the 'Nukes, Dollars, Diplomacy and the Sinister One - A Conspiracy of Global Proportions' narrative.

When they entered, they literally almost ran into Jennifer Ebanks, the young maid and assistant to Twila Bodden, the Villa Serenity cook. Jennifer had been busy running between the electric cart she drove all over the compound and a ten-foot long counter that pulled down from the war room wall. She was laying out an incredible array of food for the working lunch, but Anna and Hugh knew from past lunches with the security team by the time they left it would all be gone.

They greeted Jennifer and went about setting up. At precisely noon, all ten members of the security team arrived led by Roger and Alberto.

They entered the room, hungrily eyeing the dishes Jennifer had just finished laying out. As if in a parade formation the group walked, counter clockwise around the rectangular conference table sitting five on each side. Meetings were always held that way in this room with Anna and Hugh sitting at each end.

"Why don't you all go and get yourselves some food," said Hugh. "Anna and I will start with a bit of background on what you're going to see today and the seriousness of not only the information, but the need to keep it absolutely confidential. If throughout the presentation you want to get refills, don't hesitate. We would like lunch to be completed by the end of the first part or what we call the 'where we are' segment. The 'where we go' and 'how we get there' pieces will require not only all of our undivided attention, but your participation because it directly affects your futures."

The presentation, exactly as it was given to Alberto and Roger the previous day, took three hours. There was a lot more participation and questions since, unlike Alberto and Roger, the new eight members of the team did not know all the history. It turned into a great recap of the entire history of how Anna and Hugh Masterson got into the funds reclamation business. Not only for the new members, but also for all. It provided a great foundation for the next part.

Hugh opened the second part of the presentation. "We are going to combine the 'where we want to be' and 'how we get there' segments. As we discussed, we are not going to do anything, but strengthen our defensive capabilities and identify the vulnerabilities of Nikita and his band of villains. However, should Nikita or his people become aggressive, that will change."

"We think it is more important that all of you understand the long term plan Hugh and I have for Cayman Covert Cyber Reclamation, Ltd.," said Anna. "And this team is critical to that plan.

"Hugh continually reminds me that our business is basically stealing money from bad guys and giving it back to the good guys that had it in the first place. Now we originally recruited Alberto and Roger," at which point all heads turned to look at Alberto and Roger, "because we realized we needed people on board who knew how to stop really bad guys, a very fortuitous decision. If it were not for Alberto and Roger, in January 2008, Villa Serenity and all its then inhabitants would have been reduced to rubble.

However, as time passed since that day, we have come to realize that our business is more like modern warfare than anything else. Thus, the most suitable talent on which to build the business are young people trained in all aspects of military conflicts, intelligence, technology, weapons, etc. Therefore team, Hugh and I have decided that you are the foundation on which we will build our growth and in the event of an unfortunate end of him or me, you are our succession plan."

"If Alberto and Roger have not already told you," said Hugh, "we are taking them on as direct protégés to learn the two sides of the business.

"Alberto will work with me in tracking down the money that has been stolen from our clients and making sure the bad guys don't become a threat to us by tracking them continuously or ...other solutions." At this, the team laughed softly.

"Roger," he went on, "will work with Anna in tracking back through history and finding who or what should benefit from the recovered funds and then getting the money into the right hands, like Sister Todd on Christmas. After about a year, Alberto and Roger will switch so both of them will understand the entire business."

"Now," piped in Anna, "for the eight new members of the team, you all bring two things to the party. All eight of you are intelligent and motivated. In addition, each of you comes with a specialty. Alberto and Roger will utilize each of you in various roles in the business as needed. You will use skills that you already have and you will learn new ones, from us, from each other or if necessary, we will arrange on-line courses or send you off to school.

"The objective is to build a tight knit, successful, family business, the twelve of us being the family and therefore, the twelve of us ultimately owning it."

Hugh got up, walked to the food table, and got two bottles of water for him and Anna. As he was coming back to the conference table, he said, "We want to know if this fits in with your plans for your own futures, but before you answer there are two things you must take into consideration. First, this is going to be a lot of work and each of you will be going into areas of knowledge that you have no experience with. Kateri, Liz, Gabrielle and Louise, you're going to have to perfect your combat skills and I expect Ken, Tom, Mario and Larry to work with you in that effort. In addition, we anticipate that Kateri, Liz, Gabrielle and Louise will teach the combat specialists each of their disciplines, as well as teach each other. On top of all that, Alberto and Roger will be teaching you the business from what they learn from Anna and me.

"The goal is a group of ten young, motivated people who each know enough about each other's functions that they could take them over if necessary."

"Mr. M," said Alberto, "that is what the Marines try to make every Force Recon marine capable of and they are pretty effective at it. I, for one, think this is right down our alley."

"It's the same with the Seals," said Roger. "In fact, it is the same with all combat groups, but it is different with the girls. Since, by law, they're not combat, front line troops, they tend to become highly specialized and focused on their specialty."

"But, that's going to change with this group," said Louise.

"I'm going to make you four warriors, technology geniuses. You, in turn, are going to get me back up to speed on efficient ways to kill."

There began a series of exchanges which indicated to Anna and Hugh that their ten new partners were already getting into their roles. However, Anna wanted their commitment formally.

"OK, I know it sounds like you are already into the plan, however, you know me, I need confirmation. Therefore, do any of you want out or need more time to decide?"

Almost instantaneously, grins appeared on all ten faces around the table. Each said, at about the same time, essentially the same thing, 'When do we start?'

"We can start formally on Monday. The weekend is here and I am sure you all want to kick back...," Anna never finished.

"No way, Mrs. M. You and Mr. M start small arms training tomorrow," said Kateri, "and you are going to have some pointers from the guys who have actually done the killing. The combat team will be joining us for the training over the next week when they are free."

Anna and Hugh looked at each other, laughed and Hugh said, "Time for a swim and then dinner. We'll pick up tomorrow and start working on specific assignments. Welcome to Cayman Covert Cyber Reclamation, Ltd. everyone, we have one helluva team."

With that, they all left the war room, the ten chatting animatedly amongst themselves.

This might be a good time, in this saga, to introduce all ten members of the security team.

Original team members.

Alberto Martínez, 32; Co Team Leader; American.

A first generation American of Puerto Rican descent, from the Bronx. Spent ten years in Marine Force Recon. Assignments classified.

Roger Taylor, 32; Co Team Leader; American.

African American from the Bronx. Spent ten years as US Navy Seal. Assignments classified.

Recruited by Alberto and Roger.

Kateri Parker, 29; Small Arms Expert (Rifles, Pistols, Machine Guns, Mortars, Rockets), American.

A direct descendent of the Wampanoag Native American tribe on her mother's side. Nine years Marine Corps, five years as senior instructor Marine Combat Training Battalion (West) at the School of Infantry, Camp Pendleton, California.

Liz Buhle, 28; Explosives Expert; American.

Eight years Marine Corps, three years as senior explosives instructor Marine Combat Training Battalion (West) at the School of Infantry, Camp Pendleton, California.

Gabrielle Tompkins, 30; Dive Instructor, American.

Eight years US Navy; five years as senior dive instructor Expeditionary Warfare Training Group US Navy, Naval Amphibious Base, Coronado, California.

Louise Corone, 27; Information Warfare, American.

Nine years US Navy; three years as senior Information Warfare Officer Expeditionary Warfare Training Group

US Navy, Naval Amphibious Base, Coronado, California.

Ken Grady, 26; Combatant; American; Navy Seal, eight years. Assignments classified.

Tom Landauer, 25; Combatant; American; Navy Seal, seven years. Assignments classified.

Mario Vialli, 28; Combatant; American; Marine Force Recon, nine years. Assignments classified.

Larry Feo, 27; Combatant; American; Marine Force Recon, eight years. Assignments classified.

"I've left you alone for a week, Vladimir," said Nikita, over the satellite network to his son, who was in the family townhouse on Andreevskaya Emb, in Moscow. "Therefore, I am assuming that since you haven't called me to tell me you have our forty billion, you don't have our forty billion. Have you been drunk for the week or chasing whores around your old haunts?"

Vladimir did not strike back at Nikita. He understood that it would take years for his father to trust him. Hell, he was thirty-four years old and had been nothing more than a rich man's playboy son until two years ago. His sister had been the shining star, but she was gone so Papa had to depend on him. Vladimir was certain that idea didn't give his father a strong sense of security.

"No, Papa, I haven't left the townhouse since I talked to you last week.

"Maybe you need help, Vladimir. After all you've been unemployed for most of your life."

"God, he will never let up," thought Vladimir. However, he answered in a very controlled voice, "No, Papa, I don't think any more bodies would make it go any faster. Actually, I have not been without success. I succeeded in getting Hugh Masterson's fingerprints from the gun manufacturer's computers. Their security is very tight so it took a lot of time.

"I finally downloaded them two days ago and have been preparing them to use on the bank's access security. This morning, I started the process of signing onto the Mastersons' account at Regal Bank of the Caymans and found that they were set up to use a single fingerprint. It took me a while using trial and error to find the correct finger, but about an hour ago I was successful and a checkmark appeared on the screen meaning the fingerprint had passed security."

"What," shouted Nikita over the communicator, "you're into the account, when...?"

Nikita did not get a chance to finish his sentence, "No, Papa, I'm afraid it's really bad news. I was doing some more testing before I called you, but there is no doubt about what the Mastersons have done. After I got the checkmark symbol, I waited a few seconds expecting to be on a bank account menu. Instead, an eye appeared on the screen, the logo for Zahavy Ocular Biometrics, followed by the instructions: 'Please place your authorized eye in front of the Zahavy iris reader and click on the 'READ' button.'

I couldn't fucking believe it..." Vladimir started screaming, but didn't get far when Nikita stopped him. "Calm down, Volya, they are one step ahead of us, but we will catch up."

"Papa, you don't understand, this means...."

"I know what it means, Vladimir, we need both. The fingerprints, which you very brilliantly got and made useable and an iris map of Hugh Masterson's eyes. Is there anywhere that we can get that other than his eyes?"

"I don't think so, Papa. They're not in wide use for anything, but security access. It would be harder and take longer to hack into the security systems, of the places that use it, and that Masterson has an association with."

"Be harder and take longer than what, Volya?"

"Harder and longer than grabbing the guy with the fingers

and eyes," said Vladimir, in a much calmer voice.

"Contact Vilen and tell him we meet at the Moscow townhouse tomorrow morning at ten. I will get there about eight. Good night, Volya, you did well. We will get into that bank, one way or another, sleep well." Nikita shut down the call.

The three Russians sat on three separate sofas of the four that formed what used to be called a conversation pit in the 1970s.

It was not that Nikita's Moscow townhouse was old or neglected, quite the opposite, it was elegant and a show place where Nikita and his children had hosted many grand parties over the last ten years. However, this was the inner sanctum of Nikita's world, the private library on the second floor of the mansion where he held any face-to-face meetings that were required in his business dealings. Never had any of the many people that Nikita had lured into his conspiracies over the years ever seen the inside of this room. Hell, only a few even knew of the Moscow townhouse. This, his private jet and his treasured yacht, The Standart, were Vladislav Dubnikov's most prized and private possessions.

"Vilen, my friend, my brother-in-law, let me bring you up to date on the uncomfortable situation we find ourselves in," said Nikita, as he leaned back in the deep cushions of the sofa and sipped his black coffee.

"A week ago yesterday, Demochev demanded twenty-five billion up front before he would let the nukes leave the port in Tolyatti. He started out wanting his group's entire share of fifty billion, but that is unimportant. Twenty-five billion is probably twenty billion more than you and I could put together if we had to."

Vilen Ovinko and Vladimir sat without making any comments. They both knew better than to interrupt Nikita when he had a story to tell or a point to make. They suspected he had both on his mind now.

"I decided our only option was to get the forty billion back from the Mastersons and I gave that task to Vladimir. Much to my surprise, my son here did quite well. He not only found where the funds were deposited, he found that access requires fingerprint scanning. That did not discourage him. He found a way of getting Hugh Masterson's fingerprints off a gun manufacturer's security data base and preparing them to be used in the process of gaining access."

Vilen looked at Vladimir with a congratulatory nod. Being the boy's uncle by marriage, he was very familiar with the strained relationship between Vladimir and his father, Vladislav, over the years. He was also aware that his nephew was trying to clean up his act, particularly since his sister was gone. This acknowledgement of that, by Vladislav, was a good sign.

"However, Vilen Ovinko, yesterday Vladimir uncovered further road blocks that the Mastersons have placed in the path of achieving our goal of reclaiming my money."

With this introduction in place, Nikita went on to relate the events leading up to Vladimir's inference that grabbing one of the Mastersons to get both fingerprint and iris scan, first hand from one of the Mastersons, may be the most efficient solution.

"As you know, the ship is scheduled to leave Tolyatti in early March. Therefore, we have to have the funds available no later than the end of February. That way when Demochev tells us the nukes are ready to sail, we will have some of your people in Russia make sure he's not lying. If he's not, they will stay on board the ship. We will transfer twenty-five billion and the ship will sail, with them as watchdogs, until the shipment is turned over to Iran's people. Then Vahdani wires the one hundred billion into our accounts, neat, clean and efficient."

Now Vilen spoke, "Neat, clean and efficient...except where the hell are we getting twenty-five billion? Vahdani, sure as hell, won't put it up front."

"And I, sure as hell, won't ask him to. Between now and the end of February, we will grab one of the Mastersons, cut off their fingers and pluck out their eyes and my son will use those parts to get through the Regal Bank of the Caymans' biometric security. Then he will pluck out our forty billion."

With that comment, both Vilen and Nikita started laughing. Vladimir did not.

"What's the matter, Volya," mocked Nikita, "does it make you squeamish thinking of a Masterson or two running about with no eyes or fingers? Worry not, we will kill whichever one we grab after we cut off their fingers and pluck out their eyes," again Vilen and Nikita burst into laughter.

"No, Papa, I'm not squeamish. I have not forgotten what they did to my sister, but there are two things. First, we must act fast since they are giving money away every day. Not much now, but as soon as they get momentum, it will start to move fast. That's a far smaller problem than the second issue."

"Which is," said Vilen?

"An extracted eye scan is not reliable with iris mapping biometric security. There are slight alterations in the iris immediately after the blood stops flowing. But, they are significant enough to be seen by the scanner software and it will reject the iris scan.

"So, Papa, uncle, we need one of them alive!"

"Then we shall have one of them alive," said Vilen. I will head back to San Francisco and make arrangements. I will contact Lucile Saji's father and if necessary we will invade their fucking villa on Cayman Brac with one of her father's Mexican drug cartel's armies."

"Excellent," said Nikita, with a smile on his face, "Vladimir, I told you to relax. We will get into those bank accounts one way or another. We will not be stopped! Now let us have lunch and Vilen will return to San Francisco, I to Teheran and you stay here and keep track of the Mastersons' movements and activities."

PART TWO

It had been over a week since the strategy meeting with the team and their spirits were high. Anna and Hugh always believed that if you present ambitious people with a challenge, coupled with an opportunity, you have a winning formula.

There had been no traffic on Nikita's satellite network since January 29th when Nikita learned that Anna and Hugh's biometric security precautions were more complex than Vladimir had first thought. After Vladimir briefly touched on the idea of kidnapping either Anna or Hugh, Nikita had abruptly hung up. From his last words, it was clear he headed for Moscow and a meeting with his two closest confidantes, his son and his brother-in-law, Vilen Ovinko.

Anna, Hugh, Alberto and Roger had hashed over that last conversation a number of times speculating on how long it would take for the bad guys to figure out that they needed biometrics from both Anna and Hugh to get past the Regal Bank of the Caymans' security gate. The conclusion was always the obvious. How long it took was irrelevant, the gangsters' reaction was predictable. If they were willing to kidnap one of the Mastersons, they wouldn't hesitate to kidnap both. That always led to more intense weapons training for both of the Mastersons. It had now gone beyond the original plan of one week, pretty much because Anna and Hugh were really getting into it and were…well becoming competitive. However, not with the other members of the team, with each other.

It was late morning when the entire team assembled at the shooting range that occupied half of the basement of the security building. They were there to see a shoot out between Anna and Hugh. The targets were silhouettes of Nikita, his son and Vilen Ovinko. The silhouettes were all the same with one differentiating feature. Enlarged photos of the faces of the three villains had been affixed one each to the three targets.

There were two sets and the competition called for them to appear one, two or three at a time in both Anna's and Hugh's sector of the range. Each of the Mastersons had one load of seven rounds apiece to 'kill' their attackers. If they took too many shots at the first two attackers and their gun was empty, it was presumed the third would get through and 'kill' which ever Masterson had used up their ammunition.

There was wagering of an unusual nature among the members of the team. Such as 'you do my laundry for a month' or 'you clean my apartment for a month', but the betting had a curious consistency. The four female members of the team were betting on Anna while the four male combatants were backing Hugh. Alberto and Roger, having been with the Mastersons for more than two years, knew better and simply smiled and watched the goings on.

The weapons were very similar; Anna's Ruger LCP is a .38-caliber compact lightweight weapon and Hugh's, a Walther PPK, slightly larger and heavier, also a .38-caliber. Where they truly were very much the same was in accuracy. They both were spot-on accurate at a range up to one hundred fifty feet, extraordinary for such small lightweight pistols.

With weapons holstered, Hugh's in a shoulder holster and

Anna's in a holster in the small of her back, the two stepped to the firing line.

Hugh was smiling and looking intently and apparently adoringly at his wife, Anna, who he had never seen sporting a deadly weapon.

Anna, on the other hand, was looking intently down range apparently sizing up the possibilities.

Kateri, who was coordinating the event, told all the team to stand well behind the Mastersons, to avoid distracting the competitors, not for fear of wild shots hitting them. A comment that brought laughter from all. She then quietly said, "The competition has begun!"

The room went quiet, as both the Mastersons stood poised waiting the popping out of the silhouettes in whatever configuration Kateri had planned. Then without so much as a squeak, they were there.

In Anna's sector, the three appeared simultaneously, two from the right and one from the center. In Hugh's sector, they appeared consecutively, about one second apart, one right, one left and one down the center.

Shots rang out in rapid succession and the team all agreed that there were nine shots. The six silhouettes were brought forward for all to examine. All six had sustained 'kill hits', but a lot of speculation as to the personalities of the Mastersons would be discussed among the ten team members for a long time to come because of the very different approach to effective killing.

Hugh's three villains each sustained two successful hits about an inch apart in the center of the upper chest. In a real conflict, all three would be dead or near enough to death to be of no concern to Hugh. Hugh shot as all combatants are taught to shoot, aim for the largest mass and expend enough ammo to be effective, but not wasteful.

Anna's three bad guys told a very different story. Nikita, Vladimir and Vilen each had a single bullet hole in the center of their foreheads. Anna, on viewing the three targets, frowned and said, "I was aiming specifically for the point between their eyes. I need more practice."

All twelve then burst into laughter. However, Kateri hushed them and said, "Since all six aggressors have been dispatched, the second criteria will determine the winner. Mr. M, how many rounds do you have left in your weapon?"

"One," answered Hugh, "I fired six and had six hits."

"And you, Mrs. M," asked Kateri?

"Four, Kateri, "I fired three and had three kills."

"Therefore, based on the second criteria, conservation of ammunition, I declare Mrs. Masterson the winner." At which point Louise stepped forward with a trophy in the shape of a cowgirl firing a pistol. "We also have a cowboy, but that will have to wait for another competition," said Roger who was standing behind Louise. At which point, they all started laughing and patting the Mastersons on the back with congratulations on an effective shootout.

As the group was dispersing to go to lunch or return to their duties, Anna turned to Alberto and Roger and said, "Would you two join us for lunch in the gazebo? We have something we want to discuss with you." All four turned and headed out towards the beach and the gazebo.

~~~

The four sat talking in the gazebo as Jennifer Ebanks brought in all the essentials for lunch from her cart. After some very complimentary comments to Anna about her shooting, Alberto and Roger told a few war stories with some serious shooting incidents. When Jennifer had left to go back to the main house in her cart, Hugh said, "Anna and I have been analyzing the possible reasons for the silence on Nikita's network since he left for Moscow. From our tracking of the movement of the communicators, Nikita is back in Teheran going about his business. Ovinko is back in San Francisco and Vladimir is still in Moscow. The other seven on the network are all silent, but all the devices are on and they are all pretty much where we would expect them to be."

"Except, of course, the President, the First Lady and the UN Secretary General, all of whom are moving from one high end resort to another on 'The President Saji's End of Severe Poverty in Our Time through International Cooperation World Tour'", said Anna, with a look of disgust on her face. "These two and their two thousand closest friends have cost the taxpayers over thirty billion bucks so far. The estimate of one billion a week was a joke. The grand traveling party is costing an estimated five billion a week and climbing, it's disgusting!"

"Anyway," Hugh said, "I fear that Nikita and his buddies are busy planning some seriously aggressive moves aimed at getting back the forty billion, so the nuke deal can go down.

The President's grand tour is serving its purpose. There is not a word in the mainstream media about any of the issues confronting the United States or any other country. Afghanistan, Iraq, Pakistan and the economy are all gone from the news media. The liberal media shout praises for the sacrifices being made by the President and the Secretary General to help the down trodden folk of the world while the conservative media is howling that the world is in chaos while 'Sorosh (Nero) Saji' eats, drinks and makes merry.

"They will not be able to carry on this diversion forever. Probably the end of March is when the shit will hit the fan. People will suddenly notice that Iran, Syria, Venezuela and North Korea are all building missile silos that strangely resemble the Soviet Scud silos of the cold war. Nikita and his group must complete the transfer of nukes for money with Iran by then. They therefore need the forty billion soon, like this month!"

"With that in mind," said Anna, "we want to strengthen our security."

"Mrs. M," said Roger, "this compound is more secure than Fort Knox. What more do you think we need?"

"Not here, Roger," answered Hugh, "the Long Island compound. Anna and I want to strengthen the security there to provide protection to both the Long Island staff and the vast data files. We tend to overlook the fact that all the data we are working from down here is actually on servers in the Long Island compound's data center. If Nikita is desperate enough, he may think that he can get information from that data to give him access or a way to get access to the accounts at Regal Bank of the Caymans. The technology security is strong enough to keep him or his son out. I am more concerned about physical security.

"Alberto, I would like you and Roger to contact the people at our New York based security firm, ATO Protection Ltd., and discuss what we have there and what we need there. You and I will go to Long Island next week and work out the details.

"I want defensive weaponry there, something less dramatic than rockets since the compound is in a populated area, possibly low impact stuff. ATO will not handle any of that, but I know of a great company through the former National Security Advisor, called Pum Pang, Ltd.

They are South Korean weapons manufacturers and they make a great perimeter defense weapon, a 5.56mm, Automatic Rapid Fire Robot Sentry, called in the industry 'ARFRS'. It is small caliber and I understand it is near to the sound of a snake spitting so it would be perfect for the Long Island compound. You and Roger look into that and any other ideas you may have. Set up appointments for the week of February 15th and we will make decisions and get the work started.

"In the meantime, Roger and the rest of the team will carry on here with Anna."

With that, the lunch ended and the group left the gazebo.

Hugh and Alberto were in the front of the villa loading their luggage into the back of the Range Rover, driven by Ken Grady, with Mario Vialli riding in the front passenger seat. Both had side arms and in special concealed compartments in all four doors were Heckler & Koch MP5s. This nasty 9mm sub-machine gun could pump out bullets at the rate of seven hundred rounds per minute. Which meant, on rapid fire, the thirty-two rounds in the magazine would be gone in 2.8 seconds, but so would anyone or anything that had been in the range of fire.

Since the team became aware that Nikita and group were contemplating kidnapping, they had decided that at least two of them, armed to the teeth as they put it, would always accompany Hugh and Anna. They were now particularly on alert since there still had been no traffic on Nikita's network. They all felt that Nikita was up to something and hoped that it wasn't off the network because someone had figured out they were listening. There had been a lot of discussion about sending more security with Hugh and Alberto, but in the end, they decided that a low profile was better and that the villa was more complicated to protect so the team should stay there with Anna. Besides, both Alberto and Hugh were carrying weapons.

Alberto was saying goodbye to Roger and Kateri, who had come to see the two off, while Hugh was hugging Anna goodbye. They had realized this was the first time they had been apart in over three years. Hugh was assuring Anna he would be back in a week.

As the Rover pulled out of the compound, heading to Gerrard Smith International Airport for the charter jet that would take Hugh and Alberto on the four-hour trip to LaGuardia's Marine Air Terminal, neither one of them could have imagined the events that lay ahead.

Alberto and Hugh arrived at the Long Island compound a little before seven on Monday evening. They were met at the charter flight arrivals center at LaGuardia's Marine Air Terminal by the Mastersons' usual limousine service, but by a driver, Guda Phadkar, that Hugh didn't know. This bothered them both, so they were very much on the alert for the entire trip over the traffic snarled Long Island roadways.

Alberto got so tense when the driver announced he was taking an alternate route to beat some of the traffic that Hugh was afraid he was going to pop Guda and take over driving himself. However, the trip was uneventful. The driver dropped them off inside the compound at the front door of the main house. Megan Ferguson, the cook at the estate, had a meal waiting when they walked in.

They spent the evening physically reviewing all the security features of the compound and the buildings. They were already extensive, but almost all were passive. Hugh wanted more than simply knowing someone was breaking in, or had broken in and gone. He wanted to stop them. If not with tight security, then with effective defensive weaponry.

Both he and Alberto agreed on the use of the newly developed unmanned machine-gun equipped robotic sentry, named by its Korean manufacturer, Pum Pang, Ltd., 'Automatic Rapid Fire Robot Sentry', or 'ARFRS'.

Alberto had contacted them the preceding week to set up an appointment. Soon after, the United States distributor of the weapons had a video delivered to the Long Island compound. It was waiting for them on their arrival.

A stand alone 5.56mm machine-gun, it is equipped with two cameras with zooming capabilities, one for daytime and one for infrared night vision. Further, it is controlled by advanced pattern recognition, which can detect the difference between humans and trees. Finally, it comes with loudspeakers and a pre-recorded message to warn an intruder.

Hugh wanted the message to be "surrender or die." He wanted those exact words spoken by a woman with a southern accent. He and Alberto laughed for several minutes visualizing the surprised look, on the face of some thug, who had laughed at the warning from a sweet southern belle. When seconds after he ignored the warning and moved, he would be literally, cut in half by fifty 5.56mm rounds.

They then marveled over the technology employed in the defensive weapon and the fact that the special ammunition, coupled with the casing of the weapon, reduced the sound to little more than that made by an air rifle or a spitting snake.

They watched the video several times commenting on different qualities and capabilities. At the end, they decided to get six for the Cayman villa in addition to those needed on Long Island. At one hundred fifty thousand bucks each, the management of Pum Pang, Ltd. would be very happy indeed.

They slept soundly, woke early and were well prepared when Roger Cole and Jessica Macina, from ATO Protection Ltd., the team responsible for the Mastersons' Long Island security systems, arrived for their three o'clock meeting.

Apparently, Roger and Jessica were a bit nervous about the links to weaponry. They spent the first fifteen minutes emphasizing the fact that their systems would provide all the linkages they needed, but the actual installation of the weapons and the connection of the two components would have to be done by Pum Pang, Ltd.

Hugh assured them that ATO's people and Pum Pang's team would not even be on the compound at the same time, so they need not worry.

They spent five hours going over what Hugh and Alberto wanted and how ATO would make it happen. They agreed that the installation and upgrades would take a week and ATO's teams would start the next day at eight in the morning.

Jessica then agreed to have the schematics and specifications for the linkages to the Pum Pang 'products', as she referred to the robotic machine guns, ready for Hugh and Alberto to go over Friday afternoon in their offices on West Fortieth Street in New York City.

Hugh agreed, explaining they would be in Pum Pang's New Jersey offices in the morning and would come through the city on their way back to Long Island.

The meeting broke up with Roger and Jessica heading back to New York City.

Hugh was pleased with the way things were going. It looked to him and Alberto like the project would be completed by the following week, right on schedule.

Alberto and Hugh were once again reviewing the existing security components, protecting the Mastersons' Long Island compound, when three white, unmarked vehicles entered the grounds. Hugh recognized the driver of the lead vehicle, an SUV; it was Roger Cole from ATO, sitting next to him was a younger guy.

All three vehicles pulled into the circular area at the front of the main house and as Alberto and Hugh approached, Roger and the young guy stepped out of the SUV. "Good morning, Mr. Masterson, Alberto, this is Bryan Attwell the site supervisor for the project. The crew and all of the materials needed for the configuration we agreed on are in the trucks."

As Bryan was shaking hands with Hugh and Alberto, Roger continued, "Bryan was a counter-terrorism team leader with the US Army Special Forces in several Middle Eastern hot spots for ten years before joining ATO three years ago. Bryan specializes in our projects that have your kind of unique needs and he is quite familiar with Pum Pang's robotic sentry equipment.

"He'll oversee the project and although I must leave for another site, he'll be able to reach me at any time. You know it's our policy to keep our installations highly confidential, so I will not be able to tell you where I'll be. However, you have my cell number should you want to reach me.

"I've got to run, but I'll be in touch with Bryan throughout the day." With that, Roger got back in the SUV and drove off the property.

"Bryan, is your boss always so nervous about weaponry?"

Asked Alberto with a laugh. "Hell, he calls Pum Pang's murderous device 'robotic sentry equipment' like it was some kind of robot vacuum cleaner. At the meeting yesterday and obviously again this morning, he appears to be really jumpy acknowledging the fact that we're linking more than bells, sirens and cameras to the fantastic monitoring technology you guys have developed. I would assume with your background, Bryan, you're not so weapon shy."

"It's a company thing, Alberto," said Bryan. "They really believe these are still the good old days when intruders wanted to steal your valuables and sneak away into the night. In Europe and the Middle East, the intruder is more often on a mission to blow up a facility or a group of people and it's only a matter of time before that becomes the norm here.

"My colleagues and I are constantly trying to convince Roger and his bosses that we should enter into partnerships with companies like Pum Pang. With their weapons and our detection technology, we could go global. They're afraid of bad press from some bad guy being shot. I tell them the publicity, from having very clear videos taken by our systems of a crowd of school kids being blown up, will be a lot worse than how the parents would react if the videos were of our defensive ARFRS cutting some terrorist in half. Hell, half the parents would want one on their lawns."

"First Recon Battalion, Marine Force Recon" Alberto offered as credentials. "We were starting to use robotic defensive weapons on my final missions before I left Afghanistan," he added. "They are the wave of the future and once the bad guys know they exist and may be on the property they are intending to invade, they think twice. That's what happened everywhere we installed one. Actually, we took to advertising their presence with some creative graphics and the terrorists avoided them like the plague."

"Hey," said Bryan, "we're staying local for the week so we can pack as many work hours in as possible. Maybe we can have dinner and swap war stories."

"I'd like that," answered Alberto.

"Mind if I come along and listen?" asked Hugh. "I'll even pay for dinner."

"The more the merrier, Mr. M," said Alberto. "Bryan, I'll touch base with you later and we'll decide whose joining us and where we'll go."

"Great, I'd better get the team started. You guys have added a lot of coverage and upgraded everything you're not replacing. It's going to take all week to get it done."

With that, the group broke up and Hugh and Alberto returned to the main house.

~~~

Less than twenty-five miles away on a stretch of Long Island's Ocean Parkway, near Oak Beach, a limo was sitting with the engine running in the parking lot of what once was one of the Long Island south shore's most famous watering holes. In the limo sat Guda Phadkar, on a cell phone, speaking with a very heavy Pakistani accent. "Yes, Mr. Ovinko, I drove by less than thirty minutes ago and there are guys working on their security equipment.

"No sir, the trucks have no names on them and I can't get close enough to see the license plates."

"Yes sir, Masterson and the bodyguard are still there. If they're going anywhere, they'll call me, I guess.

"Well, that is what they said when I dropped them off yesterday from the airport.

"Yes sir, the minute they contact me, I'll contact you."

As the line went dead, Guda said to himself, "Shit, he doesn't even say goodbye. How am I supposed to know if he didn't get disconnected or the call wasn't dropped? Asshole, if it's dropped, he'll call me back. I sure ain't calling him."

"Papa, it's me," said Vladimir Dubnikov, into the satellite communicator. "Masterson is on Long Island at their north shore compound. He's there with one of the bodyguards, the Hispanic one. But, without Anna Masterson."

"When did he get there, Volya?"

"Vilen says he came in Monday night and he's been there ever since. He says there are people all over the compound working on their security systems, so he doesn't think it would be a good idea to try to grab him in the estate. If it was tough to get in before, it's impossible now. He says he has the estate being watched twenty-four/seven and the limo driver they are using is one of ours. If they move, he will tell us and we make the decision when to grab him.

"But, Papa, if he is here why not grab the wife off the Cayman Brac villa. Either one will get us into the accounts."

"Because if you think getting into the Long Island compound is tough, you have no idea what it would be like to get her off Cayman Brac. You were in a drunken stupor when we tried to attack that fucking fortress in 2008. It was like invading a country and I am sure it is worse now since we tried to blow them up then.

"No, Vladimir, he has one body guard with him and the driver of the car they travel in is ours. We will wait until the perfect opportunity. It will come.

"Get back to Ovinko and tell him to have a standard 'hit and grab' team ready, just like in the old Soviet. He'll know exactly what I mean and tell him that every time Masterson leaves the estate the entire 'hit and grab' team stays with him, even if they decide to drive to California.

"Tell Vilen I will call him and discuss our next steps. Explain to him that I can't get to him now because I have to get to a meeting with Heydar Vahdani and his Minister of Energy, Rastinpour. They want to discuss the brokering and logistics of selling the first batch of nukes to their buddies; Syria, Venezuela, North Korea and of all places Bangladesh."

"Jesus, Papa, do you see what he's up to? If Bangladesh goes nuclear, India is surrounded by countries with the bomb and if Syria goes nuclear, they could damn near roll the bombs into Israel. Same with North Korea dropping one on South Korea or Japan. He is strategically making alliances in countries that have been the weak guys on the block since the Second World War and then arming them with nukes."

"So?"

"So, Papa, his game plan is to neutralize the countries with nuclear fire power, particularly the democracies, using his own version of MAD. The way the Soviet and the US kept each other in check for fifty years. But, they just wanted to keep each other in check. I think once he has ringed the world with allies, including Venezuela, and armed them with nukes, he's going to make a move for global power and that is when the shit is going to hit the fan.

"Papa, are you sure we should be doing this?"

"Vladimir, you like all your toys and all your whores. Well, this means a clear profit to us of fifty billion US dollars, a lot of whores and a lot of toys. But none of it happens without getting our money back from those fucking Mastersons. So call Vilen and get the plan in the works."

With that, the satellite phone went dead.

Vladimir Dubnikov went to get some supper. He would wait a few hours before calling Uncle Ovinko. It was seven in the morning in San Francisco and he hated waking him up.

As he walked down the stairs to the kitchen, he was mumbling to himself, "Great, Papa, we pull this off and have our share of the fifty billion and our forty billion back from the Mastersons, but will there be any place in the world left to spend it?"

The ATO crew was ahead of schedule by Thursday evening. That made it even more important that Alberto and Hugh work out all the details with Pum Pang before the weekend. Since they were trying to squeeze in the meeting with Jessica, at ATO's offices in Manhattan that afternoon, they were up early. By eight o'clock, they were in the limo and on their way to Pum Pang's offices in Moonachie, New Jersey, with Guda Phadkar once again in the driver's seat.

Alberto didn't trust the driver and it was easy to pick up on that sentiment in both the fact that he questioned his every move and the way he questioned him. Hugh couldn't help but laugh to himself and hope Alberto was wrong. The problem was that Alberto was seldom wrong when he had a gut feeling, and did he have a gut feeling about this guy.

Well, if Guda did anything unusual, he unfortunately would be dead or incapacitated before he could explain. Hugh sat back and leafed through the prints of the Long Island compound's new security map. It had the points at which the ATO monitoring technology would meet the Pum Pang defensive weaponry. This and price is what they would discuss in New Jersey. The schema for the links would be the topic later in the day when he met with Jessica at ATO for the integration schematics.

They made good time and pulled up in front of Pum Pang's building at ten minutes before ten. As they exited the limo, Alberto instructed Guda to stay put in the parking lot on the side and said he would call his cell phone when they were getting ready to go to their next meeting. Guda asked casually, "Where is our next destination, Mr. Masterson?" Alberto damn near bit off his head, telling him he would give him the destination when they were on their way. He closed with, "Now, go park on the side and sit. If you've got to leave the car to pee, call me and ask permission," with which he slammed the door and followed Hugh into the building.

~~~

Guda Phadkar was pleased to bring the car to the side of the building where the parking lot was, it met his needs. There were no windows or doors on that side of the building, just gray brick.

Guda pulled the limo into a parking space near the middle of the building and left the engine running. It was twenty-three degrees Fahrenheit outside and he wanted to stay warm. He pulled out his cell phone and pressed a key.

"Mr. Ovinko, I am in the parking lot of Pum Pang's building at 21 Cordovan Drive, Moonachie, NJ. Masterson and the Hispanic bodyguard went inside five minutes ago for a meeting."

"Guda, do you know how long they'll be inside?"

"No sir, I don't know when they will be out. They told me to wait for a call to take them to their next appointment."

"Where is their next appointment?"

"The bodyguard pretty much told me it was none of my business. They would tell me when they were leaving. But from bits of their conversation on the way here, until they closed the glass separating me from them, I think it may be in New York City."

"Do you know anything about this Pum Pang? What they do? Who they are?"

"No sir, I don't know what Pum Pang is or does."

"OK, Guda, you just sit there. Three black SUVs will be getting to the lot in less than thirty minutes. They have been tracking you via GPS and are already in New Jersey. Guda, they are part of what we used to call in the Soviet 'Hit i Zahvat'. It was effective then, it will be effective today."

"'Hit i Zahvat', what does it mean, Mr. Ovinko?"

"Better you don't know, Guda Phadkar. You will see and understand all a little later. Just keep being the obedient chauffer and all will be good. If all goes well today, there is a healthy bonus in this assignment for you. Now, stay put and keep Masterson happy and relaxed," and the phone went dead.

"Again he just disconnects and I don't know if he is finished or I lost the connection. These fucking Russians, I will never understand them."

Guda turned on the radio to a Pakistani language station, turned up the heat, tilted the seat back and settled in to wait.

The meeting was going far better than expected. When Hugh told the Pum Pang team after they completed the Long Island installation, he also wanted a proposal to surround the perimeter of the sixteen-acre Cayman Brac villa Alberto and Hugh were treated like royalty. They wanted some information on the Cayman villa and that took time, which was not in Hugh and Alberto's tight schedule.

At twelve noon, the conference room doors opened and six servers rolled in carts laden with varied and colorful trays of Korean food for what was going to be a great, but probably long luncheon.

The group still had to finalize the details for the positioning of the ARFRS around the Long Island compound in order to get complete coverage of every inch of perimeter. The Pum Pang team had been working with Jessica, at ATO, to identify the fields of coverage of their monitoring equipment. They had a proposed schema to present to Alberto and Hugh after lunch.

Hugh suggested to Alberto that they have a working lunch. Alberto, who had spent six months in the Korean DMZ and made many Korean friends, explained to Hugh that the Korean hosts would be upset. The luncheon was a kind of sealing of the trust between the security company and the client.

Hugh, being less sensitive to these traditions, indicated that he would have to leave alone and go to ATO. If Alberto stayed at Pum Pang and worked with them to finalize the positioning of the machine guns, by the time he got to ATO, they could have gotten the specs to Jessica. Then, she and Hugh could finalize the interface specifications. That would keep the whole project on schedule. The specs could be gotten to Bryan Attwell, at the Long Island compound, and the team could start that evening with the preparations for Pum Pang's arrival on Monday.

"No, Mr. M, you don't go anywhere without me. If anything were to happen to you, Mrs. M would personally put a bullet in my head like she did the targets."

"Alberto, it'll be fine. I'll get a local limo to take me to ATO in the city and when you're finished, you take our limo and meet me at ATO. We'll have dinner in the city and be back on Long Island by ten o'clock."

Alberto kept trying to dissuade Hugh pointing out they were paying both of the vendors in this project 'big bucks' as he put it. Finally, with his concern …and voice rising he said, "They should, surer than hell, be accommodating us not the other way around. I don't want you out of my sight for even a minute."

Alberto's level of concern and stress was very apparent. It did not go unnoticed by Myon Chou, Pum Pang's senior vice president, who was hosting the meeting and the luncheon. When there was a break in Alberto's pleading with Hugh, he interjected, "You seem to have a scheduling problem. Maybe there is something we can do to help?"

Hugh explained the time line emphasizing how he wanted all the design work finalized by the evening. ATO could finish the monitoring installation over the weekend and all would be ready for Pum Pang's team on Monday. He pointed out, smiling, that Alberto's concern was his going into New York in a strange limo without the benefit of Alberto's protection, but he saw no danger in the short trip.

Besides, Alberto would catch up at ATO later, with their limo and driver, and all would be OK.

"Possibly, we can help," said Myon Chou. "Mr. Masterson, you can go to New York in your limousine and when the work is completed here, we will provide Alberto with a car and driver to bring him to ATO's offices."

"No, that's worse...," started Alberto, but Hugh cut him short. "That would be most gracious of you, Mr. Chou. Alberto is very protective of me and our current driver is new to us, so Alberto who by his nature is...shall we say cautious, does not feel comfortable entrusting me to him."

"You must be very proud to have a young man as loyal and protective in your employ."

"Proud and secure, Mr. Chou, and with all respect to his caution, I think yours is an excellent solution and one for which we are both grateful. I shall continue to enjoy your exquisite cuisine and leave for the city at one o'clock. Alberto, would you let Guda know I will be out at one and it would be good if he had the car in front of the entrance at that time."

Alberto was on the verge of continuing his objections. Before he could say anything Hugh smiled and said, "Alberto, remember I meet all challenges fully prepared thanks to you and Kateri." In that way, he reminded Alberto that he had a fully loaded Walther PPK – 380 ACP in a soft leather shoulder holster under his left armpit.

~~~

The ringing of his cell phone startled Guda awake. The combination of the warm vehicle and the lilting strains of the Pakistani music over the radio had lulled him into a shallow sleep.

"Guda here," he shouted into the phone.

"Why are you yelling, Phadkar? Did I wake you up?" said Alberto, who was making the call from a small room down the hall from the conference room. "Straighten yourself up and be in front of the entrance at five to one. Mr. Masterson will be out shortly thereafter."

"Where is he going and will you be going with him?" He realized he was asking more than he needed to know so he quickly tried to cover himself adding, "Or am I to come back for you?"

"You ask too many fucking questions, Phadkar," shouted Alberto into the cell phone. "Just be in front at twelve fifty-five" and the line went dead.

"Does everybody in this crazy country just hang up phones," he mumbled to himself as he pushed a button on his cell phone.

"Mr. Ovinko, it is me Guda."

"I know who the hell it is, Phadkar. I can see your name on the caller ID screen. What is it?"

"At one o'clock, Masterson will be leaving Pum Pang and I believe he will be alone."

"Why do you believe he will be alone, Guda?"

"The Hispanic bodyguard told me to be in front of the entrance at five to one to pick up Mr. Masterson. When I asked the bodyguard if he would be alone, he told me in a very angry tone, 'you ask too many fucking questions, Phadkar'. I figure I hit on something he didn't want me to know. That is why I think he is going to be alone, Mr.

Ovinko."

"Guda, do you see the three SUVs? They appear on my GPS monitor to be about fifty yards from you."

"Shit," Guda thought to himself, "how would I know, I've been sleeping." Coughing into the phone to buy time, he glanced all around the parking lot looking for three black SUVs and then he spotted three Hummers parked in a row on the street in front of the building.

"I'm not sure, Mr. Ovinko. None came into the parking lot, but three black Hummers are parked in a row on the street in front. They got here a little while ago."

"That's them. Ignore them and just go about your driver responsibilities and be in front of the building entrance…actually now, get moving." The line once again went dead and Guda pulled the limo in front of the entrance to 21 Cordovan Drive, Moonachie, NJ.

~~~

Hugh opened the back door of the limo, jumped in and said, "Turn left on Moonachie Road and head south, it becomes Washington Avenue. Take it to Route 3 East and go through the Lincoln Tunnel. Head up Tenth Avenue to Fortieth Street. I'll tell you the address when we get near."

Hugh pushed the button that raised the glass partition between him and Guda.

Guda did as he was told and headed towards Washington Avenue.

The three Hummers did as their Russian drivers had been briefed to do and followed the limo.

Three thousand miles away, Vilen Ovinko sat at a desk viewing a map of Moonachie, New Jersey, on a very large computer screen. As he concentrated, a tiny orange rectangle that resembled an automobile started moving along a street labeled Cordovan Drive towards another street labeled Moonachie Road.

His eye was then caught as three tiny blue rectangles, which also resembled automobiles, started moving in what on the screen resembled a silly little parade. They stayed about a block behind the orange rectangle.

Vilen Ovinko was watching the beginnings of his 'Hit i Zahvat' via a GPS tracking program. All the vehicles in this maneuver had tracking devices installed that broadcast their whereabouts and movement at all times, even when parked and unoccupied.

Ovinko pressed a key on the keyboard in front of him and the view zoomed in on all four rectangles. Only then was it evident that there was lettering inside each of the rectangles.

Inside the orange rectangle was a clear 'T1'. Ovinko was a man of simple solutions, 'T1' stood for Target 1. This was the vehicle driven by Guda Phadkar and Vilen believed carried Hugh Masterson.

The three blue rectangles were labeled 'HIZ1', 'HIZ2', and 'HIZ3'. This was a bit of Ovinko's macabre sense of humor. The 'HIZ' stood for the Russian designation of this operation, 'Hit i Zahvat'. '1' was the lead Hummer, '2' and '3' the followers.

Ovinko pressed another key on the keyboard and asked,

"Who is in the limo?"

The heavily Russian accented voice of the driver, of HIZ1, responded, "The Pakistani driver and Masterson in the back."

"That's all?" asked Vilen Ovinko.

"That is all, just the two."

"I will be back to you in a few minutes. Stay close with them."

Vilen Ovinko removed the satellite communicator, from his inside jacket pocket, and pressed a button.

"Masterson has left the New Jersey offices of the Korean weapons manufacturer, Pum Pang, Ltd., in a limo driven by one of our people. It appears they are heading for New York City and it appears he is without his bodyguard."

Nikita's two-word response before disconnecting, "Grab him."

Each of the three Hummers moving south on Cordovan Drive, a short distance behind Hugh's limo, had three occupants. A driver in the front seat and two Russian thugs in the back seat.

All nine villains wore wireless headsets so they were all in constant communication with each other. In addition, any instructions from Vilen Ovinko to the team leader, Liv Polyansky, who was driving HIZ1, reached all of them simultaneously. This avoided confusion and the waste of time relaying the instructions.

Therefore, seconds after Nikita told Ovinko to, "Grab him," Ovinko instructed the kidnapping team. "Grab Masterson and after disposing of the limo, bring him to Vladislav Dubnikov's mansion in New York City. Liv, you're familiar with where it is, but for the rest of the team, should you get separated, the address is 1011 Fifth Avenue. It is at the corner of Eighty-Second Street and Fifth Avenue, across from The Metropolitan Museum of Art. Use the private garage entrance on Eighty-Second Street.

Now as to Masterson. He can be unconscious if necessary, but not dead. Above all, don't let any damage come to his fingers or eyes." Vilen gave no other instructions, simply hung up. The gang was well prepared for this kidnapping having gone over the plan a dozen times. Regardless of where or when they would grab Hugh, the method was to be the same and the location where they would bring him always, the mansion.

Immediately on Ovinko disconnecting, Polyansky pressed a tiny button on the headset attached to his right ear and started talking. Although the entire group could hear what he was saying, his instructions were intended for the driver of a tractor-trailer parked two blocks away. At the same time, Polyansky was checking the map of the area on the GPS screen in the dashboard of the Hummer. After studying the area and the logical route for Masterson to take to New York City, Polyansky told the tenth member of the team, the tractor-trailer driver, to position himself facing Washington Avenue on Barell Avenue in Carlstadt, New Jersey, and await instructions. This was, about five miles south of where they were.

Polyansky stayed very close behind the limo, making sure that no other vehicles got between him and Hugh. "Stay close on me and let no vehicles between us," he said to the team. "The driver of the limo is on our payroll, so he is expecting us to be behind him. Since Masterson is in the backseat and has no rearview mirror, he'll have to turn around and look through the rear window, not likely."

They had gone about four miles in silence when Polyansky began talking, once again the message was for the driver of the tractor-trailer. "The limo is a silver stretch Mercedes. You can't miss it because there are three black Hummers right behind it. You know what to do," and the team went silent again.

At the corner of Washington and Barell Avenues, as the limo was entering the intersection, the eighteen-wheeler pulled across Washington Avenue and appeared to stall. Guda, driving the limo, was caught off guard since he had no idea what Ovinko had planned. All he knew was that he kept Ovinko informed of his movements with Masterson and his bodyguard. He almost slammed into the trailer section and hit the brakes so hard Hugh was thrown out of his seat in the back. He hit the console containing the refrigerator.

It was quite a different story for Polyansky and his gang. Fully prepared for what was to happen at the corner of Washington and Barell Avenues, Liv had pulled his Hummer along side of the limo. As Guda was hitting the breaks, Polyansky had already stopped the SUV and the other two Hummers had pulled in behind blocking any view of what was going on. The two thugs had exited the back seat of Polyansky's vehicle and in less than five seconds, one pulled open the driver's door. Using a silenced Russian 9mm Stechkin automatic pistol he fired a single shot into Guda Phadkar's temple.

The second Russian pulled open the back door and found Hugh Masterson struggling to get back in his seat while at the same time reaching for his Walther PPK. The gangster fired a syringe like dart into Hugh's neck, from a Russian made YAd, tranquilizer dart pistol. The syringe contained an animal anesthetic usually reserved for gorillas. The effect was instantaneous and Hugh rolled over onto the floor of the limo, unconscious.

Immediately the shooter jumped in beside the unconscious Hugh, took the Walther PPK from Hugh's hand and propped him up in the seat. Guda's assassin pushed the Pakistani driver to the front passenger seat, and got behind the wheel of the limo.

By the time Guda was pushed aside, two Russians from the second SUV had opened the door and were removing Guda's dead body. The thug, in the driver's seat, popped the trunk and the two with Guda's body dumped it in the trunk and slammed the lid. One of them got in the back next to the unconscious Hugh, while the other returned to HIZ2. Hugh was now propped up like an ordinary passenger between the two Russians.

While all this was going on, the tractor-trailer had maneuvered around and backed up to within twenty feet of the limo. Two Russians, from the third Hummer, were lowering the back door of the trailer, which became a ramp. Immediately, the limo was driven up the ramp and into the truck.

Except for the driver and two Russians with Hugh in the limo, the remaining six thugs were back in their vehicles.

The procession, which now comprised a tractor-trailer and three black Hummers, continued down Washington Avenue towards Route 3. Ironically, they would take exactly the route that Hugh had instructed, the now dead, Guda Phadkar, to take.

The entire operation had taken one minute and fifty-eight seconds.

In just over an hour, the tractor-trailer and the three SUVs pulled into a huge storage warehouse, on the corner of 39th Street and 10th Avenue, in New York City. The ramp on the back of the trailer came down and the limo backed out.

Hugh's two Russian minders lifted him out of the back seat. Since the anesthetic shot into his neck was generally used to disable gorillas for short periods, it was fast acting and not long lasting.

As the Russians placed him on the warehouse floor, Hugh began to come around and his first instinct was to reach once again for his Walther PPK. Of course, it was no longer in his shoulder holster.

Almost immediately, Liv Polyansky knelt down next to Hugh and jammed the point of a syringe through his pants and into his left thigh. "He'll be out for about four hours. That gives us plenty of time to get him to the mansion and safely tucked away. Get him into the back seat of my Hummer, between you two," he said to the two minders, "and prop him up like a passenger."

Turning to the Russian who had backed the limo out of the truck, he said, "Is Guda still in the trunk?"

The driver nodded yes.

"Good, put the limo back in the truck and you and the driver take the truck to Brooklyn, to Kulik's scrap yard in Greenpoint, you know where it is. Stay there while they dump the limo with Guda into that monster car eater they have. I want you to make sure that it dumps out those golf ball sized pieces. Is Guda dead?"

The Russian simply shrugged this time. He was obviously

a man of few words.

"When you're sure the limo and Guda are just a ton of little balls, bring the truck back here and you two go home. Your part is done on this operation."

As the warehouse doors opened and the truck pulled out, Liv turned and said, "Now we go to the mansion. Remember to use the 82nd Street garage entrance. There is nobody in the mansion, so if you get there before me wait on 82nd Street. I have the automatic opener."

With this, the three Hummers left the warehouse and headed north on Tenth Avenue.

~~~

It took them a half-hour to get to the mansion and within minutes of arriving, they had carried the unconscious Hugh to the third floor and handcuffed him. They then put a cuff around his right ankle and ran the attached chain to a ring in the wall of the cell-like, windowless room.

"He can yell his head off in here and no one will hear him, not even us," said Liv. "This room was constructed just for special occasions like this and it is triple sound proofed. Get a pail and put it on the floor near him in case he has to piss or throw up when he wakes up, no need to make a mess on the floor. I'm going down stairs and will assign the guard duty shifts. I want him watched twenty-four/seven. There are cameras in all four corners of the room so he can be monitored on the screens downstairs at all times also."

Seeing that his fellow thugs were about to question why a guard was needed, he added, "I am taking no chances with this package. There will be two of us up here in front of the door at all times and that's that. Get yourselves some chairs and whatever you listen to, read or watch. You're taking the first two hours. I'll wait here for you."

~~~

When the two got back with chairs and magazines, Polyansky went downstairs to a study on the first floor where he immediately called his boss on his cell phone. "Mr. Ovinko, it's me, Liv. I'm in the mansion with seven of my people and Masterson."

"Yes, Liv, and what condition is Mr. Masterson in?"

"Undamaged and sleeping like a baby in the third floor special room. I have two people on the door to make sure it's watched twenty-four hours a day. Including me, there are eight of us here. I'll have four teams and we will all take two-hour shifts on the door and two hour shifts watching the video from the four cameras."

"Very good, Liv, just stay there until we decide what is next. It may be a few days. Do you have enough money for food?"

"Yeah, we're good boss. I'll wait to hear from you," said Liv, Vilen disconnected.

~~~

Vilen immediately contacted Nikita over the satellite network. He had been keeping him informed of the progress of the grab from the time the group left Pum Pang's building in New Jersey.

After hearing the status and assuring himself that Hugh was undamaged and well guarded in the New York City mansion, Nikita said, "As soon as the team left the front of the Pum Pang building, I arranged for a jet to get Vladimir from Moscow to New York. He's on his way and should get to the mansion around eight o'clock. He has all the necessary equipment with him, so when he arrives he'll be ready to begin the process of using Masterson's fingers and eyes to hack into and clear out the accounts.

"As soon as we know that the money is moved and safe, have one of your people shoot the bastard and have him cremated somewhere. I want to send his ashes to that bitch he's married to with a forty billion dollar invoice marked 'paid in full.'

"While you're looking after that, I'll contact Demochev and work out the details for paying him when the nukes are on board the ship.

"Have you got people ready to get to Tolyatti and take charge of the nukes?"

"They are already there, Vladislav Dubnikov, I never doubted you would succeed. You always have."

"Until later and our success, my friend," and Nikita disconnected.

It was three hours since Hugh left and Alberto was getting very nervous. Calls to his cell phone kept forwarding to voice mail and he was making a nuisance of himself with Jessica Macina at ATO.

The last time he called, she abruptly told him, "Alberto, Mr. Masterson is probably stuck in traffic at one of the Hudson River crossings from New Jersey. Maybe he's using the delay wisely, taking a nap, and has turned off his cell phone. Since I received the design file you uploaded to our servers, I am really trying to finalize the specifications, for the points where our system interfaces with Pum Pang's system, before Mr. Masterson arrives. If you will please stop calling every ten minutes, I promise to have Mr. Masterson call your cell phone the minute he arrives. Goodbye now." Then she hung up.

Alberto thought to himself, "No way would Mr. M turn off his cell phone and take a nap. He never turned off the cell phone when he was away from Mrs. M."

Since the conference had ended when the plans were finalized and sent to ATO, Myon Chou told Alberto he should make himself comfortable in the small office down the hall that he had used when he called Guda. He had been there almost an hour and Alberto was kicking himself for letting the boss go alone. Even worse, alone with that sleaze ball, Guda. Finally, at a quarter after four, he decided he best alert Anna in Cayman Brac that Hugh was out of touch. He pulled out his cell phone and pressed the speed dial number for her cell phone.

"Mrs. M, this is Alberto."

"Hi Alberto, everything OK?"

"I'm at Pum Pang's offices in Moonachie, New Jersey. Mr. Masterson left here at one o'clock to go to ATO in the city. He insisted on going alone and he used the limo driver from Long Island. We didn't recognize him and I don't trust him. I don't know why, I can't put my finger on it. I just don't. Anyway, he never got to ATO. I can't reach his cell phone and it's over three hours. He could make that trip in under two, even in traffic, and I don't like…"

He never got to finish. Anna realized that he was seriously distressed and rambling. Alberto usually spoke in short phrases as if he were giving firing directions to artillery from the front lines of a battle. Now he was running on like a nervous kid.

"I have got to keep it together," she thought, "if something has happened to Hugh these young people are going to look to me for direction and I can't go to pieces."

"OK, Alberto, let's take it a step at a time. Hugh's gone and unreachable for over three hours and he never got to ATO, right?"

"Right, Mrs. M."

"Alberto, does he have his notebook computer with him?"

"No, he didn't bring it. In fact, I don't think he's been on it since we left Cayman, why?"

"We may have made a serious mistake. We were going to take over the monitoring of the conversations on Nikita's megaphone network from here in Cayman Brac, but Hugh said you and he would stay on it. Since the computer systems we're using for the eavesdropping are in the Long Island facility, he felt he could easily access them from his notebook. Besides, he felt you would probably have a lot of free time waiting around for the security firms to complete the upgrades and installation. I gather since he hasn't been on the notebook with you no monitoring has gone on."

"No, Mrs. M. I don't think that's been going on since we've had very little free time."

"OK, Alberto, I want you to rent a car, preferably a high end SUV just in case we need the power, speed and size. Get back to the Long Island compound, but before you go lead Pum Pang and ATO to believe everything is OK and the project is to continue as planned. ATO is to finish this weekend and Pum Pang is to install all the defensive weaponry next week.

Let them know you may or may not be around, but the project is to continue on schedule.

While you're on the way back to Long Island, Roger and I will review all of the traffic on Nikita's network since a few days before you guys left on the fifteenth. Now get going. We'll stay in constant touch and I'll get back to you as soon as Roger and I have gone through the conversations."

"Yes, Mrs. M. I'm on it…and, Mrs. M, I am so sorry that…"

"Alberto, there is nothing you could have done. If he made up his mind to be efficient, which I gather is the reason he left you at Pum Pang and went off to ATO, there is not a thing any of us could have done to change that. Don't worry, Alberto. Either we will get our Hugh back or a lot of people are going to pay a price."

"You got that right, Mrs. M," Alberto thought to himself as he disconnected.

~~~

"C'mon, Roger, we have a problem," Anna said to Roger as she entered the war room in the security building. "You and I are going to listen to Nikita and his buddies' conversations since Hugh and Alberto left on Monday."

"But...," started Roger.

Anna cut him short, "I'll explain to you in the main house. We're going to my office and learn what they've been up to."

After ten minutes, Roger knew everything Anna had learned from Alberto's phone call. This included her fears and her belief that the answers would be found in the Nikita network conversations.

After two hours, they knew the whole story and to a limited degree where Hugh was.

The satellite conversations between Nikita and his son, together with those between Nikita and Vilen Ovinko, described the plan. Even more enlightening were the updates that Ovinko gave to Nikita about every fifteen minutes. They made it clear that the operation had been a success and they had Hugh.

The problem was that all three of these villains knew the details, so no details needed mentioning in their conversations.

Vilen would say something like, "He's in the warehouse and he is in good shape and unconscious." Even though they never mentioned Hugh by name, Roger and Anna would interpret that to mean that Hugh was in a warehouse and not seriously injured. What warehouse? Where? In what city?

"The gangsters that grabbed Hugh are talking to each other in greater detail I'm sure," said Anna. "But, they're not doing it over Nikita's network. They're probably using cell phones and we're out of that loop."

Then they reached the last conversation between Nikita and Vilen. "As soon as we know that the money is moved and safe, have one of your people shoot the bastard and have him cremated somewhere. I want to send his ashes to that bitch he's married to with a forty billion dollar invoice marked 'paid in full.'

"While you're looking after that, I'll contact Demochev and work out the details for paying him when the nukes are on board the ship."

Roger was very still watching Anna's reaction. Initially she went very pale and seemed simultaneously to be both sad and terrified, but it lasted only for seconds. Then her look turned to anger and determination.

"They will not do anything to Hugh because they won't get into the accounts and they badly need that money. Apparently, Nikita's kid is doing the hacking and he'll be in the mansion they refer to around eight tonight. That means they'll know, no later than mid morning, they need two sets of biometrics. Once they scan Hugh's fingers and eyes into the system, they'll get the following message: 'Security Access User One Accepted; Please Process Biometrics For User Two'. Then the shit will hit the fan.

"At that moment, the kid will figure in order to get into the account they need biometrics from both Hugh and me. He'll keep checking for about an hour, putting off telling his father, then he'll call him on the satellite phone and tell him they need to grab 'the bitch', me.

"That should happen early tomorrow afternoon, New York and our time. Within an hour of that call, they'll start working on a plan to grab me.

"C'mon, Roger, we have less than twelve hours to formulate a plan and put together the tools we'll need.

"Let's get to the war room and get the team together. By then Alberto will be back in the Long Island compound and we can link him into the session."

They left the main house and headed across the villa grounds to the security building and the war room.

Anna had underestimated Vladimir's determination to convince his father that he was reformed and responsible.

Thanks to strong tail winds and a heavy premium paid to the Russian jet charter service, the trip from Moscow to New York's LaGuardia airport must have set speed records. Vladimir was in the mansion and setting up his equipment before eight that evening.

Liv Polyansky and the two minders on duty brought the semi-conscious Hugh to the mansion's first floor library. That was where Vladimir had set up a notebook computer and several peripheral devices including iris and fingerprint scanners.

Vladimir really wanted to impress his father. He was hoping to access the Mastersons' account at Regal Bank of the Caymans. He would then move the forty billion, or whatever was in the account, to the family accounts in Nikita's private bank, Bank Snachala Dlits'a, and report the success to his father by ten that night, New York time. It was not to be!

By nine o'clock, Vladimir knew the news he had was not going to make Papa happy. Everything went well, but turned sour real quick, pretty much the way Anna had predicted.

The sign-on process was straightforward and worked like the sign-on procedure for any other bank, except for two differences. Instead of an ID and password, the screen was a deep purple and blank except for the words in the center 'User – Scan Fingerprint Now.'

Vladimir dragged Hugh's right index finger across the

fingerprint scanner. In his earlier efforts with the fingerprint biometric, using the fingerprints he had acquired from the gun retailer, Vladimir had determined that the fingerprint was that of the right index finger, so that went smoothly.

The screen showed a whirling vortex, then the words 'Fingerprint Accepted – Please Scan Iris'. This was the point that Vladimir had realized, in Moscow, that they had to kidnap Hugh.

Vladimir grabbed Hugh by his hair and forcing his left eye open pushed his head forward against the headrest of the laser iris scanner simultaneously activating it.

The screen once again showed the whirling vortex, then the words 'Iris Scan Rejected – Please Scan Again – You Have Two Attempts Remaining Before System Lockout'.

"Shit," said Vladimir to no one in particular. He once again grabbed Hugh by his hair and this time forcing his right eye open pushed his head forward against the laser iris scanner and activated it.

The now familiar whirling vortex appeared on the screen followed by 'Security Access User One Accepted; Please Process Biometrics For User Two'. The deep purple screen with the words in the center 'User Two – Scan Fingerprint Now' appeared.

"Mother fucker," screamed Vladimir, as he closed the access screen to Regal Bank of the Caymans and bounced Hugh's head against the back of the chair he was sitting in. He shouted to the Russian minders, "take this prick back to his cell and don't leave the door until you're relieved. Shit, shit, shit!"

"What's the matter, Mr. Dubnikov, is there anything we can do?"

"Yeah, go get that bitch wife of his. In order to get through the security we are trying to break, we need his and his wife's fingerprints and eye scans."

"Where is she, Mr. Dubnikov? I'll take two of my people and we'll grab her."

"Never mind, Liv, she's probably in the Cayman Islands in the middle of a fucking fortress. I'll contact my father and find out how we go about getting her.

~~~

It was after nine-thirty, before Vladimir had gotten his thoughts together as to how he would deliver the news that now they needed to kidnap Anna. When an idea struck. Instead of grabbing Masterson's wife, why not get her to come to him right here in the mansion. Then he would have the two of them together and breaking into their accounts would be as simple as four scans.

He fished his satellite communicator out of his pocket and hit the keys to reach Nikita.

"Papa, it's me, Vladimir."

"Do you have our money, Volya?"

"No, Papa," and figuring leaping in was the best way to deliver the news, he quickly went on. "We need another set of eyes and fingers."

"What is that supposed to mean, Vladimir? If you do not have the money, tell me why."

"I learned fifteen minutes ago that access to the Mastersons' account requires both of them. We need to scan fingerprints and iris scans from both of them…" He didn't get a chance to finish.

"When does this end, Vladimir?" Nikita's voice was obviously full of stress. "First we needed to break a password code, and then you learned we needed a fingerprint so you got the fingerprints. Then you learned we needed an iris scan, so I got you Masterson and his eyes. Now you tell me you need the fingerprints and eye scan from his wife. Are you sure that is the final obstacle or will we need their dog's paw print?"

As he answered his father, Vladimir knew instinctively that his remark was wiseass, but he couldn't help himself. "Papa, everything I have researched about the Mastersons would lead me to believe that they have no pets, dogs or cats or anything…"

The explosion was worst than he anticipated, "You little, snot. Don't be a wiseass with me or I'll have those animals that are babysitting Masterson take a break and drop you into a shredder. You are too stupid and inexperienced to realize that we are dealing with vicious self-interested pricks on all sides. Masterson, Iran's President Vahdani, Demochev and his nukes, the American President Saji and even that whore-chasing mongrel of a United Nations' Secretary General, Pham Dac Kien. All of them are waiting for me, or your uncle Vilen, to make the smallest slip and they will dispose of us like yesterday's shit. If any one of them thinks they can take us out of the deal, they will, permanently. That is why I keep them all apart and they deal only through me.

"Without that money we can't make the deal and if we do not make the deal, we are dead. It is only a matter of when and who will make us dead.

"So, Vladimir, other than wisecracks do you have any real ideas?"

He would have to talk fast to get his old man calmed down, but he had a good idea. Because of his endless research, he had knowledge about the Mastersons that he believed his father didn't. "Sorry, Papa, you were right, it does seem like endless barricades, but I couldn't resist joking back about the dog paw. I truly doubted you were serious. I do think that the bitch's biometrics will do the trick because the system is looking for a second person's finger and iris scans. According to all my research, they don't completely trust one other person besides each other. It has to be her and probably only her.

"Can I completely guarantee that her biometrics is the end of the line? No, I can't. I only learn of a new layer after I get through a layer. But, it appears very logical to me that will be the final layer. More than that would make access awkward for them. Since they are generally always together, it would have been a rational approach to tiered security. I believe she is the other user and once we get her, we get into the accounts."

"Do you have any ideas on how to pull that off?" Nikita asked, with the sarcasm dripping from his tone.

"As a matter of fact I do. I don't think we should grab her as we did Masterson. By now, she knows he's missing and is probably speculating on where he is and is definitely surrounded with bodyguards, heavily armed bodyguards. I propose to tell her tomorrow where he is, who has him and what we propose to do with him, if she doesn't cooperate. I then will lay out instructions to get her to come here, to me, where I will use their eyes and fingers to retrieve our forty billion. What do you think?"

Nikita was quiet, truth be told he was taken aback by his son's plan and the way he had delivered it. After a moment, he said, "I think your assumption that she is the final layer is correct. You're right, we have no way of knowing until we get through the next layer. If it's not the final layer, your idea of us having both of them alive and in our control will make it that much easier to get through any additional obstacles they may have put in place.

"Only one change to the plan. I want Masterson out of there, when she gets there. Just in case, she brings the law or an army. Here is what I want you to do. Pack Masterson into a steel trunk and have Liv and two of Ovinko's people take him and bring him to San Francisco where they can pick up Ovinko and then fly Masterson to Hawaii. They should all get on board the Standart, which is currently moored in Maui.

"I'll meet them there and we'll take the Standart and anchor about five miles off the coast of Johnston Atoll, one of the most avoided parts of the Pacific Ocean. It once was a test site for US nuclear bombs. I think it would be fitting if we start the process there that puts nukes in the hands of anyone with enough cash. Besides, it's the last place anyone will look for Masterson.

"All of us getting to Maui, and on to the atoll, should take no more than thirty-six hours so we can be at Johnston Atoll by Sunday evening the twenty first. That will give us plenty of time to get the money back and pay Demochev.

"You work on getting that bitch to the mansion where you can have her scan her fingerprint and iris into the bank site, while we scan Masterson's from the Standart. Contact Captain Machtcenko and make sure he has the necessary scanning equipment on board before we leave Maui.

"You keep two of Vilen's people and let the rest go. How many are there now?"

"Eight, including Liv Polyansky. I'll let Liv decide who he takes to meet you with Masterson, the two he leaves with me and which three go do whatever it is they do."

"Good. Once the money is moved, we'll dump Masterson into the Pacific in pieces and you kill the bitch. Have her, and anyone or anything that came with her, shredded at Kulik's Scrap Metal place in Greenpoint."

"Maybe I won't kill her before we shred her, just to repay her for the trouble she's caused us." His father had disconnected before he finished.

Anna and Roger had assembled the security team in the war room and had set up a link with Alberto who was now back at the Long Island compound.

"I'll start with what we know," said Anna, "and then explain how we know what we know. After that, we'll discuss our next steps.

"Hugh has been kidnapped by Vladislav Dubnikov, who we know as Nikita. He had the help of his brother-in-law, Vilen Ovinko, who also happens to be the head of the Russian syndicate that imports most of the heroin into the US. Their objective is to use Hugh's biometrics, fingerprint and iris scan, to access the forty billion in money they stole over decades from United Nations' programs all over the globe. As you all know, we've recovered those funds and are in the process of distributing them to the projects for which they were originally intended. If those projects no longer exist, we identify new ones that are similar.

"We have it directly, from Nikita's mouth, he intends to move those funds into his control and immediately kill Hugh, cremate his remains, and send the ashes to me."

The room was silent, absolutely silent.

Anna continued, "There is a flaw in Nikita's plan. One that he is not yet aware of. In order to access the accounts, my fingerprints and iris scans are required as well as Hugh's. They must be input within three minutes of each other. We made this change just after Christmas last year, together with one other that I'll tell you about in a minute.

"Since the breaking into the accounts is the responsibility

of Nikita's son, Vladimir Dubnikov, Nikita has him in a jet on his way to New York as we speak.

"We know that Hugh is OK. He is unharmed and is being held at a location in or near New York City called the 'mansion'. What we don't know is where this 'mansion' is.

"It will only be a matter of an hour or two after the son arrives at the mansion, when they'll realize they need a second set of biometrics. Nothing in the access process identifies who that second person is, but these gangsters are not dumb. Within minutes they'll figure the second person is me, after which, they'll be putting in place a plan to grab me."

The silence in the room was shattered with eight of the ten committing to locking down the compound and letting no one in or near Mrs. M. The chatter centered on commitments to round the clock 'babysitting' Anna until they could find and kill Nikita. Roger was silent and very serious, as was Alberto, who was visible on the videos in the war room, viewed in video conference from Long Island. These two knew what Anna's priority would be.

Anna, smiling, was obviously touched by the loyalty and commitment of these young people.

"First," she said calmly, "I'm deeply touched by your commitment to protect me. However, that is no more Hugh's and my style than it is yours. Our strategy, from this moment on, will be offensive not defensive or hunkering down.

"By tomorrow, we'll know exactly where Hugh is being held. When I say exactly, that is precisely what I mean. We'll know his GPS coordinates.

"As I said earlier, after Christmas, Hugh and I began to take measures to add security to the protecting of the funds. We also started to consider what we would do in the event of certain aggressions on the part of Nikita, or any of the other villains we've offended, by taking back money they stole. Since kidnapping has always been a possibility and we promised each other we would not give in to ransom demands, our option would be the finding of the kidnapped Masterson by the free Masterson. Well, we looked into options and just before New Year's, Hugh and I had GPS tracking chips embedded under our skin. Where under our skin, will remain our little secret. Leave it be said, we think it will not be the first place anyone would look for a micro scar. Even though the devices are experimental and have not been widely distributed, except in animals, we've every confidence they'll work.

"The process is simple. The device is inert unless activated and it is activated remotely, presumably by the Masterson not kidnapped. By the way, Alberto and Roger were in on our decision just in case we were both grabbed simultaneously. Anyway, once activated the power supply lasts three years. It looks like we did this just in time.

"Louise and I will activate both tomorrow morning. Mine as a test and if all goes well, Hugh's. Shortly after that, we'll know precisely where Hugh is.

"I want to wait for the morning to give Hugh a chance to get his bearings. When the chip is turned on, there is a bit of pain and a strange sensation. He'll know what it is, if he is alert or near alert. He may not, if he is only coming out of a drugged state. He could overreact or forget it happened and we don't want that. To be on the safe side, we'll wait until about six-thirty tomorrow morning. That's

212

late enough that if they're keeping him unconscious, the drugs may be wearing off and he'll be alert. If they're not drugging him, all the better. He'll know exactly what we've done and he'll know we're on the case. Of course, if he is unconscious it won't make any difference.

"Hugh and I screwed up big time. We became complacent.

"While we were concentrating on the tools for offensive action, we let slide the best defensive tool we had, the eavesdropping on all of Nikita's team of villains' conversations over their private satellite network. If we had been on top of those conversations, constantly monitoring, listening and analyzing real time, we would have known this plan was in the works and exactly when the grab was going down. Vilen Ovinko relayed every step of the plan and its execution to Nikita, as it was happening, using the satellite network.

"That won't happen again. Beginning tonight, we'll put in place a system that every time a new conversation takes place Louise, Roger or I will be notified and immediately review them as they happen.

"Now, as I said, it won't be long before Nikita and his pals know they're screwed and can't get that money so they'll come up with their next step. As soon as they do, they'll talk about it over their satellite network. We'll know what it is and we're going to be prepared

"Roger, you and Alberto work with Kateri, Liz, Gabrielle, Ken, Tom, Mario and Larry and put together a fully equipped, any eventuality, rapid response team, ready to go anywhere in the world and launch an offensive raid, land or sea. I mean fully equipped and the nine of you know better than I ever would what that calls for. Collectively, you have worked with every specialty in military offensive operations. Therefore, you know what equipment needs to be acquired and how assignments should be handled. Money is no object and I mean no object. You guys know what we need and where to get it, so go to it.

"In the meantime, Louise and I will set up the alert mechanism for activity on Nikita's satellite network.

"I suggest you all get some sleep and start early in the morning. It may be the last opportunity for good solid rest for some time, so grab it while you can. All indications, from the last conversations over Nikita's network, are that Hugh is in this place they call the mansion for the night and nothing will happen until tomorrow.

"C'mon, Louise, we're going to set up that automatic alert system, then both of us are going to get some sleep.

"See you guys at breakfast. If you need me, don't hesitate to wake me up."

Anna and the group didn't know that before their meeting was even breaking up, Vladimir and his father Nikita knew they were screwed. Nikita had already set down the plan for his next phase.

Anna and the rescue team would learn all about it in the morning. Saturday, February 20, 2010 was going to be a very eventful day.

The President Saji's End of Severe Poverty in Our Time through International Cooperation World Tour had taken over all of the fifteen hundred fifty rooms in the Ottoman Citadel Hotel, in Jakarta, Indonesia. They were planning to spend most of February touring the most important of the over seventeen thousand islands that make up the archipelago nation.

Sorosh Saji and Pham Dac Kien are lunching in the Keemasan Merpati, the world-class restaurant atop the twenty-five story four-towered hotel.

Approaching their table is Clive Bauman, Saji's Intelligence Czar, and Saji's Press Secretary, Jackson Phillips.

"Mr. President," said Clive Bauman, the fifty-one year old, three-hundred plus pound former teacher of political science at Kendrew University in South Africa's Eastern Cape. "May we have a private word with you? It is quite important."

"Anything you need to say to me, Clive, can be said in front of my esteemed colleague from the United Nations. Our interests and agendas are as one now and our goal of eliminating severe global poverty is the most important of our objectives. Is your message, which by the way was so very important that you thought it necessary to disrupt our luncheon in this glorious hotel, related to the purpose of this world tour?"

"It may be, Mr. President, but I can assure you that it is of global importance and could possibly cause a disruption in this tour for both of you. However, it is very sensitive and it would be best to remove ourselves from this public place to discuss it."

Clive was attempting to deliver the sense of urgency in as diplomatic and respectful a fashion as he could, while controlling his own terror at what he was about to report to the President. He could have spared himself the effort since standing about three paces behind him was, Saji's Press Secretary, Jackson Phillips, the former publisher of 'Jeunes Nus et Dégénéré' the French porno magazine. He was rolling his eyes and making gestures indicating that his colleague was overreacting. Phillips was clearly visible to both Saji and Pham Dac Kien, but not to Bauman. Phillips' mockery unfortunately set the mood for Saji's response, not the underlying terror in the intelligence czar's demeanor.

"Spit it out," said Dac Kien, "our main course, soto betawi, is about to be served and the chef in this palace is known to make the finest soto betawi in all of Indonesia. So, quickly man, quickly."

Realizing that nuclear proliferation clearly took a back seat to soto betawi and the grand tour, Clive decided to deliver his news quickly and succinctly. Besides, he wanted to get to a table and order his own lunch of soto betawi. He too had heard of the chef's reputation.

In fact, since landing his new and quite unexpected job, one of the first intelligence gathering projects he gave to his staff was the compiling of a list of the finest chefs in the world. He wanted to know their specialties, where they performed their culinary magic and solid justification for the President Saji's intelligence czar to visit each of these regions.

Frustrated, Clive pulled out a chair at the table, sat down and simply said, "There is a crisis! Intelligence reports indicate that there is a serious escalation in the efforts by Iran's President, Heydar Vahdani, to obtain nuclear weapons. The buzz is that he has begun negotiations for a large quantity of nuclear warheads. It is rumored he has specifically chosen this time, while both of you and your entire staffs are preoccupied. The reports go on to speculate that he has made his move now, either because he is very alert and has been waiting for this opportunity, or..." Here Clive hesitated fearing the reaction to the rest of the spy chatter.

"Or what, Clive?" said Sorosh Saji, half mockingly. He was obviously looking behind his intelligence czar to the now unrestrained ridicule by the press secretary.

"Or, you two, and your two-thousand closest friends, are deliberately on this grand tour to create the distraction so he can get on with his nuclear proliferation project." Clive Bauman sat back in his chair, bit his lip, and awaited the violent response he expected, simultaneously thinking, "God, I'm hungry."

The outburst never materialized. Saji and Dac Kien, while waiting for their main course, had been consuming a great deal of a highly acclaimed Indonesian wine, a product of the Bali region, and they were both quite cheerful.

The reaction of both was calm and quite lighthearted. Dac Kien simply said "pshaw." Saji, however, was a bit more vocal since it was after all his intelligence czar bringing the news and it was definitely news they wanted to downplay.

Sorosh Saji, President of the United States, sat back in his chair, wine glass in hand and said, with a mocking look, "Remember the intelligence reports in 2002 and what they said about Saddam Hussein and Iraq? If I listen to and act on intelligence reports, I will wind up with as much egg on my face as did my predecessor. Iran is a nation trying to preserve their most valuable asset, their oil, to be sold into a global rising market. They wisely see nuclear power as the most sustainable of energy sources. Vahdani is trying to move his country's energy infrastructure towards one hundred percent nuclear and their transportation towards one hundred percent electric supported by that nuclear power.

"Those that are not so forward thinking nor have the resources to implement such an ambitious plan are jealous. They are constantly accusing President Vahdani of making bombs and ballistic missiles. I agree with my colleague here, pshaw, on these so-called intelligence reports.

"Now the real news of the day," went on Saji, "is the opportunity at hand here in Indonesia. There are almost two hundred fifty million people living in this poverty-stricken nation and this will be the first recipient of the largesse of the joint United States – United Nations war on global poverty."

"And we have this very morning outlined the plan for funding," said Pham Dac Kien jumping in with enthusiasm. "Using as a model the practice of some of the most popular religious organizations, we are going to propose a form of tithing of US private industry. Ten percent of their gross income is to be redirected to a special commission to be set up by the United Nations."

"It is very exciting," piped in Saji, as the waiter refilled both his and Pham Dac Kien's wine glasses. "Companies of every size must participate, there will be no exceptions. This will not be a tax, but rather a form of a contribution. A way to share the good fortune of the American people with the less fortunate countries of the world like here in Indonesia. It will be like a charitable contribution... but not tax deductible."

Jackson Phillips was one of the few people in President Saji's insider circle who actually knew something about business being a former entrepreneur. Granted he sold a rather seedy product, porn, but he was an entrepreneur nevertheless. He began to pay attention. "Holy crap," he thought to himself, "I hope this is the wine talking and they don't really believe they can ram a ten percent involuntary contribution to the United Nations down the throats of American businesses.

"I'm glad I have a backup plan. Lucky I didn't sell off my magazine and porn is hotter than ever. What did the French President say when I took this post, 'Don't give up your day job.' He knew what he was talking about. I guess I should say something about Indonesia and poverty. They're going to want a press release and ...well, here goes."

"Ahhmm, Mr. President, Mr. Secretary General, you may want to rethink the recipient of the largesse. Indonesia is not really a pool of poverty. Their economy's expanding at a rate more than twice as fast as the United States. If you announce this effort, a lot of Americans will think the contributions should be going the other way."

Clive Bauman, by this point, was becoming very agitated. He didn't have even a job to go back to and if this Iran nuclear thing blew up, he would be the logical goat. He could hold his exasperation in no longer and almost shouted, "Mr. President, you can't sit back and take no action in view of the fact that the source of the intelligence reports are from within Iran. Actually, they are from inside

Vahdani's inner circle by a CIA paid informer. If it is true and it does blow up, that will come out and we are up the creek without a paddle."

"You are up the creek, Mr. Bauman," thought Sorosh Saji. "You are the fat cat intelligence czar who did not impress on his boss the weightiness of this matter. Fat cat, yes Mr. Bauman, you are definitely a fat cat. This is really great wine I will have to see to a hundred cases being sent to the White House."

"Shit," thought Jackson Phillips, "I had better do my job or I'll find myself stranded here in the Pacific when they impeach this idiot." Once again, he opened with his humble interruption. "Ahhmm, Mr. President, Mr. Secretary General, in all probability this information on Iran will be in the hands of the American public within forty-eight hours. If you do nothing, the level of discontent in the US will escalate, more chaos will erupt and there will be more demands for your return or resignation. I hesitate to trouble you with this while you are working so diligently on the grand tour. A new blog has been put up by a consortium of media outlets both conservative and progressive called SajiKienResign.com and it is getting over two million hits a day."

"Pshaw, again," snickered Dac Kien. "President Saji's and my supporters are not on that web site. There will always be those nay sayers who shout against progress, either in the streets, in the media or on the internet."

"No, no, Pham, I must listen to my advisors, particularly when it comes to public opinion," said Saji. He was now so mellow from the Indonesian wine that he had what appeared to be a permanent smile.

"Listen to them if it relates to your image, but fuck their advice when it comes to a possible global nuclear war," thought the intelligence czar. "Shit! How the hell did I wind up in this mess? I used to worry about keeping my job for four years, now I worry about not getting killed in two."

"Gentlemen," said Saji, "get together with my Under Secretary of Public Affairs and my Director of Intelligence and come up with some joint statements that keep the public calm. Now good day, here comes our soto betawi. Ahh, it looks delicious. Waiter, bring us another bottle of this superb wine."

When the two czars had left, Pham Dac Kien turned to Sorosh Saji and said in a low voice, "Where the hell did you get that crap about Iran, Vahdani and renewable energy? That is so much bullshit. Vahdani wants nuke warheads for his Shahab-3 missiles and I think our boss is supplying them. Both our boss and Vahdani could give a shit about renewable energy. But you are some actor, I was beginning to believe it. Where did you get it?"

"Nikita," replied Sorosh Saji, President of the United States and full time employee of Nikita Incorporated.

It was almost another two hours before Pham Dac Kien and Sorosh Saji left the restaurant and went directly to Saji's suite. As they walked among the tables, bodyguards in front and behind them, they greeted all the well-wishers, sycophants and general hangers-on with smiles and warm comments.

When they got to Saji's suite, they instructed the bodyguards to stay outside and they went into the empty suite.

"The shit is going to hit the fan," said Pham Dac Kien. "We are both running the risk of being kicked out of our respective jobs. We appear to the rest of the world like a couple of rich school kids that have gone on an extended vacation."

"And took all the other kids in the school with us," added Saji.

Pham Dac Kien was visibly agitated as he went on. "Nikita and Vilen have got to be told whatever they're doing with nukes, for which you and I are keeping the world distracted, has got to be completed by March 31st. If it's not, we'll get dumped and people will really start to look into what the hell we have been up to."

"Calm down, Pham. I know exactly what he and Ovinko are doing with the nukes and this leak is going to make you and me very, very rich."

"What are they doing with the nukes?"

"He has negotiated the sale of four thousand nuclear warheads originally manufactured for the Scud that are presently stored in Russian Federation warehouses. The sale is to Iran who will then sell off half of them to Syria, Venezuela, North Korea, and a dozen others. This whole tour is just one more distraction to make sure their private nuclear proliferation adventure doesn't come to the attention of the US. Or worse yet, to the rest of the nations that will be directly threatened by a dozen nuclear armed pissed off countries."

"Sorosh, how do you know this is what he is doing?"

"He told me."

"So now that the cat is out of the bag, won't they back off?"

"Nikita back off? You've been in his employ longer than I have, do you think he'll back off?"

"No, but I do think I'm right that it better be wrapped up no later than March 31st. If we're not back at our desks being global leaders by then, all hell will break loose. We had better convince them of that."

"Oh, we are going to convince them of more than that, Pham. I figure they are selling these warheads to Iran for about twenty-five million apiece."

"One hundred billion bucks, are you sure?"

"No, I'm not sure," replied Saji, "but that sounds about right and would appeal to Nikita's orderly mind. Yeah, I think it's one hundred billion.

"We are going to call Mr. Ovinko and tell him it's all starting to unravel. We are nervous and we are the guys out front on this. We're going to tell him we can only keep this farce going another month or he will lose all the power he has so craftily created in you and me."

Pham Dac Kien was a global level strategist who had managed to prosper and rise from street urchin to the top of the most ruthless and corrupt political organization in the world. He didn't deal with the number two.

"No," he said, "let us call Nikita directly since it appears somebody in President Vahdani's inner group has created this mess by leaking the deal they're working on."

"Yeah, good idea, Pham. While we're at it, we'll inform him we want our future secured so he can set aside a half a billion apiece for you and me. Hell, it's only one percent of the deal…and I think I'll take a chance and tell him that. If I'm right and it is a hundred billion buck deal, it will drive him crazy trying to figure out how I know."

Sorosh Saji pulls his satellite communicator from his pocket and dials the codes for Nikita and Pham Dac Kien, who was seated on the sofa opposite Saji. Pham Dac Kien pulls his communicator from his pocket and hits 'answer'. Moments later, they hear the gruff familiar voice from Nikita in Teheran.

Sorosh indicates Pham is on the phone and then they both relate the happenings of the last two hours. Pham and Saji emphasize that in order to get eight years of benefits out of this very expensive presidency, they are going to have to appear as if they have the interests of their respective entities as their priority.

They will both start pushing for the Indonesia give away. The United States Congress and courts will never let Saji force American citizens to contribute, but that will keep everyone distracted through March.

Then Pham and Sorosh can go back to the states and start a process to make their dream of eradicating poverty with money from the G-7: Canada, France, Germany, Italy, Japan, United Kingdom, and the United States. This will escalate the chaos to Asia and Europe, but it will seem sincere and they can keep their jobs.

"It has got to be over by March 31st," says Saji, his voice rising to a shrill.

Nikita argues, but gives in.

As they are preparing to disconnect, Sorosh adds one last comment. "By the way," Saji says, "this whole thing can blow up. That's funny a nuke deal can blow up, kaboom. Anyway, if it blows up, Pham and I will take the hit. We need a retirement plan.

"Vladislav Dubnikov, please set aside one percent of this deal for Pham and I, half a billion apiece. That should upset no one and it will make Pham and I sleep much better knowing we will have sufficient to retire to a remote island somewhere if it all blows up in our faces."

Nikita hit the disconnect button, and said to himself, "They're both stupid and I would gather from the slurring, they are both drunk. A terrible combination when one is trying to extort a billion dollars from a sociopath like me."

It was lunchtime in Teheran and Nikita waved off Svetlana, his Russian cook. As was her custom, she was bringing his lunch to the study where Nikita generally was at this hour and where he now sat after the call with Saji and Dac Kien. "Svetlana, I have a call to make after which I think I will take lunch on the terrace. I'll stop by the kitchen on my way."

Svetlana Baikov blushed and quickly backed out of the room gushing apologies in a distinctly Siberian dialect. Svetlana feared Nikita because her son, a low ranking soldier in the Russkaya Mafiya, had told her that Vladislav Dubnikov was a very powerful man both wealthy and ruthless. He told her it was rumored he was responsible for the disappearance of possibly hundreds of his enemies. She should tend to her household duties and pay no attention to Dubnikov's business or people who may meet with him from time to time. Svetlana took her son's advice very seriously. She avoided looking directly at any of Nikita's guests, and always left the room when he was on a phone call particularly when he was using that strange looking little phone.

When the door had closed behind the cook, Nikita pressed the buttons on his satellite communicator to reach Vilen Ovinko.

It took a few moments, but the deep and obviously sleepy voice of Vilen Ovinko came on the line. It was one in the morning in San Francisco and Ovinko, now sixty-eight years old, went to bed at ten whenever he could.

"Yes, Nikita, what is it?"

"First, I have arranged for Masterson to be brought to the

Standart in Maui. Along the way, they will pick you up in San Francisco. We need fingerprints and iris scans from him and his wife to get into the accounts. We'll scan his finger and eye from the Standart, while Vladimir scans hers from the mansion."

"How are you getting her to the mansion?"

"Vladimir figures she will do anything to save Masterson's ass so he is going to contact her and tell her he is in the mansion. He'll make it clear to her if she cooperates and comes there, they will scan both their biometrics. After the money is moved, they can both leave. Even if she doesn't believe him, she hasn't got any other choice but to go through with his plan."

"Vladislav, of course she has other choices, she can storm the mansion with a hundred New York City cops or buy an army with your money and raid the mansion."

"And risk having him killed by us before she can get to him? No, she won't try that. However, just in case, I'm having him moved before Vladimir calls her. One; we will have him where no one can find him and two; if she comes with the police we can let them search the mansion. Vladimir will be very understanding of the distraught woman, but he will explain that he doesn't know her or her husband. Her husband certainly isn't a prisoner in the mansion."

"It sounds like it should work. Where are you taking the Standart? We certainly won't want to stay in Maui."

"Off the coast of Johnston Atoll."

"Ahh, remote and symbolic. Good choice, Vladislav Dubnikov, no one will look for him there. If she doesn't show up, we have a very powerful bargaining chip to get at your money."

"Good, I am glad you agree. Vladimir will contact you later this morning with the details of your pickup in San Francisco. If all goes well, we'll meet on the Standart on Sunday and we can cruise to Johnston Atoll. Now for the second bit of news.

"Your puppet is acting like he can cut the strings and dance on his own."

"What! I doubt that he can tie his own shoelaces without the help of his wife, Lucile. What's he up to?"

Nikita spends the next fifteen minutes relating the conversation with Saji and Dac Kien. He ends with, "I told him we would finish our business by March 31st and he could prepare to wind down the tour by then. I didn't tell him the shipment was already scheduled to be in Iran by mid March and if we didn't conclude our part of the deal by the end of February, we would all be looking for new jobs.

"Anyway, I did not react to the request for the billion dollar bonus. After he's back in Washington and Pham is back on First Avenue at the UN, I will have a conversation with them both and point out that the world already knows we're bad guys. However, there'll be a lot of surprised looks when they find out the two of them work for us.

"It will probably take less than ten minutes to reacquaint them with their roles and responsibilities and get them back on track. I believe their conversation and demands were about ten percent balls and ninety percent Indonesian wine."

The laughter was loud and long.

"Good night, Vilen, my friend. Go back to sleep. I am going to go enjoy a hearty Russian lunch. See you on Sunday in Maui," and Nikita closed down the call.

PART THREE

The sun had been up for less than half an hour, but the security team had already been up for more than an hour. Anna, after deciding the more alert eyes in the villa the better, had told the household staff that morning Hugh was missing and assumed in danger. They should be on high alert for anything that appeared out of the ordinary. If they noticed the slightest detail they felt was unusual, they should immediately tell her or any member of the security team.

Anna found Louise in the security building just finishing her breakfast. Together they went to the top floor offices in the West tower.

On entering the office, she directed Louise to Hugh's workstation and showed her how to set up access to the systems monitoring Nikita's network. Telling Louise to set up her own user name and password, she walked to her desk and opened the bottom drawer on the right hand side. She took out her Ruger LCP 380 and clipped the small holster, containing the compact semi-automatic pistol, to the belt in her jeans.

Turning, she walked to one of the windows in the tower. She looked out onto Hawksbill Bay, the site of so many happy hours spent with Hugh kayaking while the giant Hawksbill turtles played alongside them. She stared at the beautiful bay in the early morning sunrise and said softly, but loud enough for Louise to hear, "I told Hugh after learning how to really use this deadly little piece, 'when I start carrying this, you will know we are at war'. Well, my

231

partner, wherever you are, we will find you and bring you home. We are going to war!"

"C'mon, Louise, it will be much more convenient for you to work in the first floor conference room than up here. If need be, you can have multiple sessions going on simultaneously with each on a separate plasma screen on the walls. All of this was going to be part of your introduction and training. Hugh and I just intended for it to be orderly and not so rushed. I have no doubt you'll be completely on top of this within a few hours. Now that you have set up your account, sign off on Hugh's computer, turn it off and let's go downstairs."

Descending in the elevator, they went directly to the conference room on the first floor of the tower. Sitting together, Anna walked Louise through the procedures for monitoring the communications and location of the ten users of Nikita's satellite communications system. She directed the computer output to one of the LCD screens on the walls.

Louise suggests, "Mrs. M, why don't we start listening to and analyzing the conversations since the last one you and Roger reviewed. That way we kill two birds with one stone. I learn and we get caught up on Nikita's plans."

"Great idea, Louise. Go to the screen listing the files captured by date and time. The way Hugh set up the table of user and digital address we get the conversation file with the participant information linked. Therefore, that list will also show the participants in the last column. Let me show you how you get into the menu of data listing options."

As Anna instructed Louise on the process, Louise moved through the steps. In moments, on the screen appeared a multi-column list sorted descending by date and time. The most current conversation at the top of the list.

"OK, Louise, scroll down to the last item with a check in that last column. The check means we've listened to it and archived it. There it is, 'Friday, February 19, 2010, 2:47 PM – Ovinko to Nikita'. That's the last one we analyzed.

"Shit, the next one was made last night just after Roger and I stopped monitoring the activity."

"Right, Mrs. M, that was just before the meeting with all the team."

"Play it, Louise."

"Louise looked at Anna quizzically, hesitating to say anything."

Anna rolled her eyes and said softly, "I'm sorry, Louise. Thank God you're a fast learner because I certainly am not doing much teaching."

"I understand, Mrs. M. I'm anxious to get to the content also. What do I do to open up and play the conversation?"

"Just double click on the file name, next to the date, and both the audio and the voice to text routine will start."

Louise followed the instructions and they sat there and listened, first to Nikita's reaction to learning from his son that both of the Mastersons' biometric data is needed. Then they heard the plan to move Hugh to the yacht, Standart, in Maui and finally to the ultimate destination Johnston Atoll. At the same time, they would lure Anna to the New York City mansion. They also had confirmation that it was Nikita's plan to kill them both.

They continued to listen, analyze and archive the rest of the conversations right up to the call to Ovinko by Nikita at one that morning California time.

Anna was busy making notes. The outline of her plan to rescue Hugh was forming in her mind and she wanted to get it down immediately. She was so focused she failed to notice Louise's shock and the apparent horror that was obvious from Louise's facial expression.

When she had completed her notes, she looked up and realized that Louise was mesmerized by what was on the screen.

"I'm sorry, Louise, I didn't prepare you for meeting the real President Sorosh Saji. I see from the conversation file you've returned to, our illustrious President's extortion of a half billion bucks to keep the world distracted from the most horrendous proliferation of nuclear weapons imaginable is horrifying you. Believe it, Louise. This type of less than admirable self-serving actions is a way of life for Saji and his wife as well as the United Nations' Secretary General, Pham Dac Kien."

As Louise closed the file she said, "I still can't get over Lucile Saji being so involved in this cabal."

"Actually, she was on Ovinko's payroll before she married Saji. In fact before she met Saji," added Anna. "We've learned all of this from analyzing the conversations of the ten members of Nikita's gang on the network. You can catch up on all that later, after we get Hugh back. Right now, we have a whole series of things to do to get ready to grab our Hugh back from this lunatic and his gang. I think I know just how we're going to pull it off.

"I want to know where my Hugh is at all times and the way to do that is to activate the GPS tracking chip. I also want to know how accurate it is in pinpointing his exact location. I mean is it inches, feet, yards or miles. Let's get going, I have a plan."

"Now, let me set up an account for you on the GPS tracking system, then I'll show you how to activate my chip. Once we do that, you're going to track me and determine how accurate the location coordinates are."

"How are we going to check the accuracy, Mrs. M?"

"We'll get an accurate GPS reading of the coordinates of where I'm sitting after we activate my chip." Walking over to a cabinet in the conference room, she took out two handheld devices. Removing one from its case, she said, "This GPS navigator is loaded with a NASA developed augmentation system and gives a reading for both coordinates to ten decimal places. I've been told that translates to inches, we'll see." Anna switched on the GPS and activated the feature that gave her the current location. As she recited the coordinates, Louise keyed them into her computer. They appeared on one of the large wall mounted LCD screens, latitude and longitude to ten decimal places.

"Now, we'll activate my chip and test it. Then I'll leave here and go to a location on the compound. You'll take this GPS tracker with you and locate me with it." At which point Anna took the second device from its case and handed it to Louise.

She then continued, "When we decided on having the chips implanted, we ordered several special trackers. They're military and used for search and recovery. They're loaded with the same NASA augmentation system and they too give a reading for both coordinates with ten decimal places.

"Now, log onto the system and let's set the GPS tracking

software. We'll put in the chip ID, for my chip, set sensitivity to ten decimal places for latitude and longitude, and activate it. Then we'll get a reading of my location from the software and compare it to the reading from the GPS navigator. If that proves to be accurate, I'll leave and play hide and seek."

They activated Anna's GPS chip. She felt a slight sensation, but nothing further.

"What did you feel, Mrs. M?" Asked Louise. "I saw you kind of jump."

"First, a low electrical shock followed by a tickling feeling. It is a very unique sensation, which is good. If Hugh is awake when we turn his chip on he'll know exactly what it is."

"How is that possible if he has never felt it before?"

"Because of where the sensations are. They are very localized and he'll know we 'lit him up', as they say."

"Where is…," but the twenty-seven year old Louise never finished the question.

"Never mind where they are," said Anna cutting off her question, "All of you randy young warriors want to know where the chips are. Jesus, they're in one of our ass cheeks, OK. As far as which one, never mind. Now let's get on with the test."

"Yes, Mrs. M," said Louise, trying desperately to stifle a giggle.

With Anna's instructions, Louise brought up the tracking data on a second one of the LCD screens. Within minutes, the satellite, a US technology corporation's private satellite, locked onto Anna's chip and gave the exact coordinates of

Anna, in the war room, out to ten decimal places. They both looked at the two screens. The one with the coordinates from the chip embedded under Anna's skin as determined by the tracking software and the coordinates from the GPS navigator.

"Bingo," said Louise, "identical. The GPS navigator gave a precise reading of your location. The tracker software found exactly where the chip was and they match down to the tenth decimal. Now let's see if the tracker devices work as well."

"I'll go out on the property and hide. I want to see how close you get to me before it tells you that you have 'found' me. Set the sensitivity very low so you will have to get close to me for the alarm to go off."

Anna left while Louise entered the chip ID information and set the alarm activation distance to 'two inches from target'. She was familiar with the device since it was used extensively by her former employer, US Navy Intelligence.

Once set up, Louise left the main building and when she was on the terrace activated the tracking of Anna's chip.

Louise followed the directions on the screen while listening to them on a wireless earpiece. As she moved towards the jungle like area on the western perimeter of the property, she could see Anna sitting on a large rock. Since the test was for accuracy, not just finding Anna, she continued awaiting the signal from the device that she was at the chip's location.

As she moved across the sand, she wondered if setting the sensitivity to two inches was stupid and the damn thing would never go off.

As she got closer to Anna, the GPS map kept zooming to dimensions that were ever more granular until it was giving readings in inches.

She walked right up to Anna who looked disappointed since she had not heard the signal. Then realized she wouldn't hear the signal since Louise had in the earpiece. Louise realizing the same thing deactivated the earpiece, which automatically redirected the audio to the tiny speaker in the tracker.

Anna was about to move when Louise said, "Don't move, stay exactly where you are. I'm going behind you because that is what the instructions are from the tracker."

When she was within an arms length of Anna, Louise held out her hand with the tracker in it towards Anna's behind. When it was two inches away, a piercing whistle erupted from the tracker's speaker.

"What sensitivity did you have it set for, Louise?" asked Anna.

"Two inches, Mrs. M."

"It's a good thing I told you where the damn chip was."

They both laughed and returning to the conference room in the residence, activated Hugh's GPS chip.

Anna and Louise are back in the conference room, sitting at the conference table, as the GPS software activates and locks onto Hugh's chip.

"If he's conscious," says Anna, "he now knows we have activated the chip and are therefore actively looking for him. He'll know we have a lot of info from the communications we are capturing and I'm sure he hopes we'll be able to piece it all together. OK, bring up the map and the sat images and let's find my husband."

It takes only a few moments and then up on the screen comes a map of New York City and the two coordinates:

Latitude: 40.7788649248

Longitude: -73.9622515236

"Convert that to an address," shouts Anna.

'1011 Fifth Avenue - corner of Fifth Avenue and 82nd Street' pops up onto the screen and Louise zooms in on a satellite photo of the mansion with details. It runs thirty feet down Fifth Avenue and one hundred ten feet along East 82nd Street.

"That is one big house in the middle of New York City. No wonder they call it the mansion. See how accurate you can get to finding Hugh. As we found out with our experiment, the system is accurate down to two inches if we use all ten decimals. Bring up the combined screen showing the GPS point inside the overlay of the building."

Louise enters a few key instructions and the dot appears inside the building about in the middle of the structure. They watch it for a few minutes and there is no movement.

"Mrs. M, he's either unconscious or sleeping. There's no movement at all."

"Or he knows we've activated the chip and he's playing asleep," said Anna. "According to the time stamps on the monitored conversations, it has been at least twelve hours since they tried to use his fingerprint and iris scan to get into the accounts. Unless he made noise or trouble, which I doubt he did, they probably haven't drugged him since then.

"Maybe they've already stuffed him in the trunk the way Nikita told Vladimir to do. However, I don't think so. They'll probably do that just before they're going to get him on the plane to Maui. Even if they did, he could still make some movement. Nope, Louise, I think he's locked up in a room. I'll bet he will give it five to ten minutes and he'll make some movement if he can, to let us know he's alive and well and knows we're watching."

"What kind of movement, Mrs. M? All we're seeing is a dot on a grid that represents the chip. Even with the coordinates showing on the screen, in order for us to see a sign by movement, he'd have to move around the room or wherever they have him."

"Zoom in Louise; make the resolution great enough that the dot from the chip takes up about six inches on that big screen. That way if he moves two inches, with the system's sensitivity level, we'll see it. If they have him tied up or tied to a bed or chair, the movement is going to be minimal. Not something his watchers would notice, if Vladimir has goons watching him round the clock."

Louise, using the computer mouse, adjusted the resolution. The dot, yellow on a black background, was now as big as a softball in the center of the sixty-inch LCD screen and the coordinates were off the screen.

"Great, Louise, now we'll wait and see if he sends us any kind of signal or if I'm just wishful thinking."

"Mrs. M, what kind of motions could he make that would send us a signal?"

"Louise, he's a creative guy. Let's wait and see what he comes up with, if he's even awake and comes up with anything. By the way, turn on video capture. I want to record any movement in case he's sending us a signal."

About fifteen minutes passed and suddenly the dot moved quickly around the screen in a strange zigzag motion.

"What was that?" Louise shouted.

"If it was what I think it was, my Hugh is not only creative, he has a very weird sense of humor."

"What is it, Mrs. M?"

Anna went to a drawer in one of the cabinets along the walls and took out a pen like object, pressed a button and the device emitted a laser beam from its front. Shining the laser on the center of the softball like image of the chip's GPS signal, she followed the motion and started laughing.

"It's a 'Z', Mrs. M, a 'Z'. What could that mean or is he just moving around?"

"Moving around in the same pattern over and over? I don't think so. Considering where that chip is, he must look pretty funny to anyone watching him, like he's having some kind of erotic episode. No, Louise, my very strange husband went through the alphabet and figured out what letter he could make, as a sign. One that would be easy to execute, not obvious and would send a message. Hugh has just sent us a 'Z', the sign of 'Zorro'.

"You are probably too young to have ever seen the Zorro movies, but Zorro is a fictional character who crusades for justice and nets out his own form of retribution. I would interpret his booty popping 'Zs' to mean Hugh wants to be rescued and he wants revenge.

"My Hugh is OK. We're going to get him back and we are going to get him his revenge.

"I'm going to get everyone together in the security building war room. We know our targets and there will be more than one," said Anna. "We also have a lock on where Hugh is and we aren't going to lose that for a minute. You stay here and keep tracking Hugh's movements and monitoring the communications. Anything changes contact us in the war room."

With that, Anna left for the security building where she knew the rest of the team was working on putting together a strike force. She had a lot of new information to add to those preparations.

The plan in her brain was getting much more detailed and as she left the main building, she was smiling. There were tears of joy in her eyes and she was saying to herself, "My Hugh, you are alive and apparently well. We are going to get you back and we are going to have very sweet revenge. Your Anna has a plan and what a plan it is."

It was late evening in Teheran. Nikita was sitting on his terrace sipping brandy and enjoying a very large Cuban cigar. He was content with the way things were moving along.

His mind was racing, the brandy and cigar having no success in relaxing him.

His thoughts were of astronomical success. "In less than a month, the first phase of this mega-deal will be completed. Heydar Vahdani will have all four thousand nukes in his warehouse in Iran and my former Soviet buddies and I will be one hundred billion dollars richer. The best part is this is just the beginning. Vahdani doesn't know it yet, but he and I are going to be partners in the nuclear warhead business, but that will come later.

"I want this deal to happen without a hitch and I want it to happen quickly. With the forty billion recovered from Masterson and half Vilen's and my fifty billion profits on the sale to Iran, Vladimir and I will have a bankroll of over sixty-five billion. We'll be untouchable. I want the details with my Soviet suppliers wrapped up before the end of February, so they can't back out or shop the deal. I think I know exactly how that can be set up. Then all that is left is simply a matter of delivering the nukes and splitting up Iran's hundred billion."

As he looked at his watch, he did a quick calculation and said to himself, "It's a little after noon in New York. Vladimir will be getting ready to package up Masterson. I'll call him now and tell him my revised plan."

"Yes, Papa," said Vladimir, into the satellite communicator.

"Everything OK there, Volya?" Nikita said, once again using the shortened, familiar form of his son's name.

"Great, Papa, we're making sure there are no signs of Masterson having been here should his wife show up with cops when I invite her later today."

"That's why I'm calling. We won't be ready to access the account until Friday, the twenty-sixth."

"Why, what's changed, Papa?"

"I want this whole transaction to go like clockwork and I want no new surprises from Dimitri Demochev and his group in Moscow.

"First, Saji and Dac Kien are acting up." With that, Nikita brought him up to date on the interaction with the President and Secretary General, essentially repeating the conversation he had with Ovinko that afternoon. "So our schedule is tightened up.

"To make sure there are no disruptions in the process and since Demochev's group are insisting on funds in advance, I'm going to get all the parties involved, in our part of this transaction, on the Standart in Maui. When we are off Johnston Atoll and recover all our funds, I can immediately make the transfer to Demochev group's account and get his commitment while we're all there. We'll firm up all the details right from the Standart and let Demochev know our group will be aboard the ship at Tolyatti and oversee the successful transport to Iran.

"We can then contact Heydar Vahdani and give him specifics on when the nukes will arrive and he can give us specifics on when our money will be transferred."

"Who are you planning on having on the Standart, Papa?"

"I've decided on four, plus me: Boris Batkin, Cheslav Bocharkov, Demochev, and of course your uncle, Vilen Ovinko. I'll arrange for them all to get to the Standart, in Maui, by Wednesday the twenty-fourth.

"I'll get there in time to be on board when Vilen arrives with Masterson and his gorillas. How many are you sending along with Masterson?"

Vladimir toyed with the idea of reminding his father he told him that before, but decided against it. His father was in good spirits and he preferred to keep him there. He said simply, "Liv Polyansky and two of his people, three all together."

"Good, Volya. They can keep watch over him at all times with none of them having a shift longer than eight hours, that way they'll stay alert.

"And you, how many are you keeping to provide protection and to get rid of Masterson's wife's body after we scan her biometrics?"

Once again, Vladimir thought, "Papa, you must be slipping. We went over this too." He actually said, "Two Papa. Liv Polyansky assigned two of his toughest and most loyal goons to watch over me and dump the bitch's body at the end. They're here now, so I'll just keep them around until this end is wrapped up.

"Papa, do you want me to delay sending Masterson to Maui since everyone won't get there before the end of the week?"

"No, you stay on your schedule and get him out of there today. Have them pick up Vilen in San Francisco as planned. I'll get to Maui mid week and can spend some time with Vilen going over our next steps. Once this deal is sowed up and thanks to you, we've retrieved all our dough, between Vilen and us, we'll have a bankroll of over one hundred billion bucks. I plan to bring the Standart back to Maui where you can meet us and we will have a grand celebration.

"Once Masterson is out of there, give it a few hours. Go over the mansion again making sure there is no evidence of him ever having been there. Then call her. Get her to the mansion on the twenty-sixth and all will go very smoothly. The scanning of the Mastersons' fingers and eyes will be on the twenty-sixth sometime around noon your time. We'll firm that up later.

"You get to work now and get Masterson on his final journey. Then get that bitch firmed up to come to the mansion."

"OK, Papa...," but Nikita had already disconnected.

"Liv, have your guys get the coffin and bring it to Masterson's room," shouted Vladimir. He walked into the large den where Liv Polyansky and two of his hoodlums were sitting watching cartoons on the giant flat screen television. "You're sure the damn thing isn't airtight and Masterson will be able to breathe until you get airborne and can open the top for the trip, right?"

"Yeah, boss," said Polyansky, "we made the old Russian carpenter in Brooklyn get in it when we went to pick it up. We locked it and went out to dinner. We came back two hours later and when we opened it, there he was good as when we left him. Except, he was really crying."

"Yeah," said one of the goons reluctantly, tearing his attention from the cartoon. "He was crying like a baby. We gave him an extra five-hundred and told him we had to test the box somehow and now we knew it worked." All three burst into laughter.

"By the way, boss," said Liv, "this is Giorgi and Stepan. They'll be staying with you and getting rid of the bitch when you're through with her."

"Hi, boss, we'll take good care of you and her when you're through with her," said the one called Stepan. Then they all grunted and went back to the cartoons.

"What's the matter with you two?" shouted Liv. "Get the box and bring it up to your buddies watching Masterson."

"OK, OK," they both grunted and once again tearing themselves away from the cartoons left the room.

After his father had casually said, "...pack Masterson into a steel trunk," Vladimir had to figure out just how he could comply with the spirit of his father's instructions without risking questions at the three airports they would be passing through or smothering Masterson. He was quite proud of the coffin idea. No one would bother them. Rich foreigners in an expensive jet, transporting one of their beloved family members to his final resting place at sea. He contacted a carpenter Liv knew in the Russian community at Brighton Beach, Brooklyn. The carpenter told him he could build a suitable box that would appear to any curious person like a coffin, but if it was not to be airtight, it could not be sound proof. He could do one or the other.

Obviously, Vladimir elected not to have Masterson's box airtight. They would just have to drug him unconscious when he wasn't in the plane.

He went back into the study, retrieved a syringe and small bottle of a powerful sedative and headed up to Hugh's cell-like room.

He entered the room with all four thugs and two of them held Hugh, an unnecessary precaution since Hugh offered no resistance. Vladimir inserted the needle into his upper arm and emptied its contents into Hugh.

It was only seconds before the drug knocked Hugh unconscious, but long enough for him to comfort himself with the thought, "You need me alive to scan my iris so this needle isn't the end for me. But if I interpreted the sensation in my ass earlier, this may just be the beginning of the end for you. I would bet you really pissed Anna off, and let me assure you, that ain't going to be good." Then he was out like a light.

"Put him into the box, gently and securely. Move the

coffin into the SUV in the garage, the one you're taking to the airport. Treat it like it's a huge crate of eggs and your life depends on not one getting busted. Because your life depends on him arriving in Maui and on board the Standart in the same perfect shape he is at this moment. If he is in any way damaged, my father and my uncle, Vilen Ovinko, will be really angry. So be very careful."

A half hour later, Liv Polyansky and the two thugs that were picked to make the trip, were driving east on eighty-second street with a coffin in the back. They looked like typical workers from a funeral home transporting a corpse.

They were on their way to LaGuardia's Marine Air Terminal, the terminal for private jets.

As soon as Anna had left the conference room, Louise set herself up to be able to monitor the conversations over Nikita's satellite network, while keeping an eye on the GPS screen locked onto the chip embedded in Hugh. Sitting at the large circular table, she could watch closely three screens of the four in the room. One was dedicated to Nikita's network, the second to the GPS. She set up the third to immediately teleconference with the team in the war room. That way if she had new events to report, she could do it easily without leaving her post.

Anna, on arriving at the war room, immediately started a review with the eight members in the room and Alberto in New York.

They now knew, from the conversation between Nikita and Vladimir on Friday evening, New York time, that Nikita's plan is to take Hugh to a point five miles off the coast of Johnston Atoll aboard the Standart.

Anna had decided this would be the site of the rescue, for two reasons. The first had to do with Nikita who would never expect it, since he apparently thinks no one in the world would be looking there. The second was for her and the team's protection. No one will be anywhere in the vicinity to question the methods Anna intends to use to carry out the rescue.

Once the plan Anna had been working on was explained to the team, there was unanimous enthusiasm for it. The whole concept and final goal of Anna's strategy was immediately embraced by the entire team. Suggestions and refinements began to pour out from each member leveraging each of their specialties in an effort to make success guaranteed. They were succeeding, the operational plan got better with each proposal.

Their biggest challenge, of course, was time. When Anna had left Louise, the most current intelligence they had from the monitored satellite conversations set a timetable that called for them to be at Johnston Atoll ahead of the Standart's arrival, Sunday evening, February 21st.

The team would have to leave in about five hours if they were to get to Johnston Atoll in the early afternoon of Sunday, just ahead of Nikita.

It was now early afternoon and the team was working feverishly to put together an at sea strike force in time. Roger and Alberto had been on the phones, using their connections with the promise of a lot of money. They had been successful in putting together the equipment by way of the suppliers to the Navy Seals in Coronado, California. However, the logistics were a horror. They had to leave Cayman, stop at LaGuardia in New York and pick up Alberto, then onto Coronado, California to pick up the equipment. Finally, on to the airfield in the south central section of Johnston Atoll with a refueling stop in Hawaii. A trip of almost seventy-five hundred miles with three intermediate stops, and they had to be there before the Standart was in sight of Johnston Atoll. This would give them the best chance to take them by surprise late Sunday night. To get there by noon on Sunday, Johnston Atoll time, they had only twenty-four hours and almost twenty of that would be fly time. Unless, they could get one hell of a fast plane.

As they were discussing this, one of the LCD screens in the war room lit up with an incoming connection from Louise. She didn't wait for any acknowledgement, was obviously very excited and without any preamble, she burst out, "We just bought about three days till Mr. Masterson gets to Johnston Atoll. Nikita has decided to assemble the entire group of his villains on the Standart in Maui and cruise to Johnston Atoll."

Anna asked, "Who's included?"

Louise, looking at the text of the conversation on one of the screens in front of her, read clearly. "Cheslav Bocharkov, Nikita's Russian lawyer; Boris Batkin, his Russian banker; Dimitri Demochev, the guy with the nukes; Nikita, and Vilen Ovinko, plus the three Ovinko goons to guard and dispose of Hugh. The conversation between Nikita and Vladimir only refers to them by name. I cross referenced them and have added who they are."

"Fantastic," shouted Anna, "this changes everything..."

Louise interrupted, "Wait, that's not all. They know they need your biometrics and they want to get you to the mansion with Vladimir on Friday, February 26th. They'll have you access the accounts from there, while they force Hugh to access the accounts from the Standart. Then they are going to kill you and have Ovinko's goons get rid of your body.

"This is getting better by the minute, Louise. Can you tell from their communications when they expect to be off the coast of Johnston Atoll?"

"Yes, they plan to be there on Thursday, the twenty-fifth."

"Again, fantastic. As soon as they contact me, I'll agree to meet with Vladimir in the New York mansion on Friday, as they'll request. Louise will stay here to keep the communications and tracking flowing smoothly. Kateri, you'll come with me to New York and the rest of the team will mount the rescue in the Pacific.

"This change is exactly what I needed, to tie up some loose ends in my plan, and it gives us the timetable we need.

"The team is going to be on the ground on Johnston Atoll and preparing for the rescue by the afternoon of February 24th, a full day before the Standart arrives. The plane that you get there in can be well hidden in one of the air force hangars and the team and pilots can use the barracks. The facilities were abandoned intact by the military when they turned the atoll over to United States Fish and Wildlife Service, as part of the Pacific Remote Islands Marine National Monument, last year. There is no life on it now, except wildlife.

"We have time to work out the logistics and the precise timing and it will be precise. But team, when we pull it off, it will be spectacular." All agreed, spectacular it would be.

"Louise, I want equipment set up so the team and I are continuously in communication, including you and Kateri. That includes the team's ability to communicate with each other and us while they're underwater. Damn, I wish I could be there to participate in the Pacific operation, but this new info means Kateri and I will be in New York while you guys are in the sunny Pacific."

"One last thing, Mrs. M," said Louise, "Mr. M is on the move. He left the mansion about an hour ago and it appears he is in a vehicle on its way to Queens. If I were to guess, I would say they are taking him to LaGuardia Airport."

"You're probably right. That's where the private airport is, at the old Marine Air Terminal.

"Louise, I can't thank you enough for handling all this monitoring after my feeble attempt to be a teacher. Wow, you certainly learn fast. Stay on the monitoring, we want to know every detail of their plan particularly any changes in the timetable."

"I got it covered, Mrs. M, and I'll get right on the mobile communications system for the operation. I have a good idea I can get state of the art equipment through some of my old buddies at Navy Intelligence. I'll keep you informed of any activity and get back to you on the com equipment." Louise ended the teleconference session and that screen went blank.

Anna stood up, started walking around the room and talking, "We've a lot to plan and discuss and we've got to get our hands on one very fast plane that can land and take off from a thirty-five hundred foot runway. I think I know just what we need and where we can get it.

"Roger, I want you to concentrate on buying, for delivery in two hours, a Cessna Citation X – 750 fitted for a crew of two and ten passengers. It can do seven hundred miles an hour, a lot faster than Ovinko's converted Boeing 737. This will assure the team of getting to the atoll when we need them there and getting back to Hawaii, in less than two hours, if medical care is needed for Hugh.

"There's a brand new one on Grand Cayman, that Hugh and I were looking at in December, when we went to the main island for the chip implants. It was bought by the chairman of a hedge fund, based in Grand Cayman, who found he didn't have the funds to pay for it. I don't know if it's still there, but if it is, contact whoever is responsible and buy it."

"Mrs. M, it's still there. It was on the Cayman News last week. Apparently, that guy left a lot of toys around the island and there are no takers. But how much should I spend?"

"Whatever it takes, Roger. It should be about twenty-five million, but whatever it takes. Work with the island's governor for Cayman registration and identification.

"Then I want you to hire two Marine pilots, either former or current, either unemployed or with time off, for a one week mission. Tell them that the fee is fifty grand apiece and they forget they ever did the job. Let me know where you want the money sent for the plane and if you need an upfront deposit for the pilots.

"Now, with Louise's news, we've got to revise the plan, lock in on all the supplies and equipment we'll need and finalize the orders."

As the team is working out details, a call comes into the villa's general number for Anna from Vladimir. Jennifer Ebanks, the Villa Serenity maid who had been alerted to expect it, takes the call and forwards it to Anna in the war room. She redirects the call to the villa's integrated communications system, thereby enabling the entire team to listen while capturing the conversation to refer back to if necessary.

"This is Anna Masterson, Mr. Dubnikov. Please excuse me if I'm not overly receptive to your call. My husband and I are a little wary of the Dubnikov family since you, your sister and your father tried to kill us and everyone else here at the villa less than two years ago.

"What is it you want?"

"Mrs. Masterson, do you know where your husband is at this moment?"

"Yes, Mr. Dubnikov," which actually was not a lie since thanks to the GPS chip she and her team knew exactly where he was. However, that was not what Vladimir was referring to. Anna continued, "Why do you ask?"

"I don't think you do know where he is. If his bodyguard has not yet told you he is missing, let me be the first to inform you that he is definitely missing. At least as far as you are concerned."

"Mr. Dubnikov, why have you called?"

"OK, Mrs. Masterson. If you insist, I will be brief and to the point. I would venture to say the last time you heard from your husband was Friday morning and you have been frantically trying to get in touch with him. Stop wasting your time. My father and I have him and he is in a nice safe place. He has not been, shall we say damaged at all, and he will stay that way as long as you do exactly as I say."

"I don't believe you," said Anna, allowing some shakiness and emotion to creep into her voice. "Why should I?"

"Mrs. Masterson, please shut up and listen to what I have to say. Believe me you will have proof of your husband's location and condition.

"You have stolen a great deal of my father's money, a great deal. We calculate that you have over forty billion US dollars belonging to us and we want it back.

"We have tried hacking into your accounts at the Regal Bank of the Caymans. However, your introduction of iris scan biometrics has frustrated that effort. The fingerprints we could get past, but the iris scan was a showstopper. So we grabbed your husband and scanned his iris into the system and you know what we got, Mrs. Masterson?"

"A request for a second fingerprint and iris scan, Mr. Dubnikov."

"Yes, we got a request for a second set of biometrics. Actually, this is the first proof I offer you that we have your husband, Mrs. Masterson. I will give you the exact wording of the request after we input your husband's biometric scans. It read, 'security access user one accepted; please process biometrics for user two', that's what was on the screen. Can you imagine my disappointment? Here I was expecting my next act would be transferring our forty billion back into my father's accounts, instead I'm confronted with another locked gate. That really pissed me off, Mrs. Masterson.

"Then I thought who would be the logical owner of the second set of biometrics? The first name that popped up...no, the only name that popped up, was Anna Masterson. So tell me, Anna Masterson, are you the second gatekeeper of our money?"

"And if I am, Vladimir, you're fucked. Send me back my husband and we'll forget about your crazy kidnapping of him and get on with our lives."

"That would work, Mrs. Masterson, if you could wire our forty billion back to us, but you can't because you need your husband's fingerprint and eye scan to access the money, just like I do. So, here is how it's going to go down.

"I have your husband with me and next Friday, February 26th, you are going to meet him and me at a house on Fifth Avenue in New York City. There you will both scan your fingerprints and irises into the Regal Bank of the Caymans' security system. We will transfer the entire contents to my father's account and you two can go home to your pretty villa on Cayman Brac. That is, if you can still afford that lifestyle after we take back our money."

"Why next Friday, why not tomorrow?" said Anna. After a short hesitation, she continued in a weaker voice to signal Vladimir a change of attitude and the beginning of apprehension. "Look, Vladimir, I just want my husband back safe and sound. I don't care about the money. It's not ours, it belongs to the people your father stole it from. It's not even in our account. It's in a special escrow account, that's why all the security. If it means getting my husband back, you can have it. So why not do it tomorrow and you'll have your money and I'll have my husband?" Anna knew Vladimir's schedule as well as he did, but her attitude of urgency made her more believable and would keep Vladimir off guard.

"Well, for one thing tomorrow is Sunday and the wire transfer systems are not reliable, in every country, on Sunday."

"Right, of course, but why not Monday? I can be anywhere you want me to be on Monday morning. We can do it then." Anna's voice now reflected urgency and rising fear.

"Calm down, Mrs. Masterson. This will happen on my timetable not yours. It will be done at noon on Friday. You come to 1011 Fifth Avenue. It is at the corner of Eighty-Second Street and Fifth Avenue, across from The Metropolitan Museum of Art. Just come to the main entrance on Eighty-Second Street and ring the bell, it is a very large house. We call it the mansion. We will get the transfers done and you and your husband will be on your way."

"Proof, Vladimir, you said you would send me proof."

"Do you have a fax machine near you, Mrs. Masterson? I know it is old technology and that's not your thing, but it is convenient. If you have one, I will send you a picture of your husband I took this morning. Using a scene from the American movies that have kidnappings in them, I placed a copy of today's New York Post next to his head so you know it is a current photo."

Anna gave him the fax number in the war room and in minutes, she was looking at a picture of Hugh lying unconscious on a mattress. There are no features of the location other than the mattress and the copy of the Post. Smiling, she passes the fax around the room for the team to look at. They all smile. Except for his messed up clothing, he looks like he is taking a nap not being held captive by a gang of psychopaths.

Vladimir's voice breaks the silence, "Are you satisfied we have him, Mrs. Masterson?"

"Yes," was her tearful answer, "I still don't know why we can't do it Monday…," but she was cut off by Vladimir.

"My timetable, Friday at noon, you have the address, come alone. By the way, we are not there now nor will we be until Friday at noon. Don't waste your time attempting to rescue your beloved Hugh. If I find out you tried something…anything, without further communications with you, I will cut off his left arm and cut out his left eye. I don't need either of them to access the account since his biometrics come from his right hand and right eye. Another proof that we have him. Do you hear me, Mrs. Masterson?"

Now the sobbing was most pronounced, "Yes, Mr. Dubnikov. I'll be there at noon on Friday. Please take care of my Hugh."

Unlike his father, Vladimir said, "Goodbye, Mrs. Masterson. I look forward to meeting you," and he hung up.

After she disconnected, the entire team who had heard the exchange, burst into applause. Anna laughed, stood, bowed, and said, "We know where Hugh is, shithead, with a lot more accuracy than you do and we know you're daddy told you to stay put in 1011 Fifth Avenue. I never thought hiding knowledge was so difficult. Boy, I'm really thankful for my years as an actress."

The team applauded again and Anna laughed. Then turning

serious, she sat down and said, "All the ducks are in a row. Let's plan our duck hunting trip."

Giorgi and Stepan were back watching the cartoons. They looked at each other when the shouts came from the library on the first floor where Vladimir Dubnikov was. He was skipping around the room punching the air and shouting, "Yes, yes, this will get me back in Papa's good graces forever."

He took the satellite communicator from his shirt pocket and pressed the button sequence to connect with his father. He somehow overlooked the fact that it was three-thirty Sunday morning in Teheran.

Nikita answered, obviously having been awakened from a deep sleep.

"Yes?" he grumbled into the device.

"Papa, it's me, Vladimir," he cheerily shouted. "Oh shit," he thought to himself, "it's what, three-thirty Sunday morning in Teheran, oh shit. Well I woke him up, I may as well continue."

"I spoke to Masterson's bitch and it's all set up. She'll get here at noon on Friday. Since she's scared shitless we'll harm her precious husband, I have no doubts she'll be here right on time. At precisely one in the afternoon, New York time, she'll sign on from here while you use Masterson to sign on from the North Pacific. It will be exactly seven in the morning Johnston Atoll time. I'll call you Friday on this network when we are ready to start."

Pouring himself a large celebratory vodka, from the bottle on the small bar in the library, he started to recount the entire conversation with Anna. He repeated a few times the threat of what he would do to Hugh, were she not to cooperate fully.

Nikita had disconnected some time into the story and gone back to sleep, but Vladimir was so excited about his accomplishment, he didn't notice. When the large quantity of vodka had taken effect and Vladimir's enthusiasm had settled down, he realized his Papa was no longer on the other end. He shrugged, put the communicator back in his shirt pocket, refilled the glass with vodka and started thinking of what he was going to do for the next six days.

PART FOUR

Thanks to Anna's plan and leadership, coupled with the military like precision of the team, all went like clockwork. They knew that the final phase of the rescue of Hugh would be at sea, about five miles off the coast of Johnston Atoll. The weather for the next five days in the Pacific, in the atoll's area, was predicted to be calm, sunny and about eighty degrees Fahrenheit. This was important to the operation since the team would be ensconced in the facilities on the atoll, hidden from view of the arriving villains, but also five miles by open sea from the Standart's anchorage. Therefore, it was very positive news that the trip from the atoll to the Standart would be good going. At least from the perspective of the weather and the seas.

Roger had unbelievable success in getting both the plane and the pilots. When he contacted the airport manager for information on the impounded plane, he almost burst out laughing. The holder of the loan, on the plane, was none other than Regal Bank of the Caymans, the bank holding the Mastersons' billions. Roger was told he should contact Stuart Jefferson, the President. Figuring correctly that it would be much more effective to let Anna contact Mr. Jefferson, he went to her and gave her the information. By two thirty on Saturday, they owned the Cessna and a much-enhanced ground crew was cleaning, fueling and giving every system a pre-flight check. "The plane will be ready to roll by five o'clock" had been the words of both the airport manager and Stuart Jefferson.

Roger knew just who to contact for the Marine pilots. He called the Commander of United States Marine Corps

Aviation Resource Allocation. This officer knows the name and capabilities of every Marine pilot that passed through training in Naval Air Station, Pensacola, Florida. The current holder of that title was Paul Gisgombe, a childhood friend who went to high school with Roger in the Bronx. When Roger went off to become a Navy seal, his high school buddy went off to become a Marine officer and fighter pilot.

That was fourteen years ago and Roger's buddy knew the whereabouts of the Marine pilots, active or inactive, who would be interested in the unusual mission.

By three o'clock, two pilots with eight years experience, who had completed their commitment to the Marine Corp and were in Pensacola looking at alternatives to reenlistment, were en route to Cayman in a supersonic jet. They had a year to make up their minds, and the fifty grand would certainly make that process more comfortable. They arrived at Grand Cayman at four twenty and were going over the Cessna by four thirty.

The team had their transportation in plenty of time for their five thirty scheduled departure.

~~~

The eight had left Grand Cayman at precisely five thirty with personal belongings and notebook computers. Most of what they would need for the rescue had been arranged before they left. What was still on the shopping list was being arranged by Anna, Louise and Kateri from Cayman Brac.

Kateri was working on weapons systems, while Louise handled communications and GPS tracking systems. Anna handled the payment from the operations account, which fortunately had over a billion bucks in it. Anna and Hugh had transferred the Cyber Covert commission from the escrowed funds recovered account to the operations account in January. If that had not been done, as Vladimir had pointed out, Anna could not have accessed the money in the escrow account without Hugh's eyes and fingers.

All of the tools for the rescue operation were waiting upon their arrival at Halsey Field (North Island Naval Air Station) in San Diego. Assembled and delivered by Coronado Military Provisioning, LLP. The company is the primary supplier to the Maritime Special Operations Force, Sea, Air, Land, better known as Navy Seals, whose Pacific Force is based in Coronado, California.

They spent almost two days in San Diego as they familiarized themselves with all the equipment. Staying close to the provisioning company to have any last minute needs filled and to get any technical assistance that might be required.

They left Halsey Field at three thirty in the morning, of Tuesday the 23rd, and arrived at Kalaeloa Airport, Honolulu, Hawaii at nine fifty that morning, Hawaii time.

At ten thirty that morning, they sat awaiting the completion of refueling and food and drink provisioning for the stay in Johnston Atoll. The eight members of the team were in a video conference with Louise, Kateri and Anna in Cayman where it was four thirty in the late afternoon. By the end of that videoconference, the plan was firmly in place. All eleven of the participants knew their roles perfectly. The eight on their way to the atoll, Anna and Kateri on their way to New York and Louise in Cayman Brac.

Anna and Kateri were leaving that night for New York via

the Cayman Covert private jet, which was both too small and too slow for the team to use for their mission. They would pick up the communications equipment in New York, which would link them with the rest of the team and Louise for the duration of the effort. The team got theirs in Coronado.

That communications link was crucial to the timing, timing was the key to success.

Just over eighty miles northwest of where the team's Cessna sat, the 285-foot Standart, Nikita's most prized possession, lay anchored. Because of the size of the yacht, it was forced to stay about one-half mile off the coast of Lahaina.

Lahaina is the main town on the west side of Maui and serves as the port for the many cruise ships stopping at or discharging passengers for a vacation stay in Maui. There are two municipal owned tender docks for use by the cruise ships and one private dock for use by the rich and mega-rich who anchor their yachts off the magnificent west coast of Maui.

The Standart's 35-foot tender used this private dock.

When Vilen Ovinko, and the three goons with their coffin containing the drugged Hugh, had arrived at the dock on Sunday, at about six o'clock, the tender was waiting for them. They, together with their cargo, were quickly loaded onto it and moments later, they were aboard the Standart.

Hugh, still drugged unconscious, was removed from his 'casket' by Liv Polyansky and the other two goons. They half dragged and half carried him down to the level immediately above the huge engine compartment. He was placed on a cot in a cell-like room and the steel door was closed and locked. There was a small porthole, nine inches in diameter about six feet off the floor in the center of the outer wall, but only about two feet above the waterline. There was a toilet, a sink and nothing else in the room. It was truly a cell.

~~~

Vladislav Dubnikov had his yacht built to his specifications. It took two years to build, and was launched in June 2004. As a kind of ironic twist, Dubnikov named the 285-foot beauty The Standart. Irony, because the original Standart belonged to the Russian Imperial family, the Tsars.

The three hundred seventy foot Imperial Yacht, Standart, was built by order of Tsar Alexander III. She was launched in 1895 and used until their demise, at the outset of the Russian revolution, by Tsar Nicholas II and his family. She was outfitted with ornate fixtures, including mahogany paneling, crystal chandeliers, and other amenities that made the vessel a suitable floating palace for the Russian Imperial Family.

Well, even though the original Standart was eighty-five feet longer, it couldn't hold a candle to Dubnikov's Standart.

Powered by four thirty-three hundred horsepower diesels and one thirty-five thousand horsepower gas turbine, it is capable of speeds up to fifty miles per hour. More than twice that of the original.

It has on board three auxiliary vessels: sixteen, twenty-four and thirty-five foot tenders. In addition, a helicopter and mini-submarine.

However, Dubnikov stayed with the Tsar's taste for interior décor. The inside of the huge yacht looked more like the grand rooms of a European palace, of the early twentieth century, than a super, modern, yacht.

The ship, and that is what it truly is, a ship, has formal and informal dining salons, library, conference rooms, billiards room, large Jacuzzi pool, an open bar, with huge deck areas. Further emphasizing its self-contained status, there is a side garage with six varied vehicles, as well as a movie theater, ten suites and a Master's Suite. The luxury yacht provides all of its water needs by purifying seawater. This coupled with state of the art communications capability and a range of eight thousand nautical miles, it is ideal for Dubnikov's periodic extended global cruising.

Finally, although the skipper, Captain Stanislav Machtcenko, generally relied on speed to avoid distasteful encounters, if he had to stand and fight, he could do so. The Standart's armament included four pods, bow, stern, port and starboard, each containing twin Russian Kord, 108mm machine guns, capable of firing 650-750 rounds/min each. Supported by a supply of 9K38 Igla surface to air missiles on board, the modern Standart could protect itself from any non-military attack and probably a military assault from lesser countries.

~~~

Ovinko went to the huge deck area on the second level where Nikita sat talking on the satellite communicator with Boris Batkin, his Russian banker. "One moment, Boris, Vilen has just arrived."

"So, Vilen Ovinko, is Masterson aboard?"

"The host of the biometrics, necessary to access your funds, is sleeping soundly in the lower deck holding room."

Laughing heartily, Nikita said into the communicator, "Vilen Ovinko says, 'the host of the biometrics is sleeping soundly'. He calls Masterson the host of the biometrics.

"Yes, yes, Boris, we will make sure he doesn't bite off his fingertips or gouge out his eyes. I do not think our Mr. Hugh Masterson cares so much about the money, only keeping us from getting at it. He assumes his wife is safe and we cannot get all four biometrics to access the accounts.

"Yes, Vladimir has arranged for her to be in the mansion Friday around noon, New York time. We will get to the atoll late Thursday and be ready with the biometrics host when she shows up at the mansion.

"By three o'clock New York time Friday, Dimitri Demochev will have his twenty-five billion US dollars, the warheads will be on their way to Bushehr, Iran and we will be on our way to a celebration back here in Maui.

"Of course, Mr. Masterson will be dropping off along the way," said Nikita with a deep guttural laugh. I've invited Vladimir to join us, but I'm afraid Mrs. Masterson will not be accompanying him. I fear she will have gone to pieces by then."

With these comments, on the disposal plans for Hugh and Anna's bodies after they are both killed, Nikita closed with, "I will see you here tomorrow. Cheslav and Dimitri will be arriving also and we will leave Maui at about four o'clock local time. According to Captain Machtcenko, we should be at our anchorage off Johnston Atoll no later than ten tomorrow night."

The eight members of the rescue team were about to end the videoconference with Louise, Kateri and Anna in Cayman, when Louise interrupted. "Wait, don't disconnect. While we've been in conference, I've been monitoring traffic on Nikita's megaphone network and I've done some GPS back mapping.

"The yacht is about eighty miles from you, anchored off Lahaina, Maui.

"Mr. M is drugged and unconscious in some kind of a holding cell on Nikita's yacht, the Standart. Ovinko and three of Ovinko's goons brought him aboard. Nikita was already there to meet them.

"I'm continually tracking his movement, by way of the GPS chip tracking, and monitored them moving him from Kahului Airport through Lahaina and on out to the Standart. By linking the chip's position to a satellite map, it appears that Nikita's yacht is about half a mile off the coast of Lahaina. I have visual evidence of where Mr. M is located.

"Shortly after tracking showed he was on the Standart, Nikita told his banker, Boris Batkin, over the satellite network, that Ovinko just delivered Mr. M. Therefore, I also have verbal confirmation from the kidnappers.

"Cheslav Bocharkov, the lawyer, Boris Batkin, the banker, and Dimitri Demochev, the Russian with the nukes, are all scheduled to board the Standart late tomorrow. Then they'll set sail for Johnston Atoll, arriving Thursday night around ten.

"The conversation was very detailed. The funds transfer

will go down Friday, after which they plan a party back in Maui. Vladimir is flying in for the festivities. The plan is to kill and dispose of Anna, in New York, and Hugh, in the Pacific, immediately after the funds transfer."

Before Louise could relate the details of Nikita's wise cracks, about getting rid of the bodies, Anna jumped in. "This is perfect. We have the locked in schedule and, except for the three politicians in the group, all the key players will be on the yacht Thursday night. Plus, we know exactly where Vladimir will be Thursday night.

"Unless something changes radically between now and Thursday, we go with the plan very early Friday morning exactly as we discussed. You brave, young warriors must get on your way to Johnston Atoll now. Get safely on the ground, setup and ready to go long before the Standart is off the coast of the atoll. Kateri and I will be setting up in New York.

"If nothing changes, you know what to do and the next thing you will hear from me is 'New York mission accomplished'. You will get that message at exactly twelve thirty, early Friday morning, and you roll. If you hear nothing by twelve thirty-three, you roll anyway.

"God's speed, my heroes." The team could hear her voice cracking as the video conference was shut down.

While the team was making the seventy-five hundred mile trip from the Caymans to Johnston Atoll, Anna and Kateri were busy preparing for the meeting with Vladimir at the mansion in New York City. They, of course, had no intentions of going into the 'lion's den' unprepared to meet the lion. In fact, the New York City operation was totally integrated into Anna's plan and it was to be carried out with the same military like precision.

They needed certain provisions for their operation, far less than the team on its way to the Pacific, but equally as complex to come by. They arranged for a special handgun, that Kateri felt was the best for her role in the operation, and a backpack containing three boxes, each holding an unusual device used in theatrical pyrotechnics.

These two items were delivered to a hangar in Gerrard Smith Airport, the airport serving Cayman Brac, and loaded aboard the Cessna Citation, CJ2 jet, that the Mastersons kept there. Although inadequate for the team's Pacific operation, the luxurious jet accommodated six passengers and a crew of two. The Mastersons had hired two former Navy pilots who had retired to Cayman Brac and flew exclusively for them. It has a range of over sixteen hundred nautical miles affording the Mastersons the ability of flying to New York non-stop. That was exactly what Anna and Kateri were doing tonight.

~~~

They arrived at the Marine Air Terminal, at LaGuardia airport, where they were met by a man who from his attire, accent and demeanor looked to be a British investment banker. He was not. He was a master forger that the

Mastersons had encountered years earlier while consulting to the United Nations. Harold Alston, for that was his real name, had a special function in the UN's Peacekeeping organization. Occasionally, it was necessary to provide a Peacekeeping mission with personnel that due to their backgrounds, race or nationality would not be welcome in the country that asked for the Peacekeeping support. Enter Harold Alston, who in twenty-four hours could create an identity, with full documentation and historical background that would pass the scrutiny of organizations like the FBI and Scotland Yard.

Harold was waiting as they came into the arriving passenger lounge and he immediately recognized Anna. He approached her smiling, kissed both her cheeks in the standard European style of greeting, and handed her a small leather portfolio.

Anna, also smiling, handed Harold a metal attaché case.

Harold's small leather portfolio contained drivers' licenses, credit cards, library cards, passports and major medical ID cards, for Anna and Kateri, created for identities with names that matched the age and ethnic characteristics of both.

Anna's metal attaché case contained fifty thousand dollars in twenty-dollar bills.

Harold left the lounge a cheerful and somewhat wealthier man.

Anna and Kateri removed all their identity documents from their wallets and replaced them with those Harold had provided. They placed all their real identity documents into the small leather portfolio and, a few minutes later, one of the two pilots entered the lounge.

"Keep the plane here until Friday at noon," said Anna to the pilot. "We will call when we are heading back. However, if we are not back or have not contacted you by Friday noon, leave and return to Cayman Brac. Place this portfolio in the safe on the plane, get yourselves rooms and wait."

The pilot sensed what these two were up to was very serious, particularly since he knew Kateri's specialty. He also had observed that they were well armed and Anna was traveling without Hugh, a very rare occurrence. He said simply, "The luggage is in the limousine. God be with you," and left.

It was almost midnight when they finally threw their bags on the beds. They were in adjoining rooms in a small hotel on West Thirty Second Street.

They unpacked nothing but sleepwear, toiletries and their handguns.

Shortly after, there was a knock on Anna's door. Kateri came to the doorway connecting the rooms with her weapon in hand. She closed the door leaving about three inches for her to observe and if necessary react.

Anna, after being told it was a bellman, opened the door slowly leaving a clear line of vision and fire for Kateri.

"A package was left for you earlier. Sorry we didn't give it to you on check in, but here it is."

Anna took the package without a word, handed the bellman a five-dollar bill, smiled and closed the door.

Kateri and Anna looked at each other and laughed, "That's an old practice in small hotels," said Anna. "The bellman forgets to give the guest a message or a package when they bring them to the room. Bring it up later and get two tips for the arrival." They laughed again and opened the package, which they were expecting. It contained the two earpiece communicators, arranged by Louise that would put them in the network all of the team would be on during the operations.

They made a brief call to Louise who told them Hugh's location was unchanged, no new conversations had taken place, and the team had arrived safely at Johnston Atoll. They were in bed and asleep by one in the morning.

Wednesday would be a busy day with many tasks.

~~~

Anna and Kateri had packed for the uniqueness of this operation. They each had a small rolling suitcase with personal belongings, the things one would expect to find in the luggage of short-term city visitors. The suitcases and the contents were clean of any identification. However, they had a third piece of luggage, the backpack containing the theatrical pyrotechnics and until last night, their weapons, which were now in the pockets of their outer coats.

They left the rolling suitcases in their respective rooms, Kateri put the backpack on and they left for breakfast at a coffee shop on Eighth Avenue.

By nine that morning, they were on the subway heading for the Bronx and a rendezvous with a former high school girlfriend of Alberto who worked in the New York City Department of Buildings. She had taken the morning off to meet with them.

By a quarter after ten, they were in a gypsy cab on their

way to a used car lot on US Highway 46, in Fort Lee, New Jersey, just over the George Washington Bridge.

Anna and Kateri were studying the detailed blueprints of Nikita's mansion on Eighty-Second Street. A copy of the blueprints, that were on file at New York City Department of Buildings, and had been updated four years earlier when Nikita had done extensive remodeling of the mansion.

Alberto's childhood girlfriend was on her way, to the principal's office of St. Brendan's School with enough cash in her purse, to pay tuition for her five-year-old daughter for the full eight years she would attend.

~~~

The entire transaction in Fort Lee took less than an hour. Anna purchased a two-year-old Nissan Pathfinder, registered and insured it using her new identity and settled the entire transaction with hundred dollar bills. It helped that the driving record of her new identity was impeccable.

~~~

They had all the equipment they needed for their part of the operation. It was now time for detailed planning and research.

They would spend the rest of Wednesday, and a good part of Thursday, in and around the mansion, relating the exterior with the blueprints and refining Anna's plan.

They would also spend time in and around the Metropolitan Museum of Art across the street from the mansion.

It too had a role in Anna's plan!

The team left Hawaii's Kalaeloa Airport at one forty Tuesday afternoon and made the seven hundred mile flight in less than two and a half hours. By ten after four, they were taxiing towards the abandoned hangars, at the southeast corner of the field, next to the former pilots' quarters.

The Cessna stopped just short of the hangar doors. All eight members of the team jumped out and working together got the doors rolled open. They were all amazed at the great condition the hangar was in, clean and clear of any debris and still with workbenches against the walls. They were off to a good start. Now if the quarters were anywhere as neat as the hangar, the forty-eight hours they would spend planning and rehearsing wouldn't be half-bad.

After easing the Cessna into the hangar, the two Marine pilots exited the plane. They checked the securing blocks placed by members of the team. Both then joined the group as they headed for the building the pilots called home, before the military withdrew from the island in 1993.

The ten entered the building, with hesitation, not knowing what to expect, but fearing the worst. They were pleasantly surprised. The building was spotless as if there had been an inspection that very morning. Except for the sand like dust on every surface, nothing appeared out of place.

Climbing the stairs to the second floor, they found each of the twenty-four rooms in perfect order with a cot, rolled up mattress and bedding, a table and two chairs in each. However, the best discovery for the group was, the six bathrooms on the floor were all reasonably clean, but more importantly, all working.

The ten went back to the hangar, returning to the quarters with their personal belongings and each staked out rooms for themselves. Roger and Alberto told the crew they had the next hour to straighten out their quarters. They would meet in the dining hall on the first floor, at 1800 hours, and layout the schedule and duties for the next forty-eight hours.

~~~

When all eight of the team members and the two pilots were in the dining hall, Mario Vialli and Larry Feo volunteered to get dinner ready. Meanwhile, the other six positioned four tables into a square and set the chairs so the entire group was facing inward, towards each other. They then rounded up plates, glasses and utensils.

After eating a meal that was surprisingly good, as Feo and Vialli promised it would be, Alberto told the pilots it would be better for them if they knew nothing of the details of the operation. He suggested they do whatever they wanted to and then go back to their quarters for the night.

The two former Marines, who had seen some of the materials being loaded at Halsey Field in San Diego, agreed. Since their future with the Marines was still undecided, they figured the less they knew about the details of the operation, the better all would be. They left the hall.

Over the next three hours, the group went over the entire plan from entering the Pacific for their rendezvous with the Standart, to returning to the atoll and departing for Maui.

They figured they had forty-eight hours before Nikita and his gang arrived on the Standart, but they planned to have all their preparations and practice runs completed by midnight Wednesday. They would spend Thursday checking and rechecking equipment and making sure each player knew their role and the timing. Then they would relax and lay low until ten thirty Thursday night, when they would enter the Pacific for the critical phase of this do or die mission.

Breakfast on Wednesday morning was prepared by Alberto and Roger who took a great deal of ribbing when they announced to the group that they had prepared breakfast.

The food provisions, loaded on the jet in Kalaeloa Airport, were extensive and diverse enough for Feo and Vialli to have prepared an elaborate meal the night before. However, breakfast consisted of pastries, rolls, tea and instant coffee. Preparation amounted to boiling water and putting the boxes of pastries and rolls on the table. All laughed at the ribbing and Alberto and Roger announced it would be the last time they did anything nice for this group.

It was a good humored and positive way to start what was going to be a long and stressful day of repetitive practice runs.

~~~

By nine, the team and the pilots were in the hangar unloading over a ton of equipment for the next night's mission.

The pilots had been in several combat zones over the preceding eight years and recognized some of the items. However, they had to admit ignorance when it came to what appeared to be five large coils of extremely thick rope. It was thirty millimeters, almost an inch and a quarter thick, and it looked to them like a large quantity of anchor line.

It was, in actuality, the central piece of equipment to Anna's plan for the rescue.

Two hundred seventy yards of a recently developed, flexible magnesium based, explosive rope known by the brand name 'SuperStrand'. Five fifty-yard spools weighing forty pounds each plus twenty yards in a coil already in a tow pack.

The video demonstration, provided by SuperStrand's manufacturer, showed a scene where one strand was attached below the water line to the one-inch thick steel hull of a vessel via the adhesive surface on the 'rope'.

It was attached in the shape of a circle with a five-foot diameter to be triggered by a single detonator. The astonishing result, with one heat intensive low impact blast, a five-foot perfect circle of steel fell off the hull and an entry way was created in less than two seconds.

The team chose not to enlighten the pilots as to the real nature of the 'rope'. It was thought that explaining the intended function of the SuperStrand would only add to what was more and more appearing like the equipment for an underwater night invasion by US Navy Seals.

The pilots helped with the unloading and stacking of the contents of the jet's cargo hold, but asked no questions.

~~~

Besides the two hundred seventy yards of SuperStrand, the team had a full complement of tools for their mission.

Since each member of the team was to have the capability to function independently, each was outfitted with the same equipment inventory, all state of the art. Therefore, there was nine each of the following, one for each of the team and one for Hugh after they rescued him:

  Diver propulsion vehicles with flotation buoys

  Pure oxygen bubble-free rebreathers

Super light wet suits, gloves, booties and flippers

Underwater night vision dive goggles/mask

9mm Heckler & Koch MP5 machine pistols capable of firing underwater

Waterproof backpacks

Ear mounted communicators that Louise had arranged to keep the participants in both operations in constant communication

Special, ultra sensitive GPS trackers pre-programmed for Hugh's embedded chip

Standard GPS navigational units for getting to and back from the Standart

A folding all-in-one tool that included everything from needle nose pliers to small saw blades

In addition to the equipment for each individual, the general mission equipment included:

One diesel powered ten thousand watt generator for the facilities and the jet's electronics

One diesel powered compressor for refilling the rebreathers' tanks

Two pair of high-powered, tripod mounted, long-range observation binoculars

A one hundred pound collapsible mushroom anchor with a four hundred foot coil of quarter-inch, polyester rope and a buoy on the end opposite the anchor

Four underwater cargo sleds enclosed to hold equipment with flotation buoys

Fifteen detonators and four detonator remotes

Three four-man inflatable rafts with inflation canisters attached

One hundred, thirty round magazines, containing three-thousand rounds of 9mm Parabellum ammunition for the Heckler & Koch MP5s

Twenty M67 fragmentation hand grenades

~~~

The pilots left the group and went to tend to their plane, not wanting to be in the way or create any awkward situations. They were Marines and could speculate on the operation, but speculation was one thing and merely speculating afforded them the luxury of absolute deniability. Real knowledge took that comfortable luxury away. They had been told the fifty grand, they were being paid, called for them to forget the entire trip and that is what they intended to do.

The team spent the rest of the day, and half the night, packing the equipment into the underwater cargo sleds, towing the sleds fifty yards out from the beach, diving and unloading the sleds. All members performed trial runs navigating their diver propulsion vehicles, dismounting from them and attaching them to flotation buoys to suspend them twenty feet below the surface. These, plus every other aspect of the operation, were practiced repeatedly. First in daylight conditions, then in darkened nighttime conditions under which the actual mission would take place.

Alberto and Roger practiced over and over getting an unconscious body into a wet suit and other equipment while underwater, without drowning the victim. They drafted Ken Grady, one of the former Navy Seals, to play the role of Hugh. Dressing Hugh would be necessary, if he was unconscious or injured when they rescued him.

The team spent almost ten hours practicing for the rescue, six hours during daylight and four after dark.

When they finally dragged all the equipment back into the hangar and stumbled into the dining room, it was after midnight. They were exhausted, but greeted with a pleasant reward.

The pilots had put together a seafood feast having caught local fish and shellfish while the team was rehearsing and practicing.

A tired, but confident team of warriors climbed the stairs to their rooms that night.

Alberto and Roger told them to sleep in the next morning and they would meet in the dining room at eleven.

They would then go to the hangar and stay there until after dark preparing the equipment.

The two pilots would keep watch on the plane's radar for the arrival of the Standart. Once it was near, they would confirm its arrival visually. After it anchored, the pilots, using the equipment in the jet, would give the team an exact reading of its GPS coordinates.

This would be confirmed with Louise who was tracking Hugh's embedded chip. She was also tracking the location of the satellite communicators, in the pockets of Nikita and his four fellow villains, on board the Standart.

Everything was ready, the equipment and the team. It was now a matter of waiting and then a night of action.

Incredible action!

The last to arrive at the Standart was Dimitri Demochev. The head honcho, at the Russian Federation Technological and Nuclear Oversight Bureau, and the guy with the four thousand nukes. He arrived in a cab from Kahului Airport, about sixteen miles east of the port, at two thirty Wednesday afternoon.

After introductions all around, except for Hugh who was quiet in his cell below decks, the yacht set sail for Johnston Atoll at four o'clock.

While they were all assembled, Captain Stanislav Machtcenko announced the cruise would take about thirty hours. They would arrive at their destination, five miles northeast of Johnston Atoll, Thursday night at approximately ten o'clock.

Nikita had each of the four shown to their suites and said the evening would begin with cocktails on the upper deck at six thirty. At dinner, Nikita would explain what the plan was for Friday's events.

~~~

At dinner, Nikita laid out the schedule. They had given Hugh no further drugs since his flight to Maui. On Friday, they would get him up on the main deck by six in the morning. At six forty-five, they would go to the conference room on the main deck. There they would set Hugh up in front of the computer with the iris and fingerprint biometric scanners.

At precisely seven o'clock, they would access the account and sign on as user number one, utilizing Hugh Masterson's biometrics. Simultaneously, Vladimir would route the computer, in the New York City mansion, through the communications gateway on board the Standart. This would make his computer and the Standart's computer appear to the Regal Bank of the Caymans' system as originating from the same access point. Vladimir would then submit the fingerprint and iris scans of Anna Masterson in response to the bank system's request for user two.

By two minutes after seven on Friday morning, they would be into the account. Dimitri Demochev would then provide the account number and bank routing number where he wanted the twenty-five billion dollar advance sent to.

Demochev was pleased with this process since he wouldn't have to reveal any of his banking information, until he knew they were transferring the advance.

Nikita explained they would send it directly from the Mastersons' escrow account. That way if there was an investigation, after the nukes were in the hands of the Iranians, it would appear that the Mastersons were the organizers of the transaction. Since they would be dead by then, they could not defend themselves against the allegations.

Vladimir would clean out the balance of the account and transfer all monies to two accounts of Nikita's dead partners. The accounts were in Seychelles Royal Bank in the African Republic of Seychelles. Next, Vladimir would wire the balances of those accounts into the accounts of the same two dead partners at Banque Douteuse de Genève.

Nikita had kept all these accounts of his dead partners active, since their untimely demise, just for occasions like this. Their money laundering had followed this route when the partners were alive. It worked then, it would work now.

The final leg of the journey, of the billions, would be a transfer to the account of Korporaciya Finiksa. This is Nikita's holding corporation account in Bank Snachala Dlits'a, his privately owned Russian Bank.

Once this part of the transaction was completed, Dimitri Demochev was to authorize the shipment of the nukes to Bushehr, Iran. They would then notify Heydar Vahdani, the President of Iran that thirty-nine hundred ninety-nine nuclear warheads would arrive around the middle of March. The complicated sea route from Tolyatti, Russia to Bushehr, Iran taking about fifteen days.

All agreed this would be the agenda for Friday and they would simply enjoy the seven hundred mile cruise in the calm North Pacific on Thursday.

"By the way, before we move on to lighter subjects, I have one bit of very good news," said Nikita. "The distraction effort has been a huge success. There is nothing in the media anywhere on the globe except Saji and Dac Kien, the hosts of the grand world party. The main topic is what it's costing and who's paying for it. Fortunately, everyone is pissed off at both of them and nothing takes up media space more than hate gossip directed at corrupt politicians and diplomats. One British tabloid has their stay in the Ottoman Citadel Hotel in Jakarta as some sort of massive orgy. Another tabloid in New Zealand has children being flown in aboard Saji's planes for the entertainment of half the males in the traveling zoo."

"My God, is that stuff true?" asked Cheslav Bocharkov, Nikita's Russian lawyer.

"I doubt it," said Nikita laughing, "I had Heydar Vahdani's

personal PR team plant the story with a freelancer in Wellington, New Zealand. They are now working on one about five hundred male hookers being imported for the women in the tour. This one they are planting in one of the Washington, DC papers.

"The interesting thing we are learning is this scam was made much easier by the fact most of the world wants to believe these two are gutter rats. We are feeding a receptive audience. The beauty is the media eats it up. It's easy work since reporters were invited along and the public is screaming for more on the grand tour. The news organizations look no further than the tour to fill their airtime or newspapers and magazines. The last thing they give a shit about is a couple of thousand nukes being spread around to a dozen or so pissed off countries. I haven't seen or heard a word even though Jackson Phillips, Saji's Press Secretary, says it has been leaked. At least the suspicion has been leaked."

"It has been leaked," said Dimitri Demochev. "One of my partners in the deal owns most of the media outlets in Russia. He said a reporter at a small TV station brought the news people the story. Fortunately, the station manager brought it to my partner and he squelched it as being absurd. They then sent the reporter on assignment to Afghanistan."

There was laughter all around as the small group toasted their own brilliance and the inevitable success of the largest and widest nuclear weapons distribution in history.

~~~

The Standart, under the command of Captain Machtcenko, made better time than expected. By nine o'clock, over two hours since sunset, the Standart had dropped anchor five miles northeast of Johnston Atoll.

Nikita's group of villains and Captain Machtcenko were in the main salon drinking and laughing at each other's jokes, while the small crew tended to the securing of the yacht for the night's anchorage. Since it had already been determined Ovinko's three thugs would stand watch over both Hugh and the yacht, the crew quickly retired to their quarters below decks for a good night's sleep.

One by one, the partying group also retired. The last to leave the salon being Nikita.

The pilots told the team that the Standart was ten miles north of the island and cruising south at a leisurely rate of about ten miles per hour. Immediately, Mario Vialli and Larry Feo, the two Marine Force Recon vets, climbed to the top level of the airfield's control tower.

Earlier that day, they had visited the abandoned control tower and set up two pair of high-powered, tripod mounted, long-range observation binoculars.

Since the tower was glass enclosed on the level where Mario and Larry were, they could use no lights. The risk of even the smallest light being seen was too great. They worked using night vision goggles until the pilots announced the sighting of the Standart.

Each going to one of the pairs of binoculars, they began to scan the horizon to the north until Larry picked up the yacht's cabin and running lights and told Mario the coordinates. They both locked onto the light configuration. As it got closer, the form and size of the huge yacht became clearer. By the time it reached the point five miles off the northeast corner of the atoll, there was no doubt Nikita and his guests were totally secure in the belief there was no other person in sight.

The Standart was lit up like a cruise ship pulling into Honolulu.

As they watched the action on the deck, it became clear the Standart was setting anchor for the night. Once the yacht was secured, the deck crew left and disappeared below. Shortly thereafter, the exterior lights were turned off, all except the anchorage lighting.

At about nine fifteen, the lights in the cabins and salons began to go out.

Mario radioed the team, they packed up the binoculars and left to join the others in the hangar. It was not yet nine thirty.

~~~

When Mario and Larry arrived at the hangar, the other six were already in their wetsuits with their rebreather backpacks on. Their ear-mounted communicators were in place and they had begun moving the underwater cargo sleds to the water's edge. They were loaded with all of the equipment for the rescue, together with all of the gear required to get Hugh back to the atoll.

Mario and Larry got quickly into their gear and joined them in dragging the cargo sleds over the sand.

Once the sleds were in position for launching, the eight returned to the hangar and picked up their diver propulsion vehicles. These were not simply propellers in a tube, but were vehicles the diver lays in and drives. The team described them as convertible torpedoes since they were torpedo in shape, but had no top except over the control area.

Equipped with two battery-powered motors, they have a range of twenty nautical miles at a cruising speed of six miles per hour and can operate at a depth of forty feet. At the tail end of the tube is a locking tow hook to connect the tow cable for the underwater cargo sleds.

It is more like a mini-submarine. Once in the tube, everything the diver needs to know is presented on an LCD display; system status, depth, speed, underwater compass with digital chronometer and depth gauge. They measure six foot three inches by three foot six inches and the sides are two foot high. They fold to half the size for storage and transport.

Each member of the team had their weapons and ammunition, together with navigation equipment in their waterproof backpacks, which were an integrated part of their rebreathers.

At a few minutes before ten, all eight waded into the North Pacific Ocean and began the five-mile underwater voyage to the Standart. Within minutes of the team entering the water, the pilots, who had been watching the proceedings from the door at the back of the hangar, stared at each other in amazement. There was not a sign of the invasion force, not even a bubble on the surface. The team was using rebreathers to supply them with oxygen underwater. Different from the scuba tanks, familiar to all moviegoers, a rebreather provides a breathing gas containing oxygen and recycled exhaled gas. That fills two needs for a mission like this. It extends, by hours, the time the diver can spend underwater. Since the exhaled air is recycled, none escapes to the surface, thus no bubbles.

~~~

The trip took an hour. The diver propulsion vehicles, even with the sleds in tow, averaged about five miles per hour. The team moved across the five miles in a perfect triangle formation with Gabrielle Tompkins, the former US Navy Seals dive instructor, at the head of the triangle. She was followed by Alberto and Roger with Liz Buhle, Marine Force Recon explosives expert, between them.

The base of the triangle was made up of the four

combatants, Mario Vialli, Larry Feo, Ken Grady and Tom Landauer. They towed the underwater cargo sleds containing Hugh's gear, his diver propulsion vehicle, the two hundred seventy yards of SuperStrand, the detonators, mounting hardware and supplies.

They made the journey traveling twenty feet below the surface in total darkness using underwater night vision goggles and the GPS navigation equipment. Their objective was to wind up at a depth of twenty feet and ten feet away from the Standart.

It was a few minutes past eleven when they arrived and all eight knew exactly what each of their roles were. There would be no verbal communication over the com network, other than in an emergency, during the preparation phase. If any communication was necessary, it would be by way of hand signals. This was a precaution should the yacht have radio monitoring equipment on board and it was manned.

Their first act was to drop a self-opening, collapsed mushroom anchor that was on a four hundred foot coil of quarter-inch, polyester rope with a buoy on the surface end. This was set to attach the diver propulsion vehicles and the underwater sleds, so they would not drift away.

Within seconds of reaching the Standart, they had inflated the flotation buoys. They attached their diver propulsion vehicles to the twenty-foot cables and let them drop and be suspended. When the mission was complete, they would use them to return to the atoll. Roger and Alberto linked all the diver propulsion vehicles and the cargo sleds to the anchored buoy.

The team split up into three units taking what equipment

each group would need.

~~~

Unit one; Alberto and Roger using the GPS tracker locked onto Hugh's chip, headed for a porthole mid ship on the starboard side, about two feet above the water line. They stayed about five feet below the surface unpacking what they needed from the underwater tow pack, which had been in one of the cargo sleds. It contained the twenty-yard coil of SuperStrand, detonators and mounting hardware specifically for their objective.

They each took an end of the sixty-foot coil of the SuperStrand and rose slowly to the surface. Using additional buoyancy, by inflating the air-filled vest, which is an integral part of the rebreather pack, they gained enough height out of the water to peer through the porthole. The cabin was dark except for a very dim light, but thanks to the night vision goggles, they could see Hugh asleep or unconscious on a cot against the left wall. There was no one else in the small cell-like room and the only door in the room, presumably to the outside, was closed.

This was the only time, during the entire preparation phase, any of the team members would be above the surface of the dark waters surrounding the Standart. The only time they risked being spotted by anyone on deck. With this in mind, they hugged the side of the hull, which curved out above them, a factor that made seeing them from the deck less likely.

Roger placed three magnetic plates, with a ring above the porthole center, exactly two feet to the left and right of the first plate. He then did the same four feet below the porthole, about the distance from the porthole to the floor of the room.

Working swiftly with the SuperStrand, they peeled off a protective covering, along one quarter of the circumference, under which there was a powerful adhesive colored dark red.

He and Alberto then ran the SuperStrand three times through the six loops creating the outline of what looked eerily like a doorway, four foot by six foot with a window in it. They inserted two detonators, one each in the two ends of the SuperStrand. These were not timed detonators. They would both respond instantaneously and simultaneously to the remote trigger hanging from Alberto's neck.

They pressed the SuperStrand against the hull securing it tightly with the adhesive on the SuperStrand itself. They both knew a single strand would have worked, but they were taking no chances on this penetration. The strand would ignite and, to the naked eye, appear to burn white-hot all at once. Actually, the ignition rate of this super steel cutting strand is about five miles per second. Therefore, the time it took to ignite the full sixty feet of the wrapped strand was less than the blink of an eye.

The effect is somewhat like a welder, cutting out a section of the hull with an oxyacetylene torch, only really, really fast.

Alberto affixed two large magnetic plates with rings to the hull inside the outlined rectangle. As an added precaution, he smeared a waterproof, instant drying super adhesive. This adhesive is used by underwater construction crews, to hold steel girders temporarily in place, while they weld them.

They then attached two thin strands of steel cable, one each to the loops, dropped ten feet below the surface and let out the cable until they were about fifteen feet from the hull. Once their buoyancy compensators were set to an inflation level, which made their weight neutral at that depth, they would neither rise nor sink. They actually appeared as if they were suspended by some unseen cable.

Alberto made three clicking sounds with his tongue, the prearranged signal over the communications network signifying their rescue operation was ready to launch. They breathed a sigh of relief at having not been spotted and settled in to await the signal the other two teams had completed their mission.

~~~

The two units remaining unpacked the five coils of SuperStrand, the detonators, the detonator remotes and several pieces of associated hardware from the cargo sleds. They inflated the buoys, attached to the line on the bow of each, and let the sleds drop the twenty feet to the end of the lines. The last step was to attach the sleds to the anchored line, holding the propulsion vehicles, so they wouldn't drift.

Unit two was led by Liz Buhle. She took Mario Vialli and Larry Feo and headed for the bow of the yacht.

Gabrielle Tompkins, the lead for unit three, took Ken Grady and Tom Landauer and they too headed towards the bow.

Once there, they placed two ringed plates one on either side of the bow, approximately twelve feet below the surface of the water. These were similar to those used by Roger and Alberto to create the door like rectangle with a slight difference, the ring had a mechanism to lock the cord in place. They passed the end of one reel through the ring on the starboard side and the end of another reel through the ring on the port side. After letting out some of the coils, they affixed a detonator to each. These, as with the two used by Alberto and Roger, were ignited by remote triggering devices. However, they were on a completely different frequency than those used by unit one.

Liz took her team and three of the coils and started up the port side of the yacht feeding out the SuperStrand as she went. Mario, one of her team members, had the job of towing the coils and feeding out the SuperStrand as they moved along the side of the yacht. Larry, her other team member followed, removing the adhesive protective covering and pressing the cord against the hull. Thereby securing it along an imaginary line on the hull twelve feet below the surface. Approximately every twenty feet, Larry would add a piece of super strong underwater reinforcing tape to make sure the strand remained in place until used to fulfill its purpose.

At the end of the first coil, the team secured the end of the second coil using a special splice device into which was placed two detonators. One embedded into the end of the used coil and the other into the beginning of the new coil. By the end of the second coil, they had reached the stern of the Standart. There, Liz's team spliced the third coil to the expended second coil, again inserting two detonators.

The team then ran the strand along the stern heading for the starboard side where they met up with Gabrielle's team. Her team had been performing the same routine twelve feet below the surface along the starboard side of the yacht. But, they had only two coils for affixing to the side of the yacht. Cutting away the excess, they spliced the stern run SuperStrand to the end of the coil from the starboard side and inserted two more detonators.

The Standart now had over six hundred feet of a very high explosive rope, an inch and a quarter thick, completely encircling its hull twelve feet below the water line.

Liz, with Gabrielle, dove to the bottom of the stern to where the twin propellers extended beyond the bottom of the yacht. They proceeded to wrap the remaining SuperStrand around the shafts of the two propellers flush against the stern of the yacht. After splicing the two ends together, attached two more detonators.

They then rejoined the four other team members, descended to about twenty feet and backed off about fifteen feet from the yacht. After all six executed the same routine as Alberto and Roger to set their buoyancy at a neutral state, Gabrielle made five clicking sounds with her tongue. This was the signal to everyone on the network, including Anna and Kateri in New York and Louise in Cayman Brac; all was now in place for the rescue.

It was fifteen minutes after midnight. In New York, it was six fifteen in the morning. Forty-five minutes earlier, Anna and Kateri had begun their tasks in this complex mission.

By five thirty on Friday morning, Anna and Kateri had checked out of the hotel on West Thirty Second Street. On the way to the garage, they disposed of the wheeled suitcases in two dumpsters, a block apart. They picked up the SUV and headed up Madison Avenue towards Eighty Second Street.

It would be slightly more than an hour until sunrise on this very cold winter morning. They were both wearing black, hooded, frigid weather, outer coats. However, if all went as planned, they would be on their way to the warm beaches of Maui by sunrise.

Their research and rehearsals had been as complete as the Pacific team's and it was about to pay off.

At exactly six fifteen, they parked the SUV on the west corner of Eighty Second Street and Fifth Avenue. Directly in front of a small park on the south end of the Metropolitan Museum of Art.

Inside the vehicle were the three boxes containing the theatrical pyrotechnic devices. One box on the floor, in front of each of the three rows of seats. They had been described by the manufacturer, and the dealer that provided them, as 'super loud, super bright and super smoky'. Those were the only contents of the vehicle. Both wore gloves in the car, since purchasing it, thus there were no fingerprints to be traced.

On leaving the vehicle, they opened all the windows including the one in the rear door and the sunroof.

Kateri had a remote detonator around her neck with three buttons labeled clearly '1', '2' and '3', denoting the seat location for each of the boxes.

At six twenty, they were both standing in the recess of the garage entry about twelve feet to the left of the main doorway to Nikita's mansion on East Eighty Second Street. Both women had a clear view of the small landing outside this main entrance. Kateri took up the position closest to the landing. Reaching into her inside coat pocket, she withdrew the special weapon she had ordered, a Beretta 92FS fitted with a Gemtech Trinity silencer, and loaded with fifteen rounds of 9mm hollow point ammunition. She held it inside the fold of her coat. She looked at Anna who simply nodded.

Kateri pressed the button, labeled '1' on the remote around her neck.

The sound of the explosion was as if the auto containing the pyrotechnic device had blown completely apart. The flash was blinding, lighting up half the Eighty Second Street block between Fifth and Madison Avenues. The smoke rose and blew down Fifth Avenue.

It produced the result they wanted.

Ovinko's two goons, who were there to protect Vladimir and kill Anna, came running out onto the landing. They were both yelling in Russian, "CHto, chert voz'mi," which loosely translated is, "What the hell!"

As they stood in the doorway, hesitating to go further on the landing to see the carnage they expected up the block, Kateri pressed the button on the remote labeled '2'. It resulted in an instant replay of the devastating explosion. This brought the two out further…a mistake.

In one very smooth flowing movement, she withdrew the

9mm Beretta, from the fold of her coat, and fired two rounds. One each into the heads of the thugs who were facing away from her. Since she was at street level and therefore positioned lower than they were, the bullets entered each at the base of the back of the skull and traveled upwards through the brain.

Kateri had thought the mission through and elected to use hollow point bullets, which accomplished two objectives at once.

A hollow point bullet has a pit, a hollowed out shape, in its tip. It therefore expands on entering the target. This decreases penetration, but also destroys more tissue as it travels through the target.

Thus, the two bullets destroyed large segments of the two creeps' brains, while not causing havoc by coming out the other side of their skulls. The two shots sounded more like the opening of a beer can than two deadly bullets, thanks to the silencer.

The two lurched forward and fell to the landing in front of the door. They were dead before they hit the ground.

The three people walking on the block at this early morning hour noticed nothing. They were mesmerized by the explosions on the corner. There were no vehicles since the only way into the one-way street was from Fifth Avenue. No one was driving anywhere near the 'exploding SUV'. All this had been considered in Anna and Kateri's planning.

As the two gangsters crumbled to the ground, Anna was up the stairs and in the door. She was steps ahead of Kateri who headed for the two corpses.

As Anna went through the doorway, she heard what she

assumed was Vladimir shouting from a room on the first floor, "CHto, chert voz'mi."

"Well, they're consistent," she thought to herself as she raced toward the sound of the shouts, drawing her 38 caliber Ruger LCP from the outside pocket of her coat and holding it behind her. It too was loaded with hollow point ammunition, but it did not have a silencer.

As she entered the study, Vladimir was looking out one of the windows overlooking Fifth Avenue at the museum and the apparently exploding car. Anna said loud enough to be heard over the street noise, "Vladimir Dubnikov?"

He turned suddenly, startled, but then smiled. He apparently recognized her, as she recognized him from the photos of him and his father Hugh and she had assembled.

He opened his mouth and said, "You're..."

Anna's movement was as smooth as Kateri's. After all, Kateri had been her instructor.

Her right arm came from behind her, the Ruger in hand, and moved up, across and extended in front of her face. At the same time, she brought her left hand up and clutching her right, to support and steady her aim, she fluidly pulled the trigger.

The front of Vladimir's face appeared to explode, the bullet entering precisely at the meeting point of the bridge of his nose and his forehead. Simultaneously, the third pyrotechnic device exploded in the vehicle outside. Kateri shouted from the hallway outside the study, "Drag him out here. I found a staircase to throw them down into the cellar."

Anna placed the Ruger back in her pocket, grabbed the

collar of Vladimir's shirt and dragged him out of the room where she quickly spotted Kateri holding a door open.

Kateri quickly grabbed Vladimir's legs and together they tossed him down the cellar stairs where he landed unceremoniously on top of his two dead bodyguards.

As Kateri closed the cellar door, Anna looked at her watch. It was six thirty exactly. She pushed a button on her earpiece activating it and said simply, "New York mission accomplished."

As they prepared to leave the mansion, sirens were screaming all over the neighborhood. Between six twenty and six thirty, there had been three horrendous explosions on the corner of Eighty Second Street and Fifth Avenue, in front of a small park on the south end of the Metropolitan Museum of Art.

It had to be terrorists and every cop and firefighter in the vicinity was on the way to the scene.

When they arrived, they would be both surprised and perplexed to find a two-year-old Nissan Pathfinder intact with no external damage. On closer examination, they would find some serious signs of smoke and fire damage on the interior, particularly on the floor in front of each of the seats.

Anna and Kateri exited the mansion through the garage and walked to Lexington Avenue. They headed south on foot all the way to Fifty Eighth Street where they hailed a cab to LaGuardia Marine Terminal.

As the cab entered the Queens Midtown Tunnel, Anna was mumbling to herself.

"Are you OK?" asked Kateri.

"Yeah, but I keep thinking.

"Vladimir started to say something when he saw me. He only got out 'you're' and I can't help wondering what he was going to say. Maybe 'you're more beautiful in person,' or 'you're shorter than I thought', or 'you're older than I thought'?"

"Anna," said Kateri, "he probably was going to say you're early."

They both started laughing. Laughter with a little tension release in it.

"Kateri, I have one question. After I shot Vladimir, you shouted for me to bring him out to get rid of the body. How did you know it wasn't me who got shot?"

"Because I trained you!"

"Let's head for Maui," said Anna, still laughing.

The sun was just beginning to rise.

Anna's four-word message reached the earpieces of all eight members of the team at exactly twelve thirty. Within thirty seconds, Larry Feo, from Liz's unit, and Ken Grady, from Gabrielle's, joined Alberto and Roger to provide cover. Their weapons at the ready, they concentrated on the yacht's windows, portholes and decks directly above the outlined rectangle on the Standart's hull fifteen feet in front of them.

Alberto looked toward Roger to his right and got the thumbs up sign. Taking the remote hanging from a thin chain around his neck, he pushed back the red safety cover and pressed the dimly illuminated detonator button.

The results were instantaneous and precisely as Alberto and Roger had planned. The flash was a perfect rectangle, four foot wide and six foot high and the sound was like a muffled twelve gauge shotgun blast. Thanks to Gabrielle's attention to detail when ordering the dive equipment, the night vision masks had built in light compensators. Otherwise, the sun bright flash would have temporarily blinded all four.

The instant the flash dimmed, Alberto and Roger simultaneously pulled on the thin cables attached to the rings in the center of the rectangle of the Standart's hull.

The rectangle pulled cleanly away from the hull and they let drop the cables, allowing the piece of steel hull to start its three hundred foot journey to the floor of the Pacific.

Immediately, the room began to fill with water and Roger propelled himself towards the opening intending to reach Hugh in seconds and provide him with oxygen from his breather. Even though there was no chance of it filling, since half the room was above sea level. The team had anticipated the possibility of Hugh being unconscious and therefore he would not propel himself to the top of the water to keep breathing.

As Roger was about to enter the cabin, Larry Feo pulled him to the left side of the opening. One of Hugh's minders was stepping into the now flooding room through the hall doorway. The thug had an automatic weapon at the ready, but never got to react to the scene that must have appeared quite strange to him.

Directly in front of the villain, opposite the door he had come through, was a large opening into the sea and water was rushing in at about waist level. The thug had to brace himself against the doorjamb to keep from being swept out of the room. Good news for the team. As long as he was off balance, he was not firing his weapon, running or yelling, thereby not bringing more thugs to the event. Bad news for the grunt!

As Larry pulled Roger out of the line of fire from Hugh's guard, Ken Grady moved in front of the opening and fired a short burst from his 9mm Heckler & Koch MP5 machine pistol. At seven hundred rounds per minute, the one second burst placed twelve rounds in the upper chest of Vilen Ovinko's employee, who was wearing a tee shirt and jeans and no body armor. Since no trouble was expected five miles from an island and seven hundred miles from the nearest human beings, the crew was not prepared for a shootout. The magazine, one of eight that the four combat ready members of the team carried, is called a 'C-Mag'. It holds one hundred rounds of 9mm ammunition in a double drum and is virtually flawless in its ability to feed all one hundred rounds. After dispatching the guard, Ken had another eighty-eight rounds should more passengers that were inquisitive show up.

Before the dead thug floated out the doorway into the passageway, Roger entered the room and was at Hugh's side in a matter of seconds. Hugh, who had been sleeping on the cot against the wall, had reacted to the salt water that essentially covered him instants after the piece of wall in the room disappeared into the Pacific. He was attempting to get his footing while hanging onto the cot, which was wedged in the corner against the corridor-side wall of the room. It was a rough struggle since he was coughing from the water he had breathed in when the flood first hit. Simultaneously, he was trying to keep his head above the water surface and avoid being swept into the corridor, which was now also filling with Pacific water.

Roger grabbed Hugh by the shoulders and quickly jammed the backup breather mouthpiece from his rebreather, into his mouth.

Hugh turned towards Roger his eyes wide open, pulled out the mouthpiece, spit out a sizeable quantity of water and replaced the mouthpiece. All this was going on while Roger, backing out, pulled him through the newly created doorway to the Pacific Ocean.

On exiting the Standart, Roger was joined by Alberto. Between them, they took Hugh down to a depth of twenty feet and rapidly headed away from the yacht. As they swam away, they could hear gunshots apparently coming from the deck of the Standart. They kept moving, not looking back. They stopped at a point about ten yards from the yacht and continued getting Hugh into his gear.

The team was just that, a precision team. As soon as the

first shots rang out, Larry and Ken sprayed the upper deck with about one hundred and eighty-eight rounds of 9mm bullets. Just to be on the safe side, Larry and Ken paused and replaced the empty magazines with fresh ones.

Within seconds, Roger, Alberto and Hugh were joined by Gabrielle, Liz, Mario and Tom towing all the recovered equipment, sleds, and the nine driver propulsion vehicles.

When Ken and Larry caught up with the team, Alberto and Roger were just finishing getting Hugh into all his gear.

The entire operation had taken one minute and forty-four seconds.

All nine climbed into the driver propulsion vehicles and headed away from the yacht. Alberto shouted into his faceplate microphone, "Take 'em down and I mean down!"

Gabrielle and Liz both clutched the remote detonators on the thin chains around their necks and releasing the safety, pressed the dimly illuminated detonate buttons.

By this time, they were over twenty-five yards from the Standart and all eight of the rescue team stopped and turned towards the huge yacht. Roger and Alberto, on either side of Hugh, turned him around so he too was looking at the Standart.

As they watched the dark waters, a line of light, two hundred and eighty-five feet long and as bright as the sun, appeared along the entire length of the Standart twelve feet below the water line.

As the nine stared at the sight through their night vision goggles, the line, where the SuperStrand had ignited became wider. Slowly the entire bottom of the Standart, the pride of Vladislav Dubnikov, slipped away from the upper portion of the huge yacht.

They had successfully cut the two hundred and eighty-five foot yacht, Standart, in two, lengthwise.

Because of the extra charges placed around the propellers of the grand yacht, the bottom of the stern separated from the vessel at the same time. The entire ship immediately began to slip into the sea to make its three hundred foot journey to the bottom of the Pacific.

The team would all agree later that it looked like a great whale diving, graceful and with almost no ripple.

It was thirty-four minutes after midnight, Friday morning, February 26, 2010, exactly four minutes from Anna Masterson giving the 'go' signal from New York City.

The team backed off another fifty or so feet and surfaced. The four warriors, Ken, Mario, Larry and Tom, all with their night vision masks in place, made their way closer to see if they could spot any survivors splashing about. They waited three minutes assuming anyone who had escaped the craft would be on the surface by then. Anyone who had not escaped was on their way to the bottom of the ocean.

Then Ken spoke into his faceplate mike, "All clear" and Roger returned with "Let's go home, team."

Seven thousand miles away, in a cab heading towards the Queens Midtown Tunnel in New York City, Anna and Kateri heard the message in their earpieces. Kateri immediately looked at Anna and could see tears rolling down Anna's cheeks.

It took the team almost two hours to get back to Johnston Atoll, slightly longer than the trip out. They didn't run the diver propulsion vehicles full out on the return trip. Thanks to Gabrielle's pointing out various forms of undersea life indigenous to the region, the trip was pleasantly distracting. By the time they were on the beach pulling up the equipment, they were more like a group of night diving tourists returning from an excursion. Rather than a group of warriors who had just successfully rescued their boss and sunk a three-thousand ton yacht.

It took them almost four hours to clean up and pack everything into the Cessna, during which time Anna and Hugh spoke to each other at least six times.

The team went over the areas on the atoll they had occupied, twice, making sure there were no telltale signs of their having been there. They went as far as scrubbing down most of the interior surfaces to dispose of any prints or other traceable remnants.

They were not foolish enough to believe they could cover all signs of having been there, but for any visitors to the atoll, there would be no obvious indication of visitors since the military left. To uncover what tracks remained, an inquisitive investigator would have to suspect there had been visitors and be on a specific mission to find out who it was.

Short of burning down every structure on the atoll, there was nothing they could do about that.

At seven fifteen on Friday morning, the Cessna lifted off the runway on Johnston Atoll and headed northeast towards the Hawaiian Islands.

As the plane leveled off at thirty-five thousand feet, Hugh got up from his seat and went to the front of the passenger cabin.

All conversation stopped as the eight turned their heads or swiveled their seats to look at their boss. "I cannot even begin to thank you nor express the emotions I feel towards each of you for the very courageous rescue you have executed," he said looking surprisingly relaxed, healthy and cheerful, "but I am going to try."

There was laughter among the eight when Hugh went on, "However, not here, and not now. The next three hours should be used for sleeping because we are on our way to Maui. There we'll be joined by Anna, Kateri and Louise and we'll all be spending the next ten days playing, eating and generally enjoying ourselves in the Ahupua`a Manor at Ka'anapali on Maui. I guarantee you're going to love the place, so I won't waste any precious sleeping time describing it. We should be there in about three hours. Please, sit back, close your eyes and prepare for some fun. You earned it."

Of course, none of them slept, they were all under thirty-two years old, healthy and fit. They chatted, laughed and for the next three hours planned the next ten days of activities.

~~~

Hugh, his eight person security force and the two pilots were at Ahupua`a Manor and settled in almost five hours before the cab with Anna, Kateri, Louise and their two pilots arrived at the entrance to the manor. The seven thousand mile trip from Cayman Brac, where they picked up Louise, took over fifteen hours with refueling. As the cab left and they stepped into the three-story entrance hall, all five looked around in awe at the sheer size and beauty of the manor and the location. There was no one in sight. The place was so big and spread out the team had gone off in every direction.

~~~

The twenty thousand square foot mansion is decked out in Polynesian décor. There are fourteen bedrooms plus the owner's suite, two dens and twenty bathrooms. For entertainment, without leaving the four acres making up the estate, there is a big screen media room seating twenty, a billiards room, a library with bar and a huge kitchen opening onto a barbecue deck and a dining room which holds twenty. Overlooking the pool and hot tub are an indoor gym, sauna and steam rooms.

Set on a hilltop peninsula jutting out into the sea, the Manor overlooks on three sides the beautiful blue Pacific. Its waves washing up on the sands of three private beaches.

~~~

Anna hesitated for only a moment and then she began wandering around the rooms shouting, "Hugh, Hugh, where are you, my Hugh? Hugh? Seconds later, Hugh dressed in the same clothes he had on when he left Johnston Atoll, came running down the stairs from the owner's suite on the second floor, grabbed Anna up in his arms and swung her about kissing her head, her forehead, her cheeks and finally her lips.

Tears of joy and relief were streaming down both their faces. Then, arm in arm, they went up the stairs to the suite.

~~~

The next ten days were like a dream to all sixteen inhabitants of Ahupua`a Manor. Each day was filled with sailing, jet skiing, fishing, scuba, snorkeling, lying on the sand, swimming in the pool and the surf and endless meals of deliciously prepared seafood. The Manor came with a full staff including an unbelievable Polynesian chef.

For those in the entourage that wanted to get out and see other parts of the island, Hugh had arranged for four Jeep Wranglers to be on the grounds and available to any wishing to wander. Few did, the Manor just offered too much.

Anna and Hugh were serene, together again, safer than they had been in years and the future looked very bright indeed.

The ten members of the security group, the team who were now about to embark on running Cayman Covert Cyber Reclamation, Ltd., could not remember a happier time. They were infected by Anna and Hugh's contagious positive attitude and state of mind.

Things were about to get better.

The last day of the vacation, the four pilots decided to explore the island. Investigating possible career alternatives for the two Marine pilots who were between enlistments and still undecided as to their next career move.

That evening a sumptuous feast and final celebration was planned, but Anna and Hugh asked the ten to assemble on the terrace overlooking the Pacific an hour early and before the pilots returned. The purpose was a brief thank you and champagne toast to the future.

As they stood, marveling at the sun setting over the Pacific,

Anna tapped a spoon against her glass. She said, "We will only interrupt this example of God's magnificent universe for a moment. Tomorrow you all will be returning to Villa Serenity. You'll take up responsibilities in addition to those of the Cayman Covert Cyber Reclamation, Ltd. security force. Hugh and I feel it's fitting we follow the policies of both commercial organizations and the military. We've decided an appropriate celebration of the launching of our new partnership would be what the military calls a 're-up bonus' and businesses call a 'signing bonus'.

"When you get back to your rooms tonight, each of you will find an envelope under your pillows containing a check for one hundred thousand dollars. It is a small token of Hugh's and my appreciation for all you have done and a fitting kickoff to a spectacular future together. We love you like family."

There was silence, then thank you all around, emotional handshaking and back clapping and here and there, a tear filled eye.

It was all over in less than five minutes and the twelve returned to watching the glorious sunset.

It was a long night of partying and a sleepy group that boarded the two planes headed back to Cayman Brac. The team took the big Cessna and would get to Gerrard Smith International Airport, after a refueling stop in San Diego, in about ten hours.

Anna and Hugh boarded the smaller Cessna jet. It would take Anna and Hugh more than fifteen hours to make the same trip, but they wanted that time alone. They had much to talk about and to plan.

It was less than three weeks since Anna, Hugh and the entire team had returned to Villa Serenity on Cayman Brac. Although the group had already settled into their new roles with enthusiasm, there was a bit of turmoil beneath the surface.

"We have to address it," said Anna, as she and Hugh were cleaning their handguns after an hour of practice in the target range. "If we don't explain our attitude of hands off and draw them into accepting and supporting it as the only viable strategy, it will become the ever present 800 pound gorilla in the room."

~~~

They had been having the same discussion for over a week. All ten members of the team were preoccupied with the fact the President of the United States, the man running the most powerful nation in the world, was at best a con man, at worst a traitor.

This grew out of Anna and Hugh's effort to put to rest any questions the team may have had about the justification for the events of the rescue operation. Anna had arranged for Louise to put together all of the captured conversations of the ten members of Nikita's gang that shared the satellite network. Louise had spent a week creating a kind of radio show with particulars and explanations prefacing each conversation series.

Anna and Hugh had reviewed and edited it with Louise. A week ago, the twelve people that now made up the management and operational staff of Cayman Covert Cyber Reclamation, Ltd., sat in the war room for eight hours where it was listened to and discussed. At the conclusion of the session, none of the ten had the slightest doubt the kidnapping of Hugh forced them into actions. The results of which, not only got Hugh back, but stopped a process that inevitably would have changed civilization.

However, the conversations exposed a great deal. These were intelligent, experienced young people and they knew that the eradication of Nikita, and the leaders of the conspiracy, was only a temporary solution.

The nukes still existed in warehouses in Russia. A new Russian civil servant would soon replace Dimitri Demochev, as Director General of RFTABO, and that's who would determine the future of the warheads.

The President of Iran still sat safely and securely in his palace in Teheran, now with a whetted appetite for the remaining thirty-nine hundred ninety-nine nuclear warheads and a willingness to pay a great deal of money to get them.

The President of the United States and the Secretary General of the United Nations were still in their positions and nothing was apparent on the horizon, which would end that condition. Their future actions were very unpredictable.

This scenario bothered the ten because they believed it was only a matter of time before the nuke deal with the Russians would be resurrected. Once again, for the right price, Sorosh Saji and Pham Dac Kien would gladly help.

The ten wanted to do something, needed to do something, but they had no idea what.

…and that was the 'it' Anna referred to she felt must be addressed.

~~~

Hugh answered, "So what would you suggest, honey? How should we address it? You know my position and all the reasons for that stance. You believe that our strategy is not only the best one, it is the only possible one. We just proceed along that path."

"I didn't always believe it was. When we landed back here in February, I was with the team. I was ready to start planning the next steps in eradicating the problem altogether."

"I know, Anna, I remember well the morning you asked the question over breakfast. Let me get it right...'OK, Hugh, what's the plan for getting rid of the rest of the bastards in this cabal?' Yeah, that was it and I almost choked on my cinnamon bagel. You were all fired up. You and the team, the invincible eleven."

"Right, and you smiled, began talking and in less than a half hour I was saying to myself, 'He's right. It will work out. The checks and balances will hold and sanity will prevail'. After that conversation, I was with you one hundred percent. Therefore, that is what I want you to do for the team. I want you to confront their anxiety, their fears and their anger and get them onboard our strategy."

"When do you want me to do this?"

"Funny you should ask. You remember today is St. Patrick's Day? Well, Twila and I got together and planned a dinner of corned beef and cabbage for tonight. I invited the whole team to join us in a little bit of Ireland celebration. I thought that would be the perfect opportunity. What do you say? If you don't want to, I'll understand."

Smiling with his eyes closed and his head shaking, Hugh answered, "No you won't."

~~~

It was almost eight o'clock by the time Anna, Hugh and the team had finished several helpings of corned beef, cabbage, boiled potatoes and carrots. Jennifer Ebanks arrived at the beachfront gazebo in her electric cart. Ken Grady and Larry Feo both jumped up to help her bring in a large urn of coffee and a bottle of Irish whiskey for the making of Irish coffee. Jennifer carried a tray with three pie plates of apple amber. It is the oldest of traditional Irish desserts, having been a mainstay of the dinner tables in Ireland for thousands of years.

As Jennifer left, everyone helped themselves to the after dinner treats. Once they were all reseated, Hugh stood up, his coffee cup in hand, an action that brought the group to quiet. "I know there is a strong sentiment among most, if not all of you, that we should continue our successful disruption of Nikita's nuclear proliferation program. I am sure the feeling is much the same as Anna and I felt on our return home. We both felt we should continue and make sure the remaining participants cannot revive the plan. We then examined how we would go about pulling that off.

"Let me say once we tried to move from the concept and outline an actual plan, it hit us the only sure approach would call for the neutralizing, in one way or another, of two heads of state and the head of the United Nations. Not a course of action I would recommend, nor do I think we would be terribly successful.

"Once we accepted that direct action was either beyond our capabilities or would end badly, we started to examine what would the probable outcome be if we did nothing.

"Our conclusion was the people of the United States will fix the problem.

"Let me lay out how we got to that point and see if you agree. The good news is it didn't take us a lengthy analysis to arrive at that conclusion, so it won't take a long time to explain.

"First, there is the reality thirty-nine hundred ninety-nine nuclear warheads that fit Iran's Shahab-3 ballistic missiles are stored in Russian warehouses. Russian interests want to sell these little buggers and the President of Iran wants to buy them.

"Yes, Mr. M," said Liz, but Hugh interrupted her. "After our experiences together over the last twenty or so days," he said, "Mr. and Mrs. M seems a bit formal. From now on, it's Anna and Hugh."

Smiling, Liz went on, "OK, Hugh. That's the transaction we derailed. That only resulted in delaying it, not stopping it. Heydar Vahdani is going to do everything in his power to revive the deal directly, as soon as he realizes his middleman has gone missing. Even if it takes several months, the world will unknowingly be back at the brink in a year or so."

"That was our initial reaction, Liz, until we put together the Nikita clan's conversations and realized 'the cat was out of the bag'. The world will not be in the dark, if the warhead deal gets a new life.

"Think back to the conversation, February twentieth, between Saji and Nikita with Dac Kien on the line. Saji told Nikita intelligence sources had picked up on the

322

nuclear deal and had figured out the Saji grand tour was nothing but a planned distraction. Saji made a point of letting Nikita know the White House press secretary, Jackson Phillips, was present when Clive Bauman, his intelligence czar, gave him the news.

"Tell one wonk in the media and it won't be long before the world knows and that is exactly what happened. Somehow, a reporter on a small Russian television station happened on the story and although it hasn't gotten into the mainstream media yet, it's on its way.

"Anna has been searching the internet for any news or information, regarding Nikita and his colleagues, and happened onto that reporter's blog. It seems as soon as he uncovered the story, he was shipped by his employer to Afghanistan. He blames it on his theory the owner of the media group he works for, a former Soviet KGB official, is in on the deal.

"The blog is hosted on a Swiss internet service provider and although they may silence the reporter, that story will live for a very long time. It will not be long before others pick up the piece and the story goes neural."

"So very soon," said Liz, "the world will not only know about the nukes up for sale, but also that there is a suspicion that Saji and Dac Kien were in on it."

"Right, Liz," said Anna, who had now stood up next to Hugh, "and that creates the feeling amongst the American people we have a scoundrel in the White House and his partner runs the United Nations. Granted there will be a split, probably down the middle of the population. Half will believe the story is true and the other half, the story is a lie."

"However," said Hugh, "none of the participants in the conspiracy will be free to act in secret. The world press will be watching all four like hawks: Iran, Russia, Dac Kien and, of course, our own Sorosh Saji. Not because of any desire to save the globe, it may just result in the next biggest story.

"Saji and Dac Kien will be particularly sensitive to this new spotlight on their actions and therefore, will become very careful in their relations with both Russia and Iran. In fact, I would not be surprised to see a joint commission formed made up of the United Nations, Russia and the United States with the sole objective being oversight and destruction of those thirty-nine hundred ninety-nine warheads."

"We know how well Dac Kien's special programs work, Mr....I mean, Hugh," said Roger and everyone in the gazebo laughed at that. "But, I agree. It doesn't allow a lot of wiggle room for the bastards to sell off a bunch of warheads without starting one hell of a rumble."

"I think we can all agree, Hugh," said Alberto, "that the exposure of Nikita's conspiracy essentially freezes the random distribution of four thousand fifty-kiloton nukes. That still leaves us with a piece of garbage in the White House, who, as we keep saying, is a con man at best and a traitor at worst. How can we sit by and let that continue? It's almost eighteen months until the next presidential election and even if he loses, he will be in office for almost two months after that. There is also the slim possibility he could win. We have to do something to bring down his administration. I don't give a damn about Pham Dac Kien and the United Nations. On their best day, they can't get feeding hungry people right. Without Sorosh Saji and

United States money and power, the UN, under his leadership, will just fumble along until his term expires in December 2011. But, I think we have got to do something to get Saji and his gangster wife kicked out of the White House."

There was general agreement from the other nine with suggestions of everything from going to the newspapers to calling Saji and Dac Kien on the Nikita network. Telling them, "We're your new bosses and we want you to resign now or we send the whole story to the press."

"One problem, Saji or Dac Kien may choose to fight back. Then your proposals will generate a lot of investigations and bring a very bright spotlight on all of us and Cayman Covert Cyber Reclamation, Ltd.," said Anna. "Not something any of us really want."

"You're right," said Louise, "what did you mean by the people of the United States will fix the problem?"

"Well, Alberto is right about Pham Dac Kien and the UN. "Without Nikita's involvement, Dac Kien will just be another UN glad hander whether he is out in 2011 or continues for another five years. He was literally a tool to create distraction and a passive partner in various United Nations' rip-offs run by Nikita. Since there is no Nikita, there will be no action.

"Sorosh Saji is another story all together. Whether he acknowledges it or even understands it, he serves at the pleasure of the people of the United States and those people aren't too pleased with his actions. He has essentially accomplished little or nothing since being elected. His major achievements have been to increase debt, expand government interference in Americans' lives, increase unemployment and generally embarrass the United States globally. Don't forget these accomplishments were made while he was being managed by a very shrewd and calculating guy, Nikita.

"Nikita wanted chaos in the US because chaos in the US generates major global distractions and he definitely got his chaos.

"Sorosh was only effective at fulfilling this agenda because he was Nikita's puppet.

"Remember, from his childhood, eleven years old to be exact, Sorosh Saji has been not only groomed by first, Vilen Ovinko, and ultimately by Nikita. Saji has had every step of his political ascendancy managed by these puppeteers.

"What we must not lose sight of is Saji's masters have also dictated every action Sorosh Saji has taken. That includes those in every public position he has held, from community organization worker to President of the United States. Sorosh Saji has no policy plan or agenda of his own. He is the marionette, manufactured, sculpted, continually maintained, and lubricated to execute the movements dictated by Nikita.

"And therein lies the foundation of our approach. The puppeteers are dead and the puppets must proceed creating their own movements. It is our strong belief, supported by the conversations you all heard, without being directed, the future actions of Sorosh Saji would run from erratic to none at all. I believe it will take awhile for both he and Dac Kien to realize they are no longer receiving day-to-day marching instructions, after which they will attempt to find out why.

"Saji's next step will be to convince himself he can create and execute policy and change on his own. That is when the shit will hit the fan.

"You will remember from the captured satellite conversations, Nikita had both the Speaker of the House and the Senate Majority Leader on his payroll. This gave him the added power to coordinate the passing of the absurd legislation he instructed Saji to propose. Now there isn't a puppeteer for those two either. Therefore, the Executive and Legislative branches, of the United States Government, are effectively without focused direction and will commit blunder after blunder over the next eighteen months.

"They have been creating chaos for these last several months because that is what Nikita needed to distract the world from his private program of global nuclear proliferation. He knew what would work and how far to take it without getting his resources fired. His program called for Sorosh Saji to do things supported by the Speaker of the House and the Senate Majority Leader that had no other objective, but to create chaos.

"He didn't want to improve the economy or strengthen employment.

"Saji will realize, or his wife will tell him, he has to concentrate on the well-being of the United States because that is what Presidents are supposed to do. If he doesn't, he risks at best not being reelected, at worst being impeached.

"He'll overreact, make endless television appearances, and start proposing programs and implementing actions through executive order. Because he has no idea how to run the country, since Nikita was essentially doing that, he will shine a spotlight on his incompetence.

"The momentum downhill will be so powerful there will be nothing those three can do to stop it. On Election Day, November 6, 2012, the people of the United States will overwhelmingly change leadership."

"So if we just stand back and watch, it will resolve itself?" asked Larry Feo.

"Right, Larry," said Anna, "and we believe it very strongly."

There was consensus around the table and it was decided that would be the go forward strategy. They would get back to the business of expanding and perfecting the activities of Cayman Covert Cyber Reclamation, Ltd.

As the group was getting ready to leave, Kateri Parker said to no one in particular, "But what if we're wrong?"

"You'll know by November fourth of this year, Kateri," said Anna.

"November fourth?" said Ken Grady.

"On November third, all of the seats in the House of Representatives and thirty-seven seats in the Senate are up for election. The results will be published on November fourth.

"If you do not see the trend we are counting on in that election and a huge number of the President's party do not lose their jobs, we will start planning for that phone call to Saji or his wife on November fifth."

"Great, good plan, works for me" were a few of the comments of a very positive team as they left the gazebo.

Warriors like to have a fall back plan and now they had

one.

The President Saji's End of Severe Poverty in Our Time through International Cooperation World Tour had been on the road now for over two months.

To the American taxpayers who were paying for the global party, it had nothing to do with ending poverty. If it had anything at all to do with poverty, it was the growing poverty in the United States.

The economic debacle, in the once richest country in the world, was not surprising. Besides the huge costs being piled onto the backs of a diminishing number of employed citizens, there was definitely a lack of leadership to guide the country through the worst economic times in over seventy-five years.

All of this was far from the minds of the four people whose priorities for the last month had been choosing the destinations of the two thousand partiers. A group that included almost two hundred members of the world press.

They had expected, since the February 20th conversation with Nikita, instructions for ending the tour would be coming from him or Ovinko, but nothing.

Lucile Saji and Mai Thi Toai, Dac Kien's wife, took over selecting the destinations for the mob as soon as they heard about the issues that could end this dream vacation.

Since that day in February, they planned an itinerary, which called for the two thousand upscale nomads to move to a fresh five star resort in a different country every week, arriving on Sunday of each week.

This week they had taken up residence in The Palace Resort in Macao, China. Newly built and just recently opened, the all suite resort was almost completely booked well into the future. Mrs. Saji and Mrs. Dac Kien sought to reserve two thousand, of the resorts twenty-five hundred suites, for the week beginning Sunday, March 28th. Negotiating with the resort management, the duo of relentless pleasure seeking women with the deepest pockets in the world, essentially the treasury of the United States, worked out a deal. The holders of the reservations were offered up to three weeks at the resort, courtesy of the United States taxpayers, in return for surrendering their reservations for the week the two women wanted. Lucile and Mai Thi Toai got their two thousand suites.

The resort is literally a city within Macao with a twelve thousand-seat theater, four lesser theaters, thirty-two restaurants, sixty-two very high-end retail stores, pools, a world-renowned spa and gym and twenty-one bars. On top of all that, it boasted the largest casino in Macao.

According to one reporter's column, which spelled out all of the above, Mrs. Saji would not relent until she had the most spectacular suite at this location. In well-televised interviews, she explained it was for her husband's long needed rest and recuperation from his draining world poverty tour.

On this particular afternoon, the four were having lunch in the spectacular Lintin Room on the fortieth floor rooftop overlooking the harbor. The topic could be summarized in a simple question, "What do we do now?"

"Sorosh, have you tried reaching him on the satellite device?" asked Lucile.

She had not paid much attention to either her communications with Vilen Ovinko or her husband's with

Nikita or Vilen. As she waited Sorosh's reply, she thought, "Out of sight, out of mind. Why ruin this fantastic global party with distasteful demands from those two. Besides, they were probably tied up with their global nuclear proliferation program."

"I have tried to reach Nikita and Vilen at least a dozen times since last week, nothing. These damn things don't have voice mail either," he said waving the tiny satellite communicator.

"Maybe your device isn't working," said Mai Thi Toai, "or maybe the network is down."

"No," said Dac Kien, "we thought of that so I tried to reach them with mine. When that didn't get any results, we called each other to make sure both our devices and the network are OK."

"And did that work?" asked Lucile.

"Yes, of course," answered Sorosh testily. "If it didn't, do you think we would be having this conversation? Instead we would be discussing an alternative way of reaching them, not, where the hell are they."

"Well, I think Nikita, or no Nikita, we have to wrap this little party up," said Pham Dac Kien. "Have any of you seen the United States' newspapers or watched any TV news? If we don't get back to our jobs soon, I don't think we'll have jobs to get back to. Sorosh, there is a movement gaining momentum to impeach you. Haven't you seen the papers or the TV either?"

"No, I haven't. I get briefings from my intelligence czar and my press guy every morning…"

Pham cut him off, "That's pure bullshit, Saji. You haven't

had a briefing since you pooh-poohed the report that the intelligence guys and the press were onto our scam. They haven't come near you since. They're both off pursuing whatever their particular form of pleasure is. You haven't got a clue as to what's going on and how deep the shit is that we're in, do you?"

"I'm on top of everything. Did you think I wouldn't be on top of everything that's going on? I'm the President of the United States! I'm…"

Lucile cut him off, "Enough bickering, boys. If Nikita and Vilen have disappeared temporarily or permanently, we cannot appear out of control. If they're gone permanently, we have to come up with a long-term strategy. Otherwise, we just play it one day at a time. We try one last measure to get in touch with them. If that fails, we move forward as if they didn't exist."

"What's the final measure?" asked Sorosh.

"Call my father and see what he knows."

Sorosh Saji, acting like some kind of Hollywood version of a king answered, "I don't think it appropriate that the President of the United States make a telephone call to the head of the Mexican drug cartel, do…?"

It was Mai Thi's turn to cut Saji off. Looking at Lucile with her eyes wide, she said, "Lucile, your father is Mexico's heroin king? You're one of those Mendozas? Your daddy is Raul Mendoza?"

"Yes, my dear Mai Thai. Raul Mendoza is my father. The difference between you and I, Mai Thai, is I had no control over who my daddy was. You, on the other hand, choose Pham to be your husband. All of us know his unusual past and his role in Nikita's swindles.

"Let us all be very realistic and accept who we are and we are in this together like it or not."

"Who are we, Lucile?" asked Sorosh sheepishly."

"We are four opportunists who like the good life and asked no questions when a billionaire master criminal managed our rise to the top of the international political and diplomatic world. We smiled, performed as instructed and enjoyed the ride. We now find ourselves four marionettes without a puppeteer master. We had better start thinking fast and, if at all possible, smart."

"I'm the President of the United States," said Sorosh Saji, looking insulted at Lucile's remarks. "Nothing has changed in my sphere of influence, which by the way is the entire world. You call your father looking for Nikita. I don't care if he has disappeared. I don't need him to guide me. I'm going to continue on my tour and work with my colleague here, the Secretary General of the United Nations, to eradicate poverty. We…"

"It's true what's in the global media," said Lucile with a strange grin. "You really do live in fantasy land, Sorosh. We are the laughing stock of the entire world. We have been on a tour to end poverty visiting only the best of five star resorts for over two months. With two thousand, of our closest friends, carrying on like drunken college students on spring break. The big difference is our party costs over a billion bucks a week. Moreover, according to the latest speculation in the media, had the added objective of covering up the biggest arms deal in history and a nuclear arms deal to boot.

"Sorosh, you haven't seen one newspaper in two months

have you?"

"No, but so what?"

"Well, the world is laughing at us and creating cartoons starring you and your buddy, Pham, here. That is the entire world, except the United States. They aren't laughing! They're screaming for your impeachment and, the more radical, for you to be tried as a traitor.

"The tour is going to close down and we'll put out a lot of press touting its overwhelming success. We'll plan on leaving and going back to the States on Sunday when our week here is up. We'll go to Washington and Pham you go to New York.

"We'll spend the next five days getting down a plan to make it appear we knew what we were doing all along. Pretend we have several initiatives that were conceived during this two-month tour. Initiatives, which we'll start working on at once.

"Given the political climate in the US and your declining poll numbers, it's going to be very difficult to get any initiatives through Congress. Also, don't forget since the Speaker of the House and the Senate Majority Leader got their marching instructions, from the missing Nikita, they'll be wandering around not knowing what to do and trying to avoid conflict.

"All of this should result in a chaotic situation which will postpone any assault on us until it is too late. The Congress will just let Sorosh's term run out.

"Pham, yours is over December 2011, right?"

"Yes, and I will be happy to just fade into the history of the United Nations and go home to Vietnam with my pension."

"Wait one minute, Lucile. Are you suggesting I do not run in 2012 and just let the nomination go to someone else? Are you serious? I'm Sorosh Saji, President…"

Lucile had been raised by a master criminal and had been taught by her mentor, Vilen Ovinko, the secret of success as a villain was to lie to the world, but never deceive yourself. She looked at the situation for what it was. The game was over, time to move on. "Sorosh, if that is what you want to do, you go ahead. We'll arrange for a quiet divorce when we get back to the States.

"As for me, I don't want the children or me to be around when they take you out of the Oval Office in handcuffs.

Believe me, Sorosh, that is what will happen if you decide to run in 2012. The opposition will dig into that leak about nukes for Iran and they will get to this tour's real purpose. They'll bury you and probably try you as a traitor.

"You make your decision when we get back to the White House," and she rose and left the dining room.

It was a beautiful morning, in probably one of the most peaceful places on earth, and the Mastersons were taking full advantage of it. After breakfast, they had decided to spend a few hours kayaking around Hawksbill Bay. Following the ever-playful Hawksbill Turtles, the species of sea turtle that the bay had been named after. This day, the Mastersons had taken a two-person kayak so they could talk to each other more easily than from their usual separate kayaks.

Anna and Hugh never tired of being with one another and most certainly never bored of talking to each other.

Today, the conversation more closely resembled the chatter of two adolescents making plans for the summer. It sounded like that because that is exactly what they were doing. They were planning fun things to do, back at the compound on Long Island, during the summer and early fall.

In less than a week, they would leave for Long Island and would take half the team with them, leaving the other five at Villa Serenity. Then, on July 1st, the five on Long Island would switch places with the five on Cayman Brac. This would repeat itself every month through the end of the year. After which, they would all have to make some decisions as to who would stay where. The idea was to have the entire crew completely familiar with both facilities and eventually have staff operating all year in both.

The business was growing and by very large numbers. Since the first week of April, they had signed on twelve new clients from around the world representing lost funds in excess of ten billion dollars. Everyone attributed this new business to the publicity surrounding the return of funds, stolen by Nikita and his conspirators, to needy and appreciative groups on three continents.

The new contracts exceeded the funds they were capable of returning in that same period. A situation making the Mastersons even more confident their decision to bring the ten young people into the business, as partners, was a very good one.

They were even more certain it had been the right decision since the ambitious young group worked both hard and enthusiastically. They were learning the entire business far more rapidly than Anna and Hugh had expected. This good news afforded the Mastersons more time to play…like this morning.

"We are one very fortunate couple," Anna said smiling at a passing turtle. Something she always did and continued to wonder if they knew she was smiling. "Things could have been very different if the rescue had not been successful."

"Anna, have you ever focused on the fact had you not successfully broken into Nikita's network, we would probably both be dead now?"

"Not really. You mean Nikita would have kidnapped and killed us because he needed the money. We just would have known nothing about his plans. He would have probably gotten his money back, killed us and brokered the nukes.

"Jesus, Hugh, the world would be a very different place today."

"Right, Anna, and it's not. And it's all because you, with that brain and determination short-circuited his scheme. By the way, has Louise picked up any chatter on the network from the four remaining villains?"

"The Sajis, Dac Kien and Iran's President, Heydar Vahdani, are not talking to each other or to anyone new on the network, if there is anyone new."

"Are you sure it's still up and running and someone hasn't dismantled it?"

"It's running OK. Louise now tracks any attempted calls and about once a week, Lucile Saji tries to reach Vilen Ovinko. I guess her husband is frustrating her with his less than stellar actions and she wants advice from her mentor...former mentor...but, I guess she doesn't know that."

"It's funny, Anna, Nikita would be proud. Without any help from him, his puppets have managed to increase the level of chaos they're generating. Both the United States and the United Nations seem to be running in circles and it appears to be bleeding into European Union countries. Maybe the chaos has a life of its own and it will continue until the elections of 2012. Have you seen anything in the media about his running in 2012?"

"Nothing either way. He is unusually silent about 2012."

"Good news, nothing upsetting on that front. Anything on the sunken Standart or the bodies in the New York City mansion?"

"Nothing on the Standart. Louise did pick up a couple of small articles in New York papers about a Mafia style multiple murder of Russian gangsters in a mansion on Eighty Second Street. Only about four paragraphs in total and those were in early March, nothing since."

"Well, all of that's good news. Nikita's son and the goons are forgotten. If there had been any survivors of the Standart, it would have gotten press and an investigation. A three hundred foot yacht sunk five miles off a former nuclear bomb-testing site would attract a lot of snoopers from all over the world. No news is good news."

"There is one thing, Hugh, our team has asked me to bring it up. They're also very aware that Sorosh Saji has said nothing about running in 2012 and they are afraid he'll try for a run and may win.

"They asked if we could come up with anything that could bring out what he has been involved in without involving Cayman Covert Cyber Reclamation, Ltd. They're convinced we can come up with something, which would encourage him to drop out of the 2012 Presidential race."

"Well, well, that's great news," answered Hugh grinning.

"What's great news?"

"The team we're depending on, for our retirement income, is more concerned about shielding Cayman Covert Cyber Reclamation, Ltd. from damage. Now they have their priorities in the right order."

"Nice, Hugh," she said stifling a laugh, "they're now more focused on our retirement than global chaos. Anyway, do you have any ideas? I sure as hell don't."

"Yes I do, love, yes I do."

"Well, let me in on it."

"I too have been concerned this less than honorable President may squeeze through and pull off another con job on the American electorate. Therefore, I called Arthur McCauley and posed an idea to him."

"Arthur McCauley, our New York attorney? What's your idea and why him?"

"My idea is simple. I've decided to take the next several months and write a novel.

"Essentially a fictionalized version of all the events since Nikita got involved with the President of Iran and a nuke deal all the way through to …hell, today.

"A fictionalized version that will force people to think and then decide if they are willing to risk it's not fiction."

"Wow…wow! That just may do it and I know it will make the team happy. But, why did you call Arthur?"

"I am going to write it under a pen name and I wanted his advice as to how I do that without revealing my real identity."

Epilogue

Somewhere in the South Pacific on a Samoan fishing boat, an old man is cleaning toilets. After telling him to hurry, the Samoan cook is talking to his assistant about who this imbecile is they picked up in February, twenty miles off the coast of Johnston Atoll.

"It is sad, but it is his luck the Captain feels sorry for him," said the young assistant.

"He sounds Russian, but speaks gibberish. He is lucky the gash on his head didn't kill him. It's a miracle he didn't drown lying there floating on what looked like a huge desk. We should have pulled the desk aboard; maybe it would tell us something about him."

"It was too heavy and who cares. Now you don't have to clean the kitchen and bathrooms every night. You got a promotion," the cook said laughing.

The assistant, a gentle boy of seventeen, looked sadly at the old man with his dirty, straggly beard and said softly, "It would have been better, old man, if you had gone peacefully to God."

"But, he didn't and now he belongs to us," snarled the cook.

"He should have a name, a Russian name," said the Samoan boy.

"Well, you went to school and learned history. Give him a Russian name from history."

The boy thought for a few moments, and then he laughed

and shouted to the cook. "He will be known as, Nikita. I remember that Russian name most from history. I read about something he did and it made me laugh. He took off his shoe and banged it on a desk at the United Nations.

"Yes, Nikita," he shouted again.

The old man stopped his cleaning and turned towards the boy and as he did so, a strange look came over his face. Similar to the look an old man gets when he starts to come out of a long and deep sleep.

MORE OF THE

ANNA & HUGH MASTERSON INTERNATIONAL MYSTERY SERIES

by
G. Hugh Bodell

TREACHERY IN TURTLE BAY
TREACHERY IN TURTLE BAY II

~~~

FOR FURTHER INFORMATION
VISIT WWW.SPRIGMEDIAGROUP.COM